SHARDS

Kit Campbell

TDP

To my friends and family, who have always stood by my side

Chapter One

WAKING UP TO the phone ringing was probably a bad start to the day. Eva groaned and rolled over while the phone continued its ungodly noise, earning a protesting meow from her large white cat, Azrael, who had made himself comfortable across her back in an attempt to claim the rest of the bed as his own. The wisps of her dream—one that seemed to repeat constantly these days—were slow to drift away.

She had an old phone, left over from the days when phones still had cords, hanging on the wall. It'd come with the apartment and, since she couldn't justify a cell phone on her pay, she thought it was probably a good idea to have some way for people to reach her. The issue was that no one ever used it, except for charities, telemarketers, and, unfortunately, her mother.

She pushed out of bed and moved into the dining room, staring at it, debating whether or not to answer it. It wasn't that she didn't love her mother—she did. She was the only family Eva had, since her father had disappeared before Eva'd been born and her grandparents had died in a car accident before she'd started school.

If she didn't answer, her mother would probably think something had happened to her. With a sigh, Eva crossed the room and answered. "Hello."

"*Querida,*" came the overly cheerful voice of her mother. Eva winced. "It's been so long since I've heard from you. How is school going?"

Eva could almost hear the unasked questions in her mother's voice. *When are you going to switch to a real major instead of that useless religious studies degree? What do you think you're going to do to pay off your loans when you graduate, if you ever graduate? Have you found any friends, or anyone who's more than a friend?*

"It's going great," she lied. Here would be where she would elaborate, if she could think of anything to say. She furrowed her brow, searching for something, anything, to add to her original statement. "I got into that class that I really wanted."

"That's nice, *chica,*" her mother replied. "When do you think you think you'll be home next?"

When do you think you'll give up on that silly degree and return to the real world?

Eva shook her head. "Oh, probably not until break. There's so much to be done—essays and projects, and I've got to apply for some grants before next semester. Plus I got a job and I can't just leave without warning. You know that."

"Ah, yes, at that bookstore." The tone of her mother's voice let Eva know exactly what she thought about that. "You should come home. The community college is offering teaching certification now. You could take that, become a history teacher. It'd be steady work, and the pay would be enough to support you."

"Mother, we've talked about this," Eva said. "I don't want to be a history teacher."

"Well, what do you want?"

Eva groaned internally. She didn't know what she wanted. Sometimes she didn't even know why she was getting a master's degree in religious studies; she wasn't particularly religious, but there was something about the subject matter that almost haunted her. She'd taken a single class on the subject as an undergraduate, and now look where she was.

But she couldn't tell her mother that. It would just be a confirmation that Eva didn't know what she was doing. It would be a confirmation that she needed to be told what to do, and Eva would find herself stuck back in that small town teaching history to teenagers who couldn't care less. Trapped forever.

"Look, Mom," Eva said, "I'm happy here. I'm really enjoying things. Everything's great."

"Everything?" her mother asked. Eva could hear the implication in her voice. "Because you'll never guess who I ran into the other day. Do you remember Mrs. Wong's son? He's back in town, so if you transfer back to the community college, you two can spend some time together."

Oh, God. She did not have time for this. "Everything is *fine*, Mother. I'm going now. I love you, *adios*."

"Eva, wait," her mother said in that tone of voice that meant business that every mother seemed to have.

Eva sighed and waited.

"*Mira*," her mother said, sounding perfectly serious. "I'm worried about you. You used to be so friendly and happy, and now you avoid me and keep everything to yourself. I want you to really think about what you're doing. And if, at Christmas, you can't tell me that you're happy and make me believe it, I want you to come home."

Unsure what to say, Eva felt an unpleasant feeling coil itself around her heart. It wouldn't be enough time.

"And I mean it, *querida*. Well, have a good day!" And she hung up before Eva could respond, had she anything to say.

Eva slid down into her chair, dropping her head into her hands. It was bad enough that Eva didn't know what she was doing, but to have her mother constantly trying to get her to do something else was exhausting. If only she were more sure about her degree. Then she'd be able to tell her mother why she was doing what she was doing, and then her mother could be proud of her, could believe that she knew what she was doing.

And Eva could believe it too.

For a long moment she just sat there, but then she remembered that she had homework to do—two chapters to read and a paper to finish up—before lecture started. She returned to her room, searched the floor for reasonably clean clothes, and pulled her long, raven hair up into a low bun.

She cleared off a corner of her dining room table and debated, not for the first time that week, actually cleaning her apartment. It was probably a fire hazard. She half-heartedly pushed some junk mail into the trash and tossed some clothes into the bedroom, then poured herself a bowl of cereal—sans milk, because she hadn't made it to the store yet this week—and sat down with her textbook. Then she stood, crossed to the tiny kitchen window, and pulled the blinds open before sitting back down. The amount of sunlight that streamed in wasn't much, but she always worked better with some sunlight than without it.

She probably should have thought about that before she'd chosen to go to graduate school in one of the rainiest corners of the state. But maybe it hadn't been apparent before she'd had to deal with regular cloud cover.

Azrael followed her, helping himself to the newly cleaned corner of the table and batting half-heartedly at her textbook. Eva picked it up, turned to the proper chapter, and read aloud, "Before Adam and Eve: The Legend of Lilith and Why It Continues To Be Relevant."

Azrael flicked his tail and gnawed on the back corner of the book.

"Don't do that," Eva said, "I'm renting this book." She ran one hand lazily down the page, looking at the illustration and wishing her mother hadn't called. She'd been having the nicest, though an admittedly strange, recurring dream. It was always the same—a man, a very pretty man, at that, telling her that he'd be there for her forever. They would be in a desert, his long hair—and hers, for that matter—waving in a light breeze, and he'd tell how glad he was that she'd come back. Her subconscious was probably trying to tell her something, but she definitely didn't have time for dating, especially not now.

Besides, she didn't even know the guy in real life. Her brain had probably conjured him out of a combination of male models and actors or something. Eva shook her head, trying to focus on her work. Still...there was something very comforting about her dream man. Something that told her that he really did belong to her, somehow.

Azrael sprawled across the book and wouldn't move until Eva fed him.

Three hours later, she'd gotten through her chapters, and had been pleased to discover her paper wasn't actually a paper, but an activity where her professor had given them sections of the first five books of the Bible and asked them to determine which of the four accepted authors had written that particular section. That was nice; Eva felt like she did so many papers that a few more were going to put her over the edge into madness.

Eva got up to retrieve her backpack, and she returned to find Azrael had chewed the corner off her assignment. Eva managed half a glower at him before noticing the clock on the microwave. Damn, she had to run or she was going to be late to Professor Axelrad's class, and that was never a good idea. He'd probably give a pop quiz before she got there just to spite her. For a long moment, Eva considered going back to bed to spend some more time with her dream guy, but she had to finish this degree, if only so her mother would forget her ultimatum. She threw her textbooks and homework into her backpack, slung it over her shoulder, and headed out.

It was a beautiful day, not a cloud in the sky. Eva paused for just a moment to raise her face to the sun and bask in its warmth, getting some much-needed sunlight. No doubt by the time she was out of class, it would be raining again. She forced herself to keep moving toward campus, sinking into her thoughts as she went. What was she doing? How could she figure out if she was doing the right thing?

Well, one thing was sure: she definitely didn't want to teach history back in her hometown.

Eva was so deep in her thoughts that she didn't notice a sudden movement in front of her. She hit something hard and instinctively jerked back, dropping her bag and tripping over it. Luckily, something arrested her fall, and she looked up into two of the most brilliant green eyes she'd ever seen. They were almost unnaturally bright, their color reminiscent of a spring meadow just after the rain, rejuvenated and full of life.

It took her a moment to realize that the eyes were connected to a person, and that he was speaking to her.

"Are you all right?" he said, hopefully for the first time.

Eva blinked at him, but it took a few moments before her mouth seemed to decide to work again. This was not turning out to be a good day, even not counting the phone call with her mother. "Yes, sorry. I didn't, well—anyway, thank you." She pulled herself away reluctantly, as the person turned out to be a young man, probably only a few years older than herself, and the rest of his face was as pleasing as his eyes. She blushed slightly, reached for her bag, and froze.

Very slowly, she lifted the bag back to her shoulder, turning back to the man still standing there. It couldn't be—but it was the guy from her dreams. It was the same face, the same hair, though it was shorter now, cut to the base of his skull instead of long like in the dream, and, when he said, "Are you sure you're all right?" the same voice.

She'd never noticed his eyes in the dream before.

Apparently taking her silence for assent, he smiled at her. "I'm Michael, by the way." His smile was nice too, Eva noticed distractedly. He held out a hand and Eva slowly took it, suddenly shy.

"Eva," she said, accentuating the "Ay" at the beginning of her name. She'd found that people often mispronounced her name if they just looked at the spelling, and it'd become habit to overemphasize it, even in conversation. "Look, I'm really sorry, and thank you for not being a jerk about it, but I have to go." He seemed surprised, but she moved around him and half-ran down the path toward her building. That was not the way to make friends, she chided herself as she went. Especially not with dream men, whatever that meant, especially dream men that apparently went to the same school as she did. Still, she'd never seen him before, and she'd probably never see him again, so it was probably best not to dwell on it.

Eva froze, severely tempted to turn around and go back to him, if only to figure out why she was dreaming about him, but she shook her head. She had goals, and one of them was getting to class on time so she would pass and eventually get a degree and do something with it.

Crap, she was going to be late. She broke into a run.

Eva reached the classroom in record time but not, sadly, *on* time. Professor Axelrad was already lecturing at the front of the classroom, his back turned toward his students. Eva crept slowly down the aisle, sliding into a seat near the back next to Sam, one of those friends that you only ever did homework with and maybe occasionally went out for a drink with after a long project was finished. Sam was ridiculously gorgeous, with dark hair that was always somehow attractively in his eyes. Eva might have gone for him if dating fell into her plans at all. Which it didn't. At all.

Sam looked up as she settled next to him, giving her a brilliant smile. Eva returned it, pleased that she'd somehow managed to be late and not catch Professor Axelrad's attention.

"Miss Martinez," Professor Axelrad drawled, not even bothering to turn from the whiteboard, "since you've had the good fortune to join us, why don't you stand up and explain the importance of angels in Christian iconology for us?"

Eva sighed, temporarily sliding down further into her seat. So much for that. Ignoring Sam's sympathetic look, she rose to her feet. "I would argue that angels are not important to Christian iconology," she said, hoping her voice carried all the way to Professor Axelrad so this could be over as quickly as possible. "In fact, outside of Roman Catholicism and Eastern Orthodoxy, many denominations don't include them in their art or worship."

Professor Axelrad paused in his scribbling, finally turning to look out over the classroom. He leveled a look in Eva's direction, saying nothing, but even so, in that look, he managed to exude all his disdain for her answer. Eva felt her cheeks color, but stood her ground. It wasn't the first time she'd found she didn't agree with her professors, and no doubt it wouldn't be her last.

"Angels," she continued, "are just borrowed deities from other religions, incorporated into Christian mythology to placate converted people. Many of their features—such as the wings—are also borrowed from those same religions. It doesn't make sense to make a big deal out of them as Christian symbols when their origins are obviously outside of Christianity." There was no response from her professor. Eva paused, glancing around the classroom, meeting the eyes of some of her classmates. "I mean, even Michael, archangel and supposed head of the Heavenly hosts, was originally

Chaldean, and now we act like he really was working for God all along."

Eva glanced around one more time, felt her knees go weak, and sat down.

After a moment, Professor Axelrad gave the barest of nods and turned back to his scribbling. "Be that as it may," he said, "angels are an important part of Christianity, and many people throughout history have turned to them for guidance and comfort. This week we'll be looking at angels at work in the Bible. I've two different essay assignments this week, and you'll be assigned based on your last name." He pulled up a whiteboard, revealing another underneath it. Under "A–M" he'd written, "Explain the Nephilim."

Eva was half-tempted to protest and point out that the Nephilim weren't necessarily angelic in any way, shape, or form, but she generally avoided provoking Professor Axelrad, especially more than once per class period.

Luckily, Professor Axelrad ignored her the rest of class. When he finally released them, Eva packed up her bag, somewhat pleased that, despite making her defend herself before the whole class, her professor hadn't torn her statements apart. She hoisted her bag onto her shoulder before she realized he was probably saving that for her paper.

"So you don't believe in angels?" Sam pulled his own bag over one shoulder. "No Gabriel coming to Mary, no Raphael telling Noah to build his Ark, no Lucifer and his fallen angels, no snake in the garden?"

Eva frowned. "The snake was not an angel."

"Oh, wasn't he?" Sam gave her a half-smile. He seemed to do it a lot, where only one side of his mouth would twist upwards. "No choirs of angels singing Hallelujah in the heavens?"

"I get your point," Eva said. She turned and headed up the aisle, Sam falling into step behind her. "I don't know. Thinking about them makes my head hurt. Do *you* believe in them?"

"No," Sam replied. "I think people just see something they don't understand, or think they are seeing something, or simply make it up."

They'd reached the outside of the building by now. Eva paused for a moment, watching her classmates stream in all directions. The clouds were beginning to roll in, promising afternoon storms. "That's kind of a pessimistic view of things." She turned to look at him. "How'd you decide to go into religious studies with that sort of point of view?"

"You're one to talk, Mrs. No-Angels." Sam meandered off the pavement into the grass, relaxing once he had done so. "Look, you don't get things in this life from believing in things that aren't there. There's no reason to pretend otherwise."

Eva shrugged, half-agreeing with him. She glanced toward the clock tower on the Physics building. Professor Axelrad had run over, again. Now she'd probably be late for work. Her bosses might not care, or even notice, but she liked to at least pretend to be on top of her life.

"Hey, look," Sam said, drawing her attention back, "I'd be happy to discuss why two people such as ourselves went into this field at any time. And to complain about our essay assignments. At least you got the Nephilim; I've got to do one on the archangels." There was a flash of some dark emotion across his face—if Eva had to, she'd call it hatred—but it was gone as quickly as it'd come. "Say, now? We can head over to the campus coffee shop, my treat." He smiled again and brushed his hair out of his eyes again, managing to look attractive and friendly and way too tempting for his own good.

"I wish I could," Eva said, meaning every word. Some real, non-expired food would be a treat. "But I've got to get to work. Some other time, maybe."

"Sure," said Sam. His smile tightened a bit, but he held out his hand. Eva tentatively reached her own out, surprised when he reached forward and gave hers a firm shake. "Good luck on your essay. Once more into the breach, and all that. See you Friday!" Sam turned and headed across the lawn, waving one hand over his shoulder as he went.

Eva shook her head, watching him go. Then she turned and headed the other way, sending worried glances at the sky. She'd forgotten to grab her umbrella this morning.

Leaving campus, she took the underpass onto a street of shops. They were mostly aimed at the college crowd, a mixture of artsy boutiques and cheaper chains. It was packed full of people, both students heading home or to class and residents out enjoying the lack of rain, for however long it would last. As Eva weaved her way through, she wondered about the look on Sam's face. She wasn't a fan of angels either, but she didn't hate them. Maybe she'd read too much into it.

Near the top of the street was a small bookstore squeezed in between one of the ubiquitous coffee shops and a shoe store. There was no name on the outside of the building; "The Bookstore" was painted in huge letters across the large windows, but that was it. Eva pushed the door open, a bell chiming as she did so. Inside, there were several narrow rows of tall bookcases, with more books sitting on the floor and every other available surface. It wasn't the best organized, as the books tended to have a mind of their own. Eva hurried toward the counter off on the left, dumping her bag behind it.

"You're late," came a voice from somewhere in the stacks.

"I know," Eva moaned. She dropped onto the stool behind the counter, rolling her head back and relaxing her shoulders. "I've had the worst day. It started out so well, but then my mother called, and Professor Axelrad called me out, and I literally ran this guy over...I swear it's a miracle that I haven't been eaten by wolves yet."

"A guy?" Rafe, one of her bosses, stuck his head around a pile of books off on her left. He had dust everywhere, standing out starkly against his dark skin. She could have sworn his voice was coming from a different direction, but that was a frequent enough occurrence that she wasn't sure he wasn't practicing ventriloquism in some manner. Eva'd never gotten up the courage to ask him. It wasn't that she didn't get along with him—she sometimes thought that it was impossible not to like the man—but she was afraid he might laugh at her.

"It was nothing," she said quickly, trying to banish thoughts of her dream. The last thing she needed to be telling people about was how she was having dreams about some guy who was apparently not a figment of her imagination. Stalling, she took her bun out and busied herself braiding her thick hair. "I'd never seen him before, and I doubt I'll ever see him again."

Rafe sighed, wiping the sweat from his brow and rubbing the top of his bald head. He'd probably been trying to organize the old textbooks again. They were a pain, but they did keep a steady income for the store. Eva had tried a couple times to make headway herself, but they seemed to multiply when your back was turned. "I wish you'd get out more," he said. "A girl your age shouldn't spend so much time with just books and studying."

Eva shook her head. "You know I need the money, Rafe," she said. "And I need to finish school so I can get a job that will support me." *Whatever that is going to be.*

"You're always welcome to a job here, you know that." Her boss stretched, his shoulders popping. "You'd think that if you wanted a good job, though, you'd major in something other than religious studies."

Eva groaned. It was a little too reminiscent of her mother's arguments.

The office door opened and a tall, redheaded man stepped out, looking at some paperwork in his hand. "Rafe," he said, without looking up, "have you found that 1598 copy of..." He trailed off, blinking at Eva. "Are you in today?"

"She's in every day, Gabe," the other man said with a shake of his head. "Maybe if you came out of the office once in a while, you'd be more aware of our current staffing arrangement."

"Maybe," agreed Gabe, his face softening into a smile. "But, on the other hand, I get to sit and play on the computer while you do all the hard work. You will never guess how many games of solitaire I have played today."

"Ah, but how many have you won?" Rafe grinned. "Anyway, yes, I found the book and I put it on your desk an hour ago. And maybe if you had looked up from your solitaire you would have noticed when I came in."

Gabe shrugged guiltily. "It is an addiction."

"Anything else you need while you're out in the world?" asked Rafe.

"Haha," said Gabe, and disappeared back into his office.

Rafe dusted his hands off on his pants and came over to the counter. "We're expecting quite a few history majors in the near future—I guess the second-years just got some sort of major paper. I've tried to at least clump interesting events together but they'll probably just have to wade in and see what they find. I put everything from 1900 onward over behind the science fiction books." He paused, scratching at his nose, leaving a trail of gray across his chocolate skin. "I think. You'd think I'd be better at history, but truth is that I couldn't really be bothered."

"When you were in school?" asked Eva.

"Sure, why not? Oh, I found some more of those mystery novels you like and put them aside for you. They're in the office on my desk."

Eva grinned. Rafe's desk was the easiest place to find things because he never used the thing. Luckily, she'd just finished the last bunch, but then she remembered her angel essay, and the fact that there was no food in the apartment. "I don't know if I'll get to read them for a while —I really need to focus on school."

Rafe put his hands in his pockets. "Oh, honey, I keep telling you you've got to switch to an easier major, like engineering or physics or something."

"I'm not sure they'd like to hear their majors referred to as easier," said Eva, unconsciously straightening the books on display near the register. "Besides, I find the topics so fascinating—we're doing Biblical Foundations this semester, and how the Bible was put together is really great, they think that the Old Testament was…"

"I'm sure it's great," replied Rafe, holding up his hands. "Super interesting and all, but the truth of the matter is that no one knows anything and they're just making crap up. At least with science, things are slightly more concrete."

"Maybe," agreed Eva sullenly. "I don't know. Sometimes I wonder why I'm bothering. I fight with my professors all the time. But I also feel some…connection to the subject matter, I guess. Even though it drives me crazy at times, I want to know more."

Rafe leant up against the wall, crossing his arms across his broad chest. "What can you do?" he asked. "Anyway, remember that your theories are just as valid as theirs. After all, everyone who was there is dead now."

"Mmm," said Eva, feeling slightly better.

"If you need anything, I'll be being eaten by the history books." Rafe stood up again. "And if you need to do some homework here, that's fine by me, as long as you're able to help customers when they need it and do a bit of reshelving." He took a few steps, then stopped mid-step. "And don't let Gabe see you, though with his solitaire addiction, I'm not really sure he would have any room to talk. One day I'm going to uninstall it just to see what he does, though he might flood the shop, and that would be problematic." He continued back into the books, out of view in a matter of seconds, and out of hearing not long after that.

Eva wasn't sure she could picture the ever-calm if somewhat forgetful Gabe purposefully destroying anything, though the solitaire thing was pretty bad—she'd needed to get his advice on something the week before and it had taken her a full five minutes to get his attention, and then only by poking him in the shoulder, as tapping hadn't elicited a response. He'd reacted strangely too; it had been almost eerie really, the way his eyes had lit up when he'd jumped. His eyes had been green too, Eva recalled, just like her apparently real dream man. Well, Gabe was Irish, so there wasn't too much odd about that. Sometimes, when he was feeling chatty, he'd tell her tales of the Old Country, though as far as she could tell, he'd grown up here in the States.

She pulled her bag over to the stool and took out a textbook. She wasn't about to overlook permission to get some work done. She wasn't sure either of her bosses would actually care at all, though she was the only employee they kept other than themselves and the store was in a constant mess. Eva sometimes felt like she wasn't really contributing, but the pay and the company were good, so she couldn't really complain.

Eva looked down at her textbook, frowning, the words running together. She sighed, rubbing one temple. How was she going to justify her degree to her mother in a way that would satisfy her? If only Eva could be more sure herself. Maybe there was some way to immerse herself more fully in the material, to get a more complete picture. Maybe there was some way to get some sort of sign that she was doing the right thing.

Eva shook her head and forced herself to focus.

The bell on the door rang several minutes later and Eva looked up to find some very confused-looking students standing in the doorway. She couldn't really blame them; when she'd seen the "Help Wanted" sign in the window and had come in that very first time, she had very nearly walked out again. But something had told her that she should be here, and not just her need for money and her yearning for a job that was not just another stress in her life. Plus once she'd met Rafe and Gabe she'd felt right at home.

That was a bit strange, if she had to be honest with herself. Maybe she was just desperate for friendship. *And,* her brain helpfully provided, *perhaps for something a little more.* She shook her head, trying to shake the thought off. Besides, why dream about some guy she didn't know when she had a gorgeous guy who'd probably be interested that she saw all the time? If she were interested, that is.

Eva frowned down at her textbook. She'd spent entirely too much brainpower today dwelling on things that weren't going to help her. Pushing all thoughts of boys out of her mind, she glanced up to make sure the college students weren't flailing too terribly, and then set to work.

Chapter Two

THE BREAK IN the rain lasted only for a few more hours before the sky opened up again. At first it was teasing and light, but after a short while the drops were hard and constant, slapping against umbrellas and roofs.

The store had cleared out some time ago and all was quiet, except for Rafe occasionally humming or even singing out loud. The tunes varied from music she caught on the radio frequently to odd lilting tunes in languages she'd never heard before. It made her a little jealous—her singing voice was nothing to write home about, and though she had occasionally found herself humming when she tried to organize the books, she couldn't see herself singing without a care of who heard.

Gabe came out of the office, closing the door behind him. He'd pulled his long hair back into a ponytail. "We're going to get some pizza for dinner. Do you want to come?" he asked.

The bookstore closed somewhat arbitrarily, depending on the moods of its owners. Eva sometimes wondered if people liked it so much because it was somewhat of an adventure as to whether or not it would be open when you needed it to be. That would be a poor trait in most businesses, but Eva had overheard people talking on campus about it. Rafe and Gabe did try to keep it open later during finals and at the beginning of the semester, but they had short attention spans.

"I'd better not," she answered, sliding her book closed and tucking it and her notes into her bag. "I've got to work on this essay."

Gabe nodded. "That's understandable. Go ahead and go; I'll make Rafe close up the shop."

"Thanks, Gabe." Eva slid off her stool and retrieved her coat, wishing as she looked outside that she'd thought to bring a hat with her. Unfortunately her one and only hat had gone missing sometime between getting home the night before and leaving that morning, and a thorough search of her apartment had revealed nothing. Eva half-suspected her cat had eaten it, as he had seemed entirely too pleased with himself.

Her boss wandered to the window. "I love a good rain," he said, "though this is a bit much. Do you need to borrow an umbrella?"

"Could I?" asked Eva, relieved. She slung her bag over both shoulders. Luckily her apartment was just up the street, but it wasn't close enough that she wouldn't end up soaked by the time she got home, and the radiator was a bit picky about whether or not it would work at any given time.

"Just bring it back tomorrow." Gabe disappeared back into the office for a moment and returned with a large umbrella in a hideous neon green that looked suspiciously left over from a less civilized time, probably when parachute pants and big hair had also been popular. Eva weighed the wisdom of going out in public with it, but decided that she would rather not have to wring out her clothing when she got home.

"Perhaps I should burn the thing and put it out of its misery," she murmured to herself, though she suspected Gabe heard, judging by the snort he attempted to conceal within a sudden coughing attack. "Thank you. See you tomorrow. Bye, Rafe!" she called to the stacks at large.

"Bye, honey!" came the reply, somewhere off by the romance section.

With a wave, she pushed out the door and into the rainy madness beyond, pausing for only a moment beneath the awning to push the umbrella open.

The return of the rain had brought with it the wind, and almost immediately Eva found herself having to strengthen her hold on the handle, which was some sort of odd faded purple color. She moved up the street, watching the drops hit the sidewalk at her feet. It was strangely silent, the only sound the pounding of the rain and the occasional slosh as a car drove by through a puddle. It had begun to get dark, the streetlights creating odd halos about themselves. Eva found it oddly relaxing. Even with the few other people on the street, she felt alone and at peace.

She reached an intersection and hit the pedestrian button, waiting for the light to change. Maybe she could heat up something from the freezer for dinner. It wasn't particularly appetizing, but it would be quick, and maybe she'd go to bed early so she could make the best use of the daylight tomorrow.

The light changed and Eva dutifully started across the street at the permission of the walking man. The wind changed directions, and Eva found her coat and her umbrella trying to blow her further into traffic. She continued across as she fought them into submission, but as she finally got her umbrella back into a useable position where she could both see and keep out of the rain, she looked up to find a car bearing down on her, its lights off and its driver apparently intent on paying the traffic signals no mind.

Eva froze despite her mind screaming at her to take some sort of action, umbrella still up. The car seemed to be unsteady, its direction altering every few seconds. *Hydroplaning*, her mind supplied for her for all the good it would do.

Someone grabbed her arm and pulled. Eva lost her grip on the umbrella and tripped onto the curb as the car careened by, flattening the unlucky umbrella underneath it. Eva blinked at its mauled form as the rain began to drip down her face.

"Gabe's going to be so mad," she murmured. He'd probably had that umbrella for decades.

"Are you all right?"

Eva turned to find herself confronted with the young man from earlier. He stepped into the street—checking both ways first—and retrieved the umbrella and offered it back to her. She took it and sighed. The handle had snapped in half and a couple of the spokes had broken off, leaving large tears in the fabric.

He put his hands in his pockets. "I'd offer you my umbrella but unfortunately I don't have one. I can offer you a warm meal, though—I was just on my way to dinner."

Eva looked from the broken umbrella to those warm green eyes. "I need to write an essay," she said reluctantly.

"Nonsense," said the young man—Michael, was it?— and offered her his arm. "After the day you're having, I'd say you could use a good meal and some company."

She wasn't quite sure why, but she looped her arm through his and he patted her hand. He was soaked, his hair hanging heavily over his face, but his arm was warm under hers. He didn't seem to be as wet as she would have been, assuming he'd walked from the university. *Remember your goals, Eva,* she told herself, but they didn't seem terribly important at the moment. And it had been a bad day. And she had nothing to eat at home.

They walked in silence for a few blocks until Michael pulled open a random door—Eva had to admit she hadn't really been paying attention, having been more focused on the warm body so close to hers—and led her into a cozy diner, brightly lit with an odd assortment of lamps that seemed determined to match as little as possible. He took her coat and hung it with his on a coat rack next to a booth, then slid in across from her, pushing his dripping hair out of his eyes. "They have good soup here," he said, "or warm sandwiches if you prefer that sort of thing."

Eva glanced around, taking in her surroundings. The diner was small, but relatively filled with patrons, all looking warm and happy. A matronly woman with a checkered apron bustled from table to table, sharing laughs with the occupants. "I really shouldn't impose," Eva said, even as she considered staying here forever. It was certainly warmer than her apartment was liable to be.

"It's no trouble," said Michael. "Truth be told, I could use a little company myself. My roommates are never home and I haven't had too much luck making friends at school."

Eva took the menu he offered her, leaning her head on her other hand. There was no doubt about it—he was definitely the same guy as her dream. At least he was proving to be down-to-earth, providing he really existed and Eva hadn't gone insane. She decided to go with her first hypothesis for now. "So, been going to school here long?"

He smiled, looking a little sheepish. "For a while, yeah. I'm afraid I'm a chronic major jumper."

"Really? Sounds expensive." She scanned the menu. It was basic Americana, not necessarily her first choice in comfort food, but at the moment she couldn't think of anything she'd like better, except maybe a large bowl of green chile like her mother made. Actually, chili sounded pretty good, even if it would be the kind made with ground beef and beans.

He chuckled. "I guess that's one way to interpret it. I'm studying physics now, and before that I was working on religious studies." She could swear his hair was already looking dry, whereas hers was still soaked. She really hoped the radiator was going to work.

The woman in the apron made her way over, smiling widely as she saw Michael. "Well, if it ain't my guardian angel. What'll it be, dear?"

Michael blushed a strangely attractive shade of pink. "I wish you wouldn't call me that."

"Pulled me out of the way of a falling tree branch, he did," the woman told Eva.

Well, Eva probably hadn't made him up. "Bit of a hero complex?" Eva asked. A sinking feeling settled in her stomach—jealousy? Because she had hoped he'd done it just for her? Eva shook her head. She barely knew him, what was she thinking? Just because he was in her dreams doesn't mean she was in his.

Michael mumbled something and hid behind his menu.

"You're new here, aren't you, dearie? I'm Pat, the owner of this fine establishment."

"Eva," said Eva with a smile, but couldn't help over-pronouncing the "ay" again.

"Pleasure to have you here, love. What'll be?"

Eva ordered her chili and a cup of cocoa while Michael lowered his menu long enough to request a grilled cheese sandwich and some tea. Pat scribbled their order on a pad of paper and wandered off towards the kitchen, humming underneath her breath and getting distracted by another table on her way.

When Eva turned back from watching Pat, she found Michael observing her. "Eva, eh?" he said. "That's a pretty name. I would have told you that earlier, but you didn't seem to have time for a conversation."

Eva felt herself flush. "My mother claims she named me after Eva Perón—you know, Evita? Not sure why, exactly, we're not Argentinean, but then when she feels I'm not living up to my potential, she likes to list off everything that Evita managed. Though she gives me this terrible look when I point out that she also died at the age of 33." She rolled a napkin-wrapped silverware package back and forth between her hands. She suddenly felt shy. She hadn't been out to dinner in so long, and especially not with someone she didn't know well. "So what do you do, Michael, besides study whatever you feel like at the moment and rescue hapless pedestrians?"

"It doesn't happen that often," he mumbled, blushing again out in the open without the menu to hide behind. Eva thought it was rather adorable, really. The color looked nice against his eyes. Michael ran a hand through his wavy chestnut hair and sighed. "I don't know, I'm kind of boring. I like hiking, going on trips, things like that."

Pat returned with their tea and cocoa. Eva's had a generous helping of whipped cream on the top, complete with chocolate sprinkles and a cherry. She pulled the cherry off and licked the cream off before popping it into her mouth. "How does someone go from religious studies to physics? They seem to be at opposite ends of the educational spectrum."

Michael swirled his tea in his hands and shrugged. "Religious studies ended up not being what I was looking for," he said, not looking up at her. "But about your essay—do you need any help? I did get most of the way through the program before I quit, and I remember most of it." He took a sip, sucking his cheeks in at the temperature of the drink. "Even though some of the things they teach are absolutely ridiculous."

Eva focused on her whipped cream, the reminder of her schoolwork and her insecurities chasing away her thoughts about her male companion. "Yeah, I know," she said quietly, "but what can you do? No one was there that's still alive today, so all we have is theories."

An odd expression crossed Michael's face, but it was gone before Eva could identify it. "Yeah, I guess," he answered. "I'm pretty sure some of their theories are wrong. But anyway, the offer stands. I did eventually learn what they wanted, though I had learned some of it a bit differently when I was younger."

"I guess it couldn't hurt." Eva took a sip of her cocoa, the whipped cream gathering like a moustache on her upper lip. She ran her tongue along it to get at the cream, not looking at Michael. "I was thinking about going on a trip." She wasn't sure why she was telling him this; it'd been floating in her brain since that afternoon, only now forming a full idea, and surely there were more important people to tell first. She admitted to herself that she was avoiding telling her mother because she knew she wouldn't approve. But something about him made her want to open up. Maybe she was just desperate for a friend. "Over Christmas break. I'm not sure how I'll get the money yet, but I think maybe it'll help me figure out more about school. Or life, or something."

Michael was silent, his green eyes watching her closely.

Eva cupped her hands around her mug. "My thesis is on relating polytheistic religions, specifically the Greek pantheon, to Christianity, looking at how Christianity borrowed things to make up its mythology."

"The Greeks, huh?" Michael said. "Not really a standard influence."

"I know," Eva groaned. "But you know how they want you to try to come at things from a new angle, and I couldn't think of anything else. But maybe I could go to Greece, see some things in person, see if I can straighten my thoughts out and if I want to continue on my current path. I'm beginning to think I won't be able to tell until I go and have a look for myself, to see and touch things that are thousands of years old." She paused, daring to meet his eyes for a moment. "I feel like there's...almost a yearning, to go and do so. My grandmother told me once, about how old buildings have this feeling, this feeling of ancientness and power and countless lives being touched. I haven't been able to stop thinking about that since." Looking down at her drink again, she sighed.

"Money will be an issue, though. I can barely afford school as it is."

Michael reached across the table and took one of her hands in his. "I think it's a good idea," he said, eyes shining. "And I'll help you with your schoolwork if you want me to, and maybe I can help you with your trip too." He paused, cheeks coloring. He withdrew his hand. "I'm so sorry, I didn't mean to be so forward. I just—I feel very comfortable with you." He sighed, tangling both hands in his hair. "Oh God, I'm coming across as a crazy stalker, aren't I?"

His hands had been so warm. Eva was almost chilled with them gone. She examined her drink carefully—the whipped cream was slowly being absorbed into the cocoa proper—and closed her eyes. What was she doing, honestly? She didn't know anything about this guy, but there was something about him that was calming. She felt better at that moment than she had in a while, like the stress had melted away and things were clear. "Let's start with the schoolwork," she said, "and we'll see about the trip later." After all, she just had this urge, this need to go somewhere. "Though I'll have to figure out something to do with Azrael while I'm gone."

Michael spat out his tea and lapsed into a coughing fit. Pat had to come by and smack him on the back to get him to stop.

"Try to be more careful," she admonished as she wandered off again.

"You okay?" asked Eva.

"I'm sorry," said Michael. "I thought you said Azrael. As in the angel of death."

Eva smiled. "He'd probably like that title, but in this case, Azrael is my cat."

"Oh." Michael took a careful sip of his tea. "Interesting choice of name."

"It fits. He's a large, white monstrosity who believes he's in charge." Eva leant her head on one hand. "He probably is. Very intelligent, can open doors and the like. All I wanted was a nice fluffy companion, and I got an aloof troublemaker. He's only loving when he wants something."

Michael smiled. "Not unlike most people. Still, didn't you consider more mundane names, like Horace or something?"

"Horace?" Eva laughed, and it felt nice, to just be sitting around and chatting without worrying about anything. Her essay weighed on the back of her mind, but for the moment it didn't seem to matter. "Has anything been named Horace in the last fifty years?"

"There was that horse in the early Disney cartoons." Michael paused, taking another sip of his tea. "I think."

"Az appreciates his name. It makes him feel important."

Pat reappeared, plates expertly balanced on her arms. "Grilled cheese for the angel, chili for the lovely lady," she said with a wink. "Let me know if you need anything else."

Eva gave her a smile in thanks and scratched behind her ear. Her hair was still somewhat damp, even though

Michael looked like he hadn't been out in the rain at all. The chili was warm and a pleasant aroma whiffed off of it. Eva leaned forward, letting her face soak in its warmth.

"Pat's a good soul," said Michael around a bite of sandwich.

"Hmm," said Eva noncommittally, though she agreed. She ate a spoonful of chili, savoring the warmth, then pointed her utensil at Michael's plate. "Grilled cheese doesn't seem to be a very manly choice," she said teasingly.

Michael rolled his eyes and took another bite.

They ate in relative silence. The chili warmed her from the inside out, and by the time she was finished, she was cozy, dry, a little sleepy, and content. It was a good night. Maybe Rafe was right, and it wouldn't hurt her to socialize a little more than she did. Belatedly, Eva wondered if this counted as a date. She couldn't remember the last time she'd gone on one, but she remembered them being awkward and horrible. Plus she didn't date. It didn't fit into her plans. No, not a date, then. Just two friends spending some time together.

Then Michael turned those eyes on her and she found herself hoping that maybe it was.

Michael paused mid-bite. "You okay?"

Eva realized she'd been staring, her spoon suspended in the air. She gave her head a shake and forced herself to slowly, calmly place the spoon back on the table. "Sorry, just got lost on a train of thought. So, um, you said you'd help with my schoolwork. I have an essay right now, so I don't know how that'll work."

"Let's meet on Friday and we can discuss the subject, so you can get your thoughts all in order." Michael finished his sandwich and wiped his fingers on a napkin. "After that, all you have to do is write it down, and one of my roommates is a grammartarian or whatever he likes to call himself, so maybe he can look it over for you and catch any spelling mistakes or odd wordings."

Eva beamed. "That would be great. I tend to do a lot of research and then I can't ever seem to put anything in a coherent order. My mother says I stuff in too much information. She compares it to having the whole family over for Christmas dinner and how it takes forever to get anyone to do anything because there are too many inputs."

"Your mother sounds like a smart woman." Michael waved Pat over and offered her a credit card without even looking for the bill.

"About some things, sure." Eva didn't expand, despite Michael's questioning look. Part of her mind rejoiced at the thought of a free meal, but her pride made some complaints. "Oh no, I can pay for my half." She wasn't sure that was true, but she was fairly sure it was rude to dig out her wallet and check.

Michael shook his head. "No, no, I insist."

Eva leaned back against the back of the booth. "You save me from becoming a traffic statistic, offer to help me with my homework, and buy me dinner. I'm beginning to agree with Pat that you are an angel."

The tips of Michael's ears turned pink and he let out a strained laugh, but he looked pleased. Eva smiled.

"It's the least I can do," he said as Pat returned with the receipt, "for the honor of your company."

Eva's mouth dropped open. Did people actually talk like that? Was he serious? She couldn't tell.

Michael gave her a half-smile. "Weird and stalkery again, isn't it?"

"Oh no," Eva breathed more than said, unsure if he would hear her, but his smile became more genuine as he bent over the receipt and flowingly signed his name.

"Do you need an escort home?" he asked as he finished.

Eva didn't honestly mind if he came home with her—quite frankly, the whole evening had been a bit of a novelty that she wasn't sure she wanted to end—but she imagined her mother's face if she learned her daughter had invited a man over whom she'd just met and barely knew. A little moderation was no doubt the responsible thing to do. "No, thank you," she said. "I only live a short distance away."

If he was disappointed, Michael didn't show it. He helped Eva back into her coat and backpack and retrieved Gabe's mangled umbrella for her before putting on his own coat and tucking his hands in his pockets. He followed her out of the restaurant and gave her a small smile. "See you Friday," he said before turning and walking back down the street.

It was still raining a bit, but nowhere near as hard as it had been earlier. Eva watched him disappear into the mist, wondering if she was missing an opportunity she should have taken, and then made her own way home.

IT WAS MORE of a struggle than Michael expected to make it to the end of the street without turning around, and when he finally did, Eva was nowhere in sight. He sighed, letting his shoulders drop. He was getting much too old for this sort of thing. Every part of his brain said to leave this girl alone, and yet his actions said they weren't even trying to pay attention to the plan.

Well, this morning had been pure accident. And he wasn't about to just let someone get run over by a car. But he should have stopped it then. Made sure she was all right, sent her on her way. But no, he had to invite her to dinner. And even then, he could—should—have ended things. Wished her well on her essay and on her trip. But no, he hadn't. Something about just being around her eased a long-seated ache in his soul that he'd never thought would lessen.

There was something about her, something almost familiar, but he couldn't put his finger on exactly what it was. But whatever it was called to him, and that was dangerous and needed to be stopped.

Well, after Friday.

Michael tucked his hands in his pocket and wandered toward his own apartment, letting his mind drift. He hoped his roommates would be home when he got there so he wouldn't be alone with his thoughts.

"Well, you're the last person I expected to see walking in the rain."

Michael froze, slowly lifting his head to peer through the light rain toward the source of the voice. There, leaning up against a darkened storefront, fire-red hair perfectly coifed, face as lovely as ever, green eyes almost glowing, was someone he had not seen in a very long time. "I find it grows on you, over time," he said.

She pushed away from the building, as graceful as a tiger, and sauntered toward him. "Come, Michael," she said, "you haven't really been here that long."

He shrugged, unwilling to fight about it. "Why are you here, Lily?"

"Look at you," she replied. She stopped right in front of him, peering up at his face. "Where's your fire, Michael? You're as timid as a field mouse."

He was too tired for this, too confused from dealing with Eva earlier. With a shake of his head, he turned and headed back in his original direction.

Lily caught his arm. He let her turn him back around. "Can't you muster up anything more than that? For me? I used to be able to make you burn—in more ways than one." She opened her eyes wide, pleading.

Michael sighed. She really was quite beautiful, but he knew better now than to fall into her trap. "Lily, if you're not going to tell me why you're here, then I don't want to bother with all this. It's not worth it anymore."

She seemed disappointed, maybe even a little sad. "Fine," she said. "I'm here because Sam asked me to come."

"I didn't know you were still in contact with Sam." He'd been vaguely aware that Sam was here—had seen him across campus, sometimes felt his presence elsewhere in town—but his presence was so rare that Michael had never given it much thought.

"Oh, you know," she said, flashing a flirty grin. "He calls me up every few decades when he's bored and needs something to do."

Michael stared down at her, trying to decipher what she meant. It was entirely possible that she meant what she said at face value, but only someone who didn't know her would take Lily at her word. She liked to layer in innuendos and hints without coming straight out about anything.

"Michael," she said, suddenly serious, "you know I regret what happened. And I wanted to let you know that I'm here, if you want a second chance." She pressed up onto her toes, lightly laying her lips against his cheek. "You'll know where to find me if you want me."

With that, she disappeared back into the shadows, out of the reach of the cheerfully lit streetlights. She was gone as quickly as she'd come, without even a hint that she'd ever been there.

Rubbing his cheek, Michael was left to puzzle about the meaning of that last statement as well.

Chapter Three

"YOU KNOW what you look like you need?" Eva looked up at Sam, who was draped over the back of the chair next to her. He continued, "You look like you need something to take your mind off of schoolwork. I have just the thing."

Eva smiled and shook her head. As she packed her bag, she watched several of her fellow students swarm Professor Axelrad, no doubt looking for help on their essays. Poor souls.

"Come on," Sam said, "you're not going to blow me off again, are you? I happen to know that you don't have to get to work quite yet."

"Fine," Eva said, twisting in her seat to look at him. "What do I so desperately need, Mr. Payne?"

"You need distraction. A hobby. Something not related to world religions." Sam waved one hand to demonstrate. He leaned in closer, resting his head on his arms. "I am starting a group. You should join it. We're going to change the world. Plus, as of now, it's a standing motion that there will be ice cream at every meeting."

"Hm," said Eva.

"Because so far it's just me, and maybe you," Sam elaborated, "so we can do whatever we want. What do you say?"

Eva shook her head again. "You know, I think a lot of religions would say their goal is to change the world. How do I know you're not starting a cult? Charismatic leader with the ability to convince people to do his bidding, and all that."

Sam laughed, a loud, pleasant noise that caused several of their classmates to look in their direction. "Well, I promise it won't be a cult. How's that?"

"I don't know, Sam." Eva stood, slinging her backpack over one shoulder. She needed to get to the library soon to meet Michael, and every time she thought about that, she felt nauseated. In the light of day, with reality staring her in the face, she wasn't sure what she'd been thinking. "Politics isn't really my thing."

Sam stood, laying a hand on her shoulder. "Come on, Eva," he said earnestly, "haven't you ever felt out of place? Like you don't quite fit into this world? Have you ever lain in bed in the morning wondering what your purpose is and why it's so hard to find it, and why it seems like everyone else has?"

Eva stared at him, unnerved by how each question touched something somewhere inside her and gave a little twist. After a moment, she forced herself to laugh. "I don't know, I'm leaning toward charismatic cult leader."

Sam smiled, indulging her poor joke. "Just think about it, will you? Now, as you don't have to work quite yet, how about that coffee I promised you?"

She hated to say no once again. "I can't," she said, trying to stuff all her regret into her voice so he'd know that she really meant it. "I've got to work on that essay." Sam probably already had his done. He never seemed to be worried about schoolwork.

"I'll come too," Sam replied, pulling his own bag over his shoulder.

"I'm...meeting a friend," Eva said quickly. But then that sounded...mean, or something, like she didn't think he'd get along with her friend, or, more simply, that she didn't want him along. She winced.

"Oh, hey," Sam said, smiling even though it was obviously fake, "no worries. I get it." He turned, heading up the aisle, the slump in his shoulders showing how hurt he actually was.

"Wait, Sam," Eva called after him. When he turned around, she continued. "Maybe next week we could get coffee before class sometime? Then we won't have to worry about me having to get to work."

He grinned, a brilliant smile that put his usual one to shame. "Awesome! Let's do Monday, so you can't figure out a way to sneak out of it. The coffee shop by the engineering building? I'll meet you there at 10:30." Before Eva could get a word in edgewise, he was gone, half-skipping up the stairs and out of the room.

"Well," she said out loud.

Students were starting to trickle in for the next class, so Eva hurried outside, pondering the sudden shift in her life over the past few days. Sam had asked her to hang out before, certainly, but he seemed to be pursuing the idea more determinedly recently, and then there was Michael. Since she'd met him, the dream had changed. Now his hair was the same as it was in real life, and he'd smiled more, held her more, and Eva was a little concerned about her subconscious and what it was trying to imply.

For a moment, she paused just outside on the quad, looking across the expanse of grass toward the library. She could turn and walk away, and never see him again. Who dreamed about some random guy that turned out to be real? And who continued to dream about said guy in a romantic fashion after meeting the real one?

Still, there was something...something familiar, something right. And what Sam had said earlier was true; she did feel out of place, like something was missing, a lot. And maybe spending more time with Michael would be a good thing. Maybe she'd figure out why things seemed...better ordered...when he was around.

And she'd disappointed one guy already today.

Straightening, Eva pulled her bag up, and then started toward the library. It's not like it was a date, after all; it was just homework. They had decided on the library because it was centrally located on campus, near the University Center. Michael was no doubt coming from some very exciting physics class, where problems had exact answers and it was impossible to get in trouble for having theories that disagreed with the professor's preconceptions of things. He liked the study rooms on the second floor and so they were to meet there, though Eva had never used one.

The library itself was made of granite or marble in some sort of neoclassical style, with impressive columns out front, trying to look respectable and elegant and belonging to an era that it most certainly didn't. Eva pushed her way through the revolving door and headed toward one of the many staircases. She suspected that the interior hadn't been updated in several decades. The carpet was an odd, faded yellow color, and the walls were blindingly white without anything hanging on them, except for the few unmatched paintings that sprang up in the stairways.

The second floor was easily reached, but as she'd never been to these study rooms, she wasn't exactly sure where they were. Her heart began to beat hard against her sternum as she moved through the stacks in search of them. It wasn't a date, she reminded herself again. Homework was never a date. Unless it was some weird grad-student mating ritual she was completely unaware of because she hardly ever worked with other people.

She finally found the study rooms on the other side of the floor, of course, and she was a good fifteen minutes late before she found Michael seated in one. He had a stack of books on the table and was sitting with his hands folded together in front of him, though he seemed to be lost in his thoughts. Eva almost didn't want to disturb him. Her heart fluttered in her chest.

Taking a deep breath, Eva pushed open the door and gave him a smile as he looked up. "Sorry I'm late. Turns out I don't actually know the layout of the library very well."

Michael blinked at her for a moment, then shook his head and smiled. "Sorry, I'm afraid I spaced out there. It's just—no, never mind."

Curiosity rose in Eva but as she stepped in and caught sight of the titles of the books he'd brought, the thought was driven from her mind. "What are these?" She picked one up, running her finger along the binding. "Wow, how did you get this? I looked on Amazon and eBay and I haven't seen a copy yet."

"Believe me, it took some effort." Michael took the book from her. "I have some connections in the bookselling industry, though, so I did get it eventually, though not in the time frame I had hoped. I was done with religious studies long before I found a copy, but I did read it and I found it very interesting." He gestured at the books. "I thought maybe we could use them as references if we needed to."

"It's nice of you to bring your own reference materials along," said Eva as she slid into one of the other chairs. *Who brings along their own books for someone they hardly know?* She wasn't sure whether to be impressed or not, so she opened her bag and added her own books to the pile on the table. "So for this essay, we're supposed to explain the Nephilim."

Michael nodded slowly. "Are you supposed to defend one of the popular theories, like that they were offspring of fallen angels and human women, or the one where the phrase 'sons of God' refers to men from Adam's lineage and the 'daughters of men' are from Cain's, or are you supposed to make up your own?"

"The exact wording of the assignment is 'Explain the Nephilim,' so it sounds like you could put forward any theory on the matter that you would like, but I think I've learned my lesson by now." Eva leaned forward, resting her elbows on the table. "I was leaning more toward the second one, the lineage one. The angel theory seems farfetched to me. After all, angels are kind of an interesting topic. Some texts assert that angels have no free will and have to do what God intends them to, and that doesn't seem like something God would want, especially since the Nephilim then supposedly go around tearing up the countryside and have to be wiped out with the flood. And then some scholars say that angels are genderless, and then one wonders how exactly they're procreating with anything, and that brings up a whole genetic sort of argument, like are angels and humans able to breed with one another in the first place? How many chromosomes do angels have?"

Michael laughed. "I'm not sure anyone has ever asked that question before."

"And," continued Eva, "what if angels are made of spirit to begin with? How does a non-corporeal being mate with a corporeal one and create offspring?"

"All very good points," agreed Michael, "though I like to think of angels as corporeal, gendered beings with free will. How does that figure into your argument?"

Eva ran her fingers along the binding of one of her books. "Assuming that angels are corporeal, gendered beings with free will, I suppose it would be possible, but you'd think that it wouldn't have been a one-time thing then. Sure, the first bunch was supposedly imprisoned by Michael—where was it now..."

"In a valley, to await the end of the world, if I remember correctly," said Michael. "And I might not, it has been a while."

"Anyway, they're locked up and the Nephilim are destroyed in the flood—though I kind of wonder how Noah kept them away from the ark, if they were really such a menace—but it seems to me that in the many thousands of years since then, surely there would have been other angels who thought they'd have a go, someone who thought they could get away with it on the sly or something." She paused, scratching behind her ear. "Plus, you know, there's no guarantee that angels even exist. There have hardly been any miracles in recent times that have been attributed to them at all."

"So you don't want to go for the angel angle," said Michael.

"No," said Eva, "and even though it's a popular theory I suspect the whole Adam/Cain thing will get me in trouble in the end, but I just...I don't know if I could do the angel theory justice. It just seems a bit silly to me, and I would be tempted to add in snide remarks as I wrote it, and then I'd forget to take them out again, and I'm not sure it would actually get me a better grade in the end."

Michael nodded. "So, the other theory."

"Right," said Eva. "So, from what I understand, you've got Adam and Eve, kicked out of the Garden of Eden, and they have two children, Cain and Abel. And, oh man, I can never get which of the two of them is which—Cain is the shepherd and Abel is the farmer, maybe?—anyway, God approves of Abel's offering and Cain kills him in a jealous rage and dumps the body in a pit."

"Bad times all around," said Michael. "And Adam and Eve find him and Cain is exiled and wanders off."

"Right, and then, even though Adam and Eve are supposedly the first people, Cain manages to find other people and reproduce and so forth, and Adam and Eve have more children who also have children, and the idea is that the children of Adam are the sons of God because they're favored by God, whereas the children of Cain are of man because they are not."

After a little more back and forth, Eva decided to go the Adam and Cain route. The discussion went on for some time, and she found it very helpful. Michael listened to her thoughts and never interrupted her or told her she was silly, though every now and then that odd smile he had would flash across his face. Eva wondered what exactly that meant, but she'd be distracted moments later by some other thought. She made a long list of notes as they went, and when it got to be around 3 o'clock, she gathered up her books—and one of Michael's that she was going to borrow—and thanked him for his help.

Michael blinked. "Already?"

"I've got to get to work. It's best that I don't delay giving my boss his umbrella back any longer, when it will only cause more pain."

"It is truly lamentable when an umbrella goes to its doom," said Michael. He gathered up the remaining books, sliding them into a blue shoulder bag. "I did want you to meet my roommate, though, the one who likes grammar so much. He's kind of solitary, but I think he'd like you and be willing to help."

"Maybe for the next essay," said Eva with a smile. "My professor is very fond of them, after all, and I'm sure we'll turn the current ones in and barely make it to our seats before we've got another one to do."

Michael stood. "Maybe for the next one, then. But I think I'll go and see him anyway. I'd talk to him if he was ever at home, but he tends to lose track of time and wander in at odd hours." He looked toward the door, and Eva realized that they were going to have to say goodbye and she wasn't quite sure how to go about doing so.

"Well, I do appreciate your help," she said again. "We'll do this again sometime, I guess." She didn't know what to say. She wouldn't mind spending more time with him, that was certain, but she couldn't construct a reason to see him outside of school. To be honest, she didn't do much in the realm of extracurricular activities.

Rafe would tell her to try something new, but nothing sprang to mind.

"I could give you my cell number," offered Michael, "and then you could call me if you wanted help again."

Eva gave a wan smile. "I'm afraid I don't have a cell at the moment." She could offer him her home number, but she had a system, and if she actually thought someone she wanted to talk to might call, then it would screw everything all up.

"Ah. Well," replied Michael. He rubbed at the back of his head uncomfortably. "Email then? You must have email, the university gives that terrible web-based email to everyone."

"Email! Yes," said Eva. She set her bag down and pulled out her notebook, ripping out a blank sheet of paper. She tore it in half and gave one piece to Michael, then jotted down her own email address on the other and offered it to him. "It probably is the best way to get a hold of me other than random meetings on the street."

Michael took the offered piece and returned the other. Eva glanced at it briefly; his handwriting was very neat, easily readable and more formal than she would have expected. She slid the paper into one of her books where it wouldn't easily fall out somewhere.

That awkward silence descended again. Eva fidgeted with the zipper on her bag, but still the ideas did not come. Sighing, she gave up. "Well, I'd better go."

"Yes," said Michael, quick to latch on to something other than that awful silence. "I'll walk you out."

They left the study room and moved through the stacks of books, Michael leading the way in the confident manner of those who had been there before and knew exactly where they were going. There was something warm about his mere presence, and Eva found herself keeping close to him just to feel it against her skin.

It had started drizzling and Eva pulled the hood of her sweatshirt up. Hopefully the rain wouldn't get any heavier before she made it to work.

"Which way are you heading?" Michael asked, digging an umbrella out of his bag. His was blue with butterflies on it. Eva stared. "It's my roommate's," he explained with a shrug of his shoulders. "Man loves an oddly colored umbrella, and I couldn't find mine this morning so I just grabbed one of his." He put it in his pocket. "No sense using it quite yet, but it helps to have it handy, just in case."

Eva pointed in the general direction of the bookstore.

"I'm going that way too." Michael offered Eva his arm and she took it, curling her fingers around his warmth. It was oddly comforting.

Campus was relatively empty, it being Friday afternoon. What few students were left walked at a leisurely pace between the buildings, the light rain not being enough to worry about. It was the end of the week, after all, and even though many people would have to spend a significant amount of their weekend on homework, it was still a cause for celebration and relaxing.

"Just let me know when we need to part ways," said Michael. He patted her hand on his arm and gave her a smile. Her heart missed a beat.

Don't get so excited, she chastised herself as they started up the street the bookstore was on, the same street he'd saved her on a few nights previously. She wondered where he lived, to have been out in this area as late as she had been. It couldn't be too far from her apartment.

She almost missed the bookstore, being so caught up in her own thoughts. "Oh!" she said. "This is it."

Michael blinked at her. "Really? You work here?"

Eva nodded, ducking her head a little. "I know. Nerdy, isn't it? But I really enjoy it." She pulled her arm out of Michael's, a little disappointed at the sudden chill of the air. "Thank you again for everything." She reached for the handle of the door at the same moment Michael did. Their fingers touched and Eva felt a little shock. She pulled her hand back reflexively, only half-noticing Michael do the same.

He was staring at her, his green eyes incomprehensible, but Eva thought perhaps he looked slightly confused.

"Sorry," she said. She felt her cheeks burning, though she wasn't quite sure why, so she reached for the door again and pulled it open.

To her very great surprise, Michael followed her inside. The bell chimed but there was no sign of either Rafe or Gabe, the register left unmanned. Unsure what to do about Michael, she automatically went behind the counter, dropping her bag next the stool. Michael stayed just inside the door, hands in his pockets, brow furrowed.

"Hey, darling!" came Rafe's voice from somewhere in the vicinity of the history textbooks.

That seemed to wake Michael up. A slow smile spread across his face. "I hope you're not talking to me," he said.

Rafe let out a loud laugh. After a moment he emerged from the shelves, a large amount of dust spotting his t-shirt, which only got worse as he wiped his hands on it. "Well, bless my soul, if it isn't my wayward roommate." He clapped Michael on the back. "Well, no, I was referring to the pretty lady by the register, but I suppose you can be a darling too if you really want."

"I think I'll pass," said Michael. "Where's Gabe at?"

"No doubt in the office playing solitaire," replied Rafe. He shook his head. "You'd think by now he would have gotten sick of that silly game."

"Gabe is a man who can really get behind something," said Michael. "I'll just let myself in then?"

"Let me introduce you to our lovely employee on the way," said Rafe. "Eva's been with us for a few months now, which you'd know if you ever bothered to come by. Physics cannot possibly be that interesting."

Michael colored slightly. "I actually already know Eva. We walked here together. And physics can be that interesting, thank you very much. There are new developments all the time, and it's nice to be exposed to something new."

Rafe looked from Michael to Eva. "Hmmm, really. Forget the physics, how long have you known Eva? Lovely girl, needs to get out more." He waggled his eyebrows.

"Rafe!" protested Eva.

Michael turned a brighter shade of pink and punched Rafe in the shoulder. "God! I forgot why I don't hang out with you."

Eva took a moment to glance between the two men. Gabe and Rafe had always seemed oddly timeless to her, but she'd place them in their early 30s if asked. Michael seemed younger, somehow—she'd thought he was only a few years older than herself—but if they were all roommates, he probably wasn't.

"You need to get out more, too," said Rafe, placing his hands on his hips. "Seriously, do you ever do anything other than study? The world is passing you by."

Michael groaned, clenching and unclenching his fists. "We're not going to fight about this again, Rafe. Especially not right now. Listen, I'm just going to go talk to Gabe, okay?"

"Suit yourself," said Rafe. He watched Michael as the latter pushed through the office door and disappeared. Then, shaking his head, he joined Eva behind the counter. "Sooooo," he said.

Eva sighed. "Maybe you're the one who needs to get out more, Rafe, so you stop living vicariously through other people."

Rafe grinned. "This is why I keep you around. The witty banter. Plus you add a nice, feminine touch to the shop."

Eva looked around. She couldn't see it. "Uh-huh," she said.

"Anyway, spill it. If I'm going to live vicariously through other people, I need details." Rafe pulled up another stool and stared intently at Eva, opening his eyes wide in an exaggerated manner.

His eyes were green too, she realized in surprise. Surely she should have noticed that before, since that wasn't common in people of his race, but she admittedly wasn't in the habit of gazing into her boss's eyes. What were the odds of all three roommates having green—and what looked suspiciously like the same shade of green—eyes?

"Eva?" asked Rafe, forehead furrowing.

"Your eyes are green," she said.

Rafe grinned again. "A true statement. Eyes are the gateway to the soul, you know." He accompanied this statement with a flutter of his eyelashes. The action looked very strange on him, and Eva couldn't help laughing. "Now, anyway, talk."

"There's not really that much to tell," she said, looking away. "I met him at school, and then I ran into him the other night and we had dinner and," she paused, "oh, I forgot about Gabe's umbrella."

"What?" Rafe blinked.

Eva unzipped her bag and pulled out the mangled umbrella. "Some car tried to run me over but luckily it only got the umbrella."

Rafe poked at the umbrella. "Wow, that's pretty bad. Gabe will get over it, though; it's not like he doesn't own a couple dozen of the things. I think he likes the sound the rain makes on them, or something. He also has a thing about galoshes."

"Are they bright green?" asked Eva. "So, Michael's your roommate, huh? I thought it was just you and Gabe."

"No, it's all three of us," said Rafe, leaning against the counter. "We offered to have Michael come into the business with us but he loves school. He gets bored pretty easily, and he'd probably have set the store on fire by now if he was trapped here day in and day out. Which would be pretty funny, actually." Rafe tapped a finger on his cheek. "I'll have to remember that one. There's not enough pyrotechnics in life these days."

Eva raised an eyebrow. "Sometimes I don't have any idea what you're talking about."

Rafe patted her on the shoulder. "Don't worry about it, hon. I think the dust gets into my brain sometimes. Anyway, yes. The three of us have been together for a long time."

"How long?" Eva tried to imagine the three of them as children, playing in a sandbox. Rafe would probably be trying to get everyone else to eat sand.

"Long as I can remember," replied Rafe. "Though Michael moving in with us is a more recent development, but he's always been nearby."

The office door opened and Michael stepped out, followed by Gabe. The latter caught sight of the umbrella and let out a cry.

"I'm really sorry, Gabe," Eva said as the tall redhead gingerly took the bright-green, mangled monstrosity.

"It's not her fault," said Michael. "I'm afraid it's mine."

"Anyway, I'll pay for it," said Eva.

"No," said Rafe and Michael in unison. They looked at each other, and then Michael continued. "It's not your fault, Eva. Anyway, I think we'll all agree that we'd rather that the car got the umbrella instead than you."

"Still, I feel responsible," replied Eva. "Isn't there something I could do?"

"No, no, don't worry about it," said Gabe, though he looked miserable. "Maybe I could have Sam look at it? He's good with metal, isn't he?"

Rafe wrinkled his nose. "Ugh."

"I don't think he's as good with the alloys," replied Michael, sounding faintly disapproving. "Plus really, I wouldn't trust him. Not after that last bit."

"The last bit?" echoed Eva, wondering if it was the same Sam she knew. After a second, she dismissed the thought. Her Sam seemed like a perfectly nice person, and it was a fairly common name. "What did he do that was so bad?" She was vaguely aware that perhaps she should keep her mouth shut—after all, this was none of her business, and she would prefer to keep these people as friends—but curiosity got the better of her.

The three men blinked at her, then looked at each other. Michael stuck his hands back into his pockets and kicked one foot at the floor while Gabe unconsciously clasped his umbrella tighter. Rafe glanced at his roommates, then crossed his arms across his chest. "He stole Michael's girlfriend," he said.

Michael's mouth dropped open. "Rafe!"

"And," continued Rafe, "then he tried to steal his friends too, but luckily Gabe and I are not susceptible to such crap. Well, I am not susceptible to such crap, and Gabe is too distracted to focus on such things."

Michael groaned and hid his face in his hands.

Rafe laid a hand on Michael's shoulder. "I know you didn't want her to know, but it's better this way, I promise."

"I'm going home," said Michael. "Let me know if you need any more help, Eva, and I'll see you around." Without another word, he disappeared out the door into the rain beyond.

"Help?" said Rafe, rubbing the back of his bald head.

"He was helping me with my homework," replied Eva, leaning on one hand.

"Not dating, then?"

"Not at the moment, no," said Eva. "Perhaps never, if you're going to traumatize him. He'll probably just sit in his room and read about physics."

"Bugger," said Rafe, tapping a finger against his temple. "Well, I guess I'll apologize later tonight when I get home. Or tomorrow. Not sure how late we're staying open yet tonight, and, contrary to popular belief, I have a date myself tonight." He accompanied this last statement with an eyebrow waggle at Gabe, who rolled his eyes.

Eva tapped her fingers on the counter. "Stole his girlfriend, you said?"

"Dreadfully tragic affair," said Rafe. "Michael really had a thing for her. Though we were never really sure if she went of her own accord, if you know what I mean. We try not to be too friendly with Sam. The guy's kind of a loose cannon, has an odd idea of what is acceptable."

"Now, now," said Gabe, waving his umbrella at Rafe, "no reason to talk behind his back. After all, maybe he's changed."

Rafe snorted. "I don't believe that, and neither do you."

Gabe shrugged. "Anyway, can we all get back to work now?"

"I don't call solitaire work," said Rafe, grinning.

Gabe bristled. "I am doing things other than that too." He scowled at Rafe and returned to the office, slamming the door behind him. A couple books on the shelves behind the counter toppled over.

Rafe shook his head. "Now I have angered both roommates. I'm having a fine day. At least you're still with me, hon." He patted Eva on the shoulder and headed back towards the books.

"Rafe," called Eva after him. He stopped and raised an eyebrow at her questioningly. "I'm...I'm thinking about taking a trip soon. Over winter break, maybe. Try to figure out where I'm going, what I want to do."

He nodded slowly. "Don't worry about taking time off or anything; Gabe and I will be okay by ourselves for however long it takes. Mental health is more important than anything else in this life, so you do what you need to do." With that, he continued on into the books, humming an unknown song to himself.

Eva leaned back in her stool with a sigh, trying to process the new information she'd learned this afternoon. Why did Michael's presence make her heart beat and her soul sing?

Chapter Four

At 10:30, as promised, Eva was waiting at the coffee shop by the engineering building. She'd never been on this side of campus before. She couldn't help but stare at the engineering building, which was a large monstrosity of a structure and looked more than a little like an evil lair whose denizens were secretly planning world domination. Maybe they were. Eva didn't actually know any engineers.

Sam was late, which in itself was not odd, because Eva had noticed that he liked to test the limits of what he could get away with, and that included timeliness. But she had thought, what with how persistent he'd been lately about hanging out, that he'd at least make an effort for her.

"Eva!"

She turned, smiling, but her smile froze almost immediately. Sam was walking toward her, waving, but right behind him, and obviously accompanying him, was a gorgeous redhead Eva had never seen before. For a moment, she was awash in confusion, unsure of what she had expected and what she had thought the point of them hanging out was. Sure, he'd never said anything about it being just the two of them—except for that whole thing about ice cream—but still, she'd thought...what? That he was interested in her? She must have read too much into things. Probably from being out of practice.

She forced the smile back into being as Sam and the redhead reached her. "Good morning," she said.

Sam grinned, taking one of her hands. "Eva, this is Lily. Lily, Eva."

Eva nodded at Lily. "Nice to meet you."

"The pleasure is mine," Lily said, taking Eva's other hand. "Sam's told me so much about you."

"Has he?" Eva glanced between the two of them. Sam brushed his dark hair out of his eyes—his green eyes, and now Eva could see that they were very similar in color to Gabe's, Rafe's, and Michael's as well—smiling widely. Lily was also smiling, almost demurely, and she kept her attention entirely on Eva. Her brilliant hair was carefully curled in a manner that made it look effortless, though it had probably taken hours, and she was wearing an unseasonable sundress, but didn't seem to be cold. "I wish I could say the same." Lily's eyes were definitely the same color as Sam's. What on Earth was with everyone she knew having green eyes? She hadn't thought they were that common.

Sam's expression faltered a bit. "Something wrong?"

Eva realized she'd been staring. "Sorry, it's just—I was just noticing that your eyes were the same color."

Lily laughed, then leaned forward conspiratorially. "We're cousins. Runs in the family."

Something relaxed in Eva's chest a little. "Oh. Cousins." Aside from the eyes, they didn't look similar, but hey, weirder things were true.

"I asked Lily to come help me get my group going," Sam said, patting the redhead affectionately on the shoulder. "She's good at that sort of thing."

"And I wasn't doing anything that couldn't be put on hold, so here I am," Lily concluded.

"Anyway," Sam said, gesturing to the shop, "I believe I promised you coffee."

As Eva turned to go in, she caught a look that passed between the two of them. It was momentary, hardly noticeable, but Sam glowered at Lily and she smirked, both looks completely at odds with the front they'd been putting up a moment earlier. Eva shook her head, putting it out of her mind. Family was weird. It was probably about something completely unrelated.

Once inside, Eva looked up at the menu boards. Coffee was something she didn't have very often, both because she didn't have the budget for it and because she preferred to time her being awake with the sun, so she wasn't terribly familiar with the offerings.

"It's on me," Sam said, all smiles and good cheer again. He held up a hand when Eva opened her mouth to protest. "No, I insist."

The three of them placed their orders and then retreated to a small table in the corner. Eva found herself seated in between Sam and Lily—not that she wouldn't have been, with only three of them—but they both seemed much closer to her than to each other. "So, Lily," Eva said, feeling less threatened now, "did you really come just to help Sam with his group?"

Lily leaned forward, resting her head on top of her hands. It put her face almost uncomfortably close to Eva's, and she had to resist backing away. "I love Sam's schemes, and this one promises to be an excellent one. Should be the best we've had in, oh, years."

"It is not a 'scheme,'" Sam interjected, narrowing his eyes.

"But to answer your question," continued Lily, ignoring Sam completely, "I think I shall also take this opportunity to visit some old friends."

Sam sat up straighter at that, obviously surprised, and the look he gave Lily said that he definitely didn't approve. But a moment later, it was gone again, replaced by his smile. "I still say you should join. It's going to be fun. And we're going to make a difference."

Eva sighed. "I really don't know, Sam. Between school and work, I'm pretty full."

"Aw, now, don't be like that," said Lily in a low, sultry voice. It was almost calming, in some way. Eva looked at her in surprise. "You should give it a try before you make a decision. After all, you know what they say?"

"What do they say?" Eva found herself focusing on Lily's lips and forced herself to look away, blushing.

"Don't knock what you haven't tried," replied Lily. She straightened as their order was called out, watching as Sam stood to retrieve it. Her eyes lingered on him for a moment, but then she turned back to Eva, leaning in again. "Sam means well. And I worry about him, sometimes. He doesn't have a lot of friends here at school. It would mean a lot to him if you'd come a few times at least. And who knows? Maybe you'll find that you like it." She leaned away again, playing idly with a few of her copper curls. "Besides, there is the free ice cream I hear about."

Eva looked up, meeting Lily's eyes, and for a moment, she couldn't look away. But then Sam returned, setting Eva's drink down in front of her. "I hope you weren't talking about me," he said, grinning, "unless it was only good things."

"Mmm," said Lily noncommittally, still looking at Eva.

"I was thinking," Sam said, taking a sip of his own drink, "that we'd have mint chocolate chip at the first meeting. How much should I get, Eva?"

Eva glanced between the two of them, both watching her eagerly, knowing smiles on their faces. "Fine," she said, "I'll come. When is it?"

"Thursday," Sam replied immediately, obviously anticipating her response. "11 o'clock in the study rooms in the library. You know where those are?"

Well, she did now. Her thoughts momentarily strayed to Michael, but she forced them back on track. "How will you have ice cream in the library?"

"I'll bring it," Lily said. "I have my ways."

Eva was tempted to ask what said ways were, but there was something about Lily that made her distinctly uncomfortable. Maybe it was that the other girl was a little too friendly. Instead, she took the opportunity to look around the coffee shop, taking note of the other students present, many of whom seemed to be working on homework. She caught sight of a clock hanging on the wall and groaned; it was almost time for class. "We'd better go," she said to Sam.

"Aw, don't let ol' Axelrad get to you," he said, but he obediently stood, slinging his bag over his shoulder and picking up his coffee. He brushed his hair out of his eyes again, then waited for Eva to lead the way out. Once outside, he fell into step on Eva's right side, while Lily settled in on her left.

"Are you coming with us to class?" Eva asked, feeling slightly trapped, though she couldn't quite identify why.

"No, but I'll walk over there with you." Lily shuddered. "Ugh, I can't imagine anything worse than that religious rot. I don't know how you stand it." She directed this last comment directly at Sam, who flushed and looked away. Eva watched him for a moment, wondering why the comment got to him, but was distracted when Lily took her hand. Lily's hand was frigid against hers, to the point where it was almost painful to touch. "Eva, darling, I feel like I already know you so well. Perhaps we were friends in a past life."

"Uh," said Eva.

"Sam too," Lily continued. "Can't you feel it? Once upon a time, we knew each other and were friends."

Eva glanced over at Sam, to see if he was buying this, when there was a flash of something...a lush garden, surrounded by sand in all directions. And a forest, ancient and wild, lost to history, and a sense of being alone and lost and utterly confused.

She stopped mid-step. Sam and Lily continued another pace beyond her, both turning to look at her, surprised.

"Eva?" Sam asked after a moment. "What is it?"

Eva forced herself back into the present, shaking her head slightly to clear it of the...vision? Memory? Hallucination? Both Sam and Lily were still watching her, but Eva wasn't willing to share. "We'd better hurry," she said instead, gently freeing her hand from Lily's. She straightened her bag and hurried on, not waiting to see if the others would follow.

MICHAEL STARED at the front of the bookstore, not quite sure why he was there. Yes, he had nothing better to do at the moment, but he still wasn't sure why here was where he'd ended up, especially since he didn't usually come to visit Gabe and Rafe at work. It tended to remind him of how he was all alone.

I know why you're here, whispered a voice somewhere in his mind, but Michael ignored it. Well, he couldn't stand outside forever. People were beginning to stare. He squared his shoulders, then pushed the door open.

The bookstore was in its usual disarray. Rafe was nowhere to be seen, but Gabe, to Michael's surprise, was seated behind the counter. The taller man leaned forward as Michael stepped inside, setting his elbows on the counter and then his head on his hands. "Ah, Michael. Good. I want to talk to you."

Michael knew that tone of voice all too well. He glanced at the door, seriously considering running for it.

Gabe straightened and sighed. "Don't be like that."

"Like what?" Michael replied, though he was aware he was fooling no one. Aside from Gabe and himself, the bookstore seemed deserted, though he assumed Rafe was lurking somewhere.

"She's not here," Gabe said.

"I wasn't looking for her," Michael said, and again, that tiny, traitorous voice said, *weren't you?*

"Anyway," Gabe said. He stood, pushing open the door to the back office. "Why don't you come in? There's something we should discuss."

Giving the door one last, forlorn look, Michael followed Gabe into the office. As he went, the redheaded man pulled out a chair, but Michael ignored it. This was probably going to be unpleasant enough without feeling like Gabe was looming over him.

"Shut the door behind you," Gabe said. He leaned against his desk, crossing his arms over his chest. He stared at Michael expectantly.

Michael stared back.

"So, Eva," said Gabe, finally.

"What about her?" replied Michael.

Gabe gave him a look. "Are we seriously going to do this?"

Michael groaned, running his hand down the back of his head. "What do you want me to say, Gabe?"

"You don't necessarily need to say anything," his roommate replied. He sighed, uncrossing his arms and pushing himself off the desk. "I just want you to be careful."

"What should he be careful about?" Rafe had thrown the door open and barged in from wherever he'd been hiding, dust covering what seemed to be every inch of his clothes and much of his bald head.

Gabe gave his clothes a severe look. "Eva."

Rafe stole the chair meant for Michael and flopped down into it, snorting. A cloud of dust flew up around him. "Why should he be careful about Eva? She's a sweet girl. And to be honest, Michael could stand a good dose of 'move the hell on, dude.'"

"Because she's human," Gabe replied, "and Michael, of all people, should know what happens when our kind gets involved with theirs."

"So what?" Rafe said. "He could do worse, honestly."

Gabe glowered at him. "That is not the point. And you know Michael doesn't do anything without putting his full heart and soul into it. The whole situation smells of trouble."

"I am right here," Michael said. "You're allowed to talk to me instead of just about me. And, Gabe, no one said anything about Eva except for you."

"Look, Michael," Gabe said, laying a hand on his shoulder, "I get it. She kind of feels like one of us. But she's not."

"It's not that," Michael protested. "It's...there's something familiar about her, more than that. And I feel...I feel like I did when...*she* was still alive." He stopped, surprised at himself. Ignoring Gabe's startled intake of breath and Rafe's sudden coughing attack, he shook his head, trying to get his thoughts into order. "It's like, from the first time I saw her, I just wanted to follow her around and keep her safe. And I don't know anything about her, but when I'm with her, it's like...something is right again, and the pain doesn't hurt so much." Now he kind of wished he'd taken the chair when he had the chance. "Oh God, Gabe, that's so wrong. She should be irreplaceable."

"It's been over a century," said Rafe from his chair.

"Two centuries," Gabe corrected. "But here you see what I'm talking about. You are, under no circumstances, to enter into a relationship with her."

"No one said anything about a relationship either, Gabe."

"Don't give me that, Michael, I know you. And I know how stubborn you get about things like this, and I can read the signs. So do what you need to in order to nip this in the bud before you can't help yourself."

"Oh, she's *definitely* interested," Rafe interjected. "Come on, Gabe, one little romp isn't going to hurt anybody."

"Michael has never done a 'romp' in his life."

"I offered to help her with her trip," Michael said, willing to say anything to distract his roommates from their current subject. It was a road he did not want to think about. Because nothing was happening. Even if she did haunt his thoughts on an entirely too constant basis.

Both Gabe and Rafe paused, mouths open.

Rafe recovered first. "You know, Gabe," he said, "this is beginning to not sound like a romp." He pushed himself off the chair. "Look, Michael, if you're going to go all googly-eyed over her, maybe you should go. Come back in another decade, when she's moved on to somewhere else, hopefully settled down with someone else."

"If I had somewhere else to go, do you think I'd still be hanging out with you two?"

They ignored that statement. "Why don't you go see Thor?" Gabe said.

Michael stared at him. "Wow, this must be bad. You hate it when I spend time with Thor."

"That's because you burned down Rome that one time," Rafe said, "which was awesome, by the way. Oh, and there was the time when you two—"

"Raphael," said Gabe in a low voice, "you are not helping."

Rafe had helped with Rome, if Michael recalled correctly. Gabe probably didn't know about that. Michael filed that away as potential blackmail material.

"Anyway," Gabe started.

Michael held up his hands. "Look, guys, will you just hear me out? I don't want to go, I don't want to hide. I will admit that there is some sort of weird connection, but I don't think it's anything I can't work past. Is it so wrong to want a little bit of respite, after all these years?

Is it so wrong to want to spend time with someone who reminds me of when things were good?" He focused on Gabe, knowing Rafe would most likely go along with whatever he decided. "Please, Gabriel. I'm not asking for much."

Gabe exchanged a look with Rafe before sighing. "This is a bad idea, Michael."

It was as much permission as he was going to get. "Thank you." He turned to go.

Gabe grabbed him by his upper arm. "Remember what happens, though, when we mix with them."

Michael met his eyes. "How can I forget? I used to administer the punishment myself."

Chapter Five

EVA STOOD IN her dream desert, letting the warm wind blow through her hair. The garden she'd gotten a glimpse of, just for a second, lay in front of her, massive and green and thoroughly impossible looking. The sands seemed to weave around it, leaving it untouched. Eva closed her eyes, feeling the warmth of the sun, sucking up its light.

"Eva," said dream Michael from behind her. She turned, as she always did, but here was yet another change to the dream. Normally he would smile at her, tell her how he'd waited for her, but now he looked sad, heartbroken. He did not reach for her, as he had before. "You have forgotten me."

"Of course I haven't," she said. "You're right here."

"You know that's not what I mean. You have forgotten me. You have forgotten yourself." He stepped up beside her, staring down at the garden. "How many lifetimes have you been trapped in a mortal shell? Remember, Eva, so you can come back to me." He twisted his gaze to her face. "I will wait for you forever. But it becomes...lonely."

His face held such pain that Eva could not help herself. She wrapped both arms around him, laying her head on his chest. "I'm here now."

She could feel rather than see him shake his head. "Not quite," he said. "Not yet. But it has begun."

Eva pulled back, looking up at him. "I don't understand."

Dream Michael pointed down toward the garden. "Go and seek knowledge from the garden. Now it is yours to have."

And then he was gone. He didn't walk off, or fade away, or anything one might expect someone to do, even in a dream, but simply ceased to be, like he'd never been. Eva slowly lowered her arms and turned back to the garden. There didn't seem any reason not to go, especially now that she'd lost her companion.

The sand slid beneath her feet as she made her descent. The garden grew in size as she approached, but she could not be sure that she was getting any closer. There seemed to be someone waiting for her at the edge, and she sped up, convinced that she must reach him before she woke up.

Sam and Lily materialized out of nowhere, directly in her path. Eva slid to a stop.

"Eva, darling," Sam said. "I was hoping I'd find you out here." He crossed the distance between them, ran his hands up her neck, and kissed her. It was long and lazy, as if they'd done it a million times and were familiar with the process. Sam pulled back first, smiling down at her. "Where were you going?"

"I must get to the garden," Eva said, peering over Sam's shoulder. It seemed farther away now, like it had shrunk in size.

"There's nothing there for you," Sam said, taking her hand. "I know a better garden. We'll go immediately." Without waiting for her to say anything, he linked his arm around hers and led her in the opposite direction. Soon, almost impossibly soon, a second garden appeared, oversaturated in its lushness. Where the first garden had drawn her in, this one was almost repellent. But she did not protest when Sam led her inside. Lily trailed behind them, but it was like she wasn't really there, just a ghost of herself, the briefest hint of her existence.

"I don't understand," she said again. "Why is this one better than the other?"

"My dearest," Sam said, "gardens bear fruit, and you must be sure you pick the right one." He led her to a fruit-bearing tree, plucking one from the branches and placing it in her hands. "The fruit of this garden will be more...palatable."

Eva looked down at the fruit in her hands. She was not sure what it was, but it smelled sickeningly sweet and the skin was slimy to the touch.

"Go ahead," dream Sam said. "Have a bite."

There did not seem to be any reason not to. Eva took a bite, wincing at the sweetness and the way the juice ran stickily down her fingers.

"There," Sam said, though he and his voice seemed faded. "See how nice that is?"

There was a sharp pain in Eva's stomach, and she bent over, dropping the fruit as the garden seemed to both expand and contract around her, making her dizzy. She shut her eyes for a moment, and when she opened them, she was somewhere else, a different garden, because this one did not have the too-much-ness of the first garden. This one could be real.

"Ah, there you are," came Sam's voice from behind her, and Eva wanted to say that of course she was here, he led her here, but when she turned, it was not the same Sam as before. He seemed...younger, somehow, despite looking more or less the same as always, except his hair was longer, pulled back at the nape of his neck, and he was wearing some sort of strange, flowy garment. "I have been looking for you."

Eva blinked and took a moment to wonder at the strange reversal this dream had taken. It felt weird to hear dream Michael's normal words coming out of Sam's mouth.

This new Sam reached her and ran his hand tenderly down her cheek. "I want to show you something. Come with me." Without waiting for an answer, he reached down, taking her hand, and led her into a large copse of trees, their branches waving gently in the breeze. He produced a flower out of seemingly nowhere and handed it to her, then led her past the trees and out to the other side, to the very edge of the garden, which looked out on a large expanse of sand. In the distance, so far Eva could barely make them out, there were what looked like tents. "Do you see them?" Sam whispered in her ear. "They have never been so close before. It is almost like they are looking for us. Like they want us to be their gods."

Eva frowned. Something felt weird. It didn't feel like a dream anymore, though she couldn't say why. And she felt like she was supposed to say something, but she didn't know her lines.

"And you, my sweet," Sam continued after a moment, taking both her hands, "you will be their most beloved. Will you not come with me?"

"Why?" Eva asked. When Sam frowned, she elaborated. "Why will I be their most beloved?"

"Why wouldn't you be?" Sam smiled at her, as brilliantly as ever. "How could they resist your light?"

"Plotting again, Sammael?"

Eva and Sam both turned to see Michael, though like Sam this was not her normal dream Michael, nor did he that closely resemble the real Michael. There was something rough about him, and he did not smile. He was dressed similarly to the Sam beside her.

Sam looked absolutely shocked. "Why are you here? You are not supposed to be here."

"I could say the same for you," replied the new Michael. He approached them, never taking his eyes off Sam. Sam took half a step back, and Michael took the opportunity to free one of Eva's hands from the other man. "Eva," he said, finally looking at her. "You have been led astray. You have eaten the wrong fruit."

"Who are you to—" Sam started, but Michael ignored him.

"Wake up," he said, and Eva did.

She was in her own bed, lying on her back. Az had taken up residence on her chest, purring happily to himself, and her left hand—the one the dream Sam had been holding—was tangled in her sheets. She could tell, even without looking, that it was still early, much earlier than she would normally get up. No sunlight was streaming in through her curtains, and she couldn't get up the motivation to move.

She pet Az absently, trying to hold onto the dream, but it had begun to fade. All that remained clear were Michael's eyes as he warned her and told her to wake up. Still, it had been very strange. That sensation did not go away. Why had the dream—which had been so consistent—changed so much in the past week? And should she read anything into it? Or was she merely spending too much time on homework?

Sleep did not seem to be forthcoming again, so she got up, took a shower, and tried to work on her homework, but she got no real work done until the sun came up. And it wasn't until she was halfway through a comparison exercise on polytheistic pantheons that she remembered she was supposed to be meeting Sam and Lily for their first meeting. With a sigh, she gathered up her schoolwork and shoved it into her bag. She wished she hadn't said she'd give it a try. She didn't even know what Sam was trying to do, other than "change the world."

Her stolen hat was still nowhere to be found, so she ventured out into the cold without it. The day was already becoming overcast, and Eva knew she'd be miserable. She zipped her coat up farther and hurried toward campus, and the library, as quickly as possible.

She was thoroughly grumpy by the time she reached the study rooms. Sam was waiting outside, leaning against the wall, looking as friendly and gorgeous as usual, and Eva kind of wanted to punch him. But she forced herself to calm down and smile back. It wasn't Sam's fault that the weather sucked. She had a flash of recollection, just a shard of memory, of her dream and the rotten fruit, but she shook her head to clear it away. It probably didn't mean anything.

"Glad you could make it," he said. He held the door open for her, then followed her inside. Lily was lounging at the table, feet up on it, and the promised ice cream was slowly melting and forming a puddle in the middle. Sam pulled a chair out for Eva opposite Lily and waited for her to get settled before he started.

He had a bowl of ice cream for himself, and indicated she could serve her own, but it was too cold and too early for Eva to bother. "Anyway," Sam said, once it was clear that neither she nor Lily were going to join him in ice-cream partaking, "thank you, everyone, for coming to our first meeting. We have a great group and I'm sure we're going to be able to get a lot done."

Charismatic cult leader, Eva thought again.

"Our first order of business is to discuss our goals."

"I vote for world domination," Lily said.

"We can make that our long-term goal," Sam replied, "but I was thinking about something a little more immediate."

Eva glanced around the table. If she didn't stick around, and Lily went home, Sam would be all on his own. "Maybe we should recruit more members."

"No need." Sam pulled out the chair at the end of the table and settled into it. "I've got everyone I need right here. I'll deal with minutiae, Lily's great at the behind-the-scenes stuff, and you, Eva, will be our beacon of light, drawing the masses to our message."

"Which is?"

"We'll have to figure that out." Sam smiled again, and Eva felt herself smiling in return. "I propose a thought experiment. I propose that we plan out our ideal world, and then think about the changes that would be necessary to make it happen."

"And then what?"

"Then we make it happen." Sam sprang back out of the chair. "Just imagine what the world could be if it wasn't run by hu—idiots. We could have cities powered by green energy and people living on the bottom of the sea."

Eva scratched her chin, both amused by his enthusiasm and wondering why she was here. Axelrad's silly Nephilim essay was due the next day, and she still had to write her conclusion. "So you want to make this club just to pretend to play God?"

"I know what you're going to say, Eva," Sam said, "and I know that you think the idea is silly and that you have better things to be doing, but give it a chance, will you? After all, the world can never change if someone doesn't picture a new one first. And it'll be a nice change of pace. There are no expectations here."

Eva paused, further objections dying unsaid. It would be nice to do something, just for fun, with no obligation for it to ever go anywhere.

"Come on," Lily said, leaning forward, "what's the first thing you would change about the world?"

Eva's thoughts drifted to Michael, just for a second. "I guess I'd make it so cars drove themselves, because people drive like idiots."

Sam laughed and Lily smiled, and Eva smiled too.

The next hour passed much quicker than Eva expected it to. Sam and Lily were attentive and appreciative of what she had to say, and it was kind of fun to think about what she would change if she could, though she thought they'd gotten a bit silly at times— and Sam's humor had a dark element to it—but that was okay, too.

Finally, she had to go to class, so they wrapped up, did their best at cleaning up the now-thoroughly-melted ice cream, and promised to meet again whenever they could manage it. Eva picked up her bag and slung it over her shoulder, pushing the door open.

"Eva, wait up," Sam said, joining her. "I really appreciate you coming." He leaned forward, giving her a quick peck on the cheek. "I'll see you tomorrow." He smiled at her for a moment before disappearing back into the study room with Lily, shutting the door behind him.

Eva turned and headed for the exit, humming to herself, but when she stepped outside into the rain, it was like a fog cleared. Her hand went to her cheek. What had just happened? She'd been so content in the study room, but now she had a vague, uneasy feeling, and she couldn't say why.

IT'D BEEN almost a week since Michael had spoken to Gabe about Eva, and he hadn't seen her since. That didn't mean that he hadn't been thinking about her; she haunted his dreams and he found his thoughts straying to her on a fairly regular basis.

He started across campus. It was early afternoon, just a little after lunchtime, but he hadn't eaten yet and he should. He should probably just grab something quick, though, because he had a presentation to give the next day and it still needed a little bit of work.

His path took him across a large expanse of grass and around the front of the library.

"Michael," said Lily. He hadn't even noticed her as he passed. She was perched on one of the stone walls which edged the front stairs, looking resplendent in tight jeans and a sweater, her hair pulled up in a messy bun. "How lovely to see you again."

Michael's hand tightened around the strap of his backpack. "Lily, hello. Enjoying the weather?" Lily had always liked it a bit chilly. Which made him wonder why they'd gotten along for as long as they had, quite honestly.

She pushed herself off, joining him at the base of the stairs. "It is quite nice here. I can see why Gabriel chose this city to settle in for the time being." She looked pointedly at the sky, which was not currently deluging them, but looked like it might at any second. "Not sure why you stay, though."

"You know why," he replied, his voice low.

Lily tsked. "Because of Gabe and Rafe? Michael, my dear, dear Michael, you can't lean on them *forever*." She reached a hand up, running it around the back of his ear. Her hand was frigid and Michael pulled away instinctively.

"Why are you here?" he asked to change the subject.

Lily frowned. "Didn't we already have this conversation once?"

"No, I mean, why are you here, in the middle of campus? Libraries were never really your style."

"Ah!" Lily said. "I am here for nefarious purposes."

Michael didn't doubt that. "Nefarious for whom?"

She grinned, just the tiniest hint of a smile. "Oh, I'm pretty sure it will be nefarious for everyone."

Michael had dealt with Lily enough over the years that he knew it would be impossible to get detailed information out of her when she was in this sort of mood. It would probably be best just to leave her to it and go on his way. But the subject of Lily's plans must have arrived, because her eyes opened gleefully as she stared over his shoulder.

She leaned in conspiratorially. "Stay," she whispered, her breath cold on his ear. "I think this will amuse you as much as it amuses me."

Turning, Michael saw Eva headed toward them. She looked beautiful, with her long, dark hair streaming loosely behind her. Following directly behind her was Sam. Michael's eyes narrowed, but Sam was obviously surprised—and not happy—to see him. Michael glanced at Lily, who was smiling innocently beside him.

As they got closer, Michael noticed that Eva looked between him and Lily, but he wasn't sure what conclusion she came to. Sam reached out for Eva's arm. "We'd better go straight in," he said, "no reason to interrupt Lily's conversation." Eva, Michael noted to his pleasure, avoided Sam's arm so masterfully it almost looked like she hadn't even seen him move.

"Michael," Eva said, "I wanted to thank you."

Sam stopped dead in his tracks. "Wait, you know Michael?"

"Sure," Eva replied. "He's been very helpful lately." She stopped next to them, acknowledging Lily with a nod. "My essay went very well, thanks to you. I think that not even Professor Axelrad will be able to find major fault with it."

Michael found himself smiling in reply. "It was my pleasure to be of service." He caught Sam glowering at Lily out of the corner of her eye; Lily looked entirely too pleased with herself.

Eva glanced between him and Lily again. "Well, I don't want to interrupt anything. I was just going to get some research material for the next essay."

Michael knew he should let her go, but it was so hard when she was right there in front of him. "Oh, you're not interrupting. Lily and I weren't talking about anything in particular, were we?"

"Oh, indeed, no," purred Lily. "The more the merrier."

"Lily," said Sam. There was an underlying tone to his voice that made Michael's skin crawl. "Maybe you and Michael should continue your conversation elsewhere."

"Oh, no, we're quite done," she replied.

"Okay, then maybe you and I could have a quick word," Sam growled. He took Lily by the arm and led her several paces away, where he began to whisper angrily, gesturing violently. Michael strained his ears, trying to hear what they were saying, but they were too far away.

"So," Eva said, drawing his attention back to her, "you know Sam and Lily too, I take it." She smiled wryly and Michael's heart skipped a beat, which was frankly ridiculous because it was just a smile.

"Oh, yes, we go way back." Michael grimaced. "And I'm afraid we don't have the best history."

Eva glanced over at Sam and Lily for a moment, then moved her attention back to him. "You seemed pretty friendly with Lily there." Michael thought he heard a hint of jealousy in her voice, but he was probably imagining it.

"Lily..." Michael paused, trying to think about how best to phrase it. "Lily doesn't really put any stock in the past. If something happened that's not convenient to what she's trying to do in the present, then it doesn't matter." Sam and Lily were still arguing, though Lily was an active participant now, her eyes flashing with a strange mixture of anger and amusement. "I'm not quite sure what she's trying to do at the moment, but apparently we're being civil to each other for whatever purpose."

"And Sam?"

"What about Sam?"

Eva frowned at him, but the sudden silence behind him told Michael that the argument was over, and Eva didn't seem willing to pursue her line of questioning with the person in question present.

Sam and Lily rejoined them, Sam looking sullen and Lily almost bouncing. She discreetly elbowed Sam in the side and the other man plastered on one of his fake smiles. "We're going to go for coffee, if you'd like to join us."

"Oh, no, I can't," Eva said. "I really need to work on this essay. Sorry." And she did seem honestly sorry. What was happening here? How long had Eva been friends with Sam and Lily, and what was their goal? Michael didn't believe for one second that either of them would befriend a human without some benefit to themselves.

Just like that, all thoughts of leaving vanished. Michael reached out for Eva's hand, and she smiled up at him. "I'll help you," he said to her. He nodded slightly to Sam and Lily. "See you around." Without releasing

Eva's hand, he led her into the library. She came willingly, and Michael managed to see the mask fall off Sam's face when they left. He looked furious, and he shot Lily a betrayed look out of the corner of his eye.

Once inside, Michael released Eva's hand and sighed, rubbing his temples. He hated dealing with Sam, could hardly stand to look at the other man. There was too much bad blood between them, and there was nothing in this world that would ever be able to make up for what Sam had taken from him.

EVA WATCHED Michael physically calm himself, surprised at how tightly he was wound. She glanced toward the entrance. That whole thing had been...strange. Sam had one of the most even composures she'd ever seen, and he'd obviously been just as rattled by the encounter as Michael had been.

"I'm sorry for prying," Eva said just as Michael turned to her and said, "You don't have to let me help you." They both opened their mouths a second time. Eva laughed, then slipped her hand back into Michael's, hoping she wasn't being too forward. "I'd love your help."

Michael smiled at her, a warm, bright smile, and his hand was warm in hers. "Well, then, I am yours for about an hour, and then, sadly, I must do my own homework." Still holding her hand, he led her toward the basement. At first Eva was surprised that he knew where she needed to go until she remembered that he'd been a religious studies major himself.

The chairs in the basement were all remnants of the seventies, an odd mustard-yellow plaid tweed with bits of stuffing popping out along the seams and wherever else it could manage to escape.

"You don't have to apologize," Michael said quietly, and for a moment Eva couldn't remember what she had apologized for. "Sam, well. We don't get along. We never have. And he took something from me that was very dear to me."

"Your girlfriend?" Eva asked, remembering what Rafe said.

Michael pursed his lips, nodding. "I'm not really sure what exactly happened there, but I know Sam was involved somehow."

Eva was half-tempted to ask him why he'd never tried to contact said girlfriend after the fact, if he needed closure, but there was something about his stance that made her think that, maybe, something worse had happened to her. "What was her name?"

Michael looked at her, surprised, then forced out a laugh. "Would you believe," he said, "that I've avoided mentioning her for so long that I almost forgot? Gabe and Rafe too—we never call her by her name anymore, if we talk about her at all." He trailed off, and was silent for so long that Eva assumed that he wasn't going to answer the question. "It was Eve."

Eva wasn't quite sure why she wanted to know, or what to think now that she had the information. "I'm sorry." She wasn't sure what she was sorry for, exactly, but it seemed the right thing to say.

Michael shrugged, but the action was forced.

She gave his hand a squeeze. "And, if it makes you feel better, thank you for happening to be right there. Sam's always trying to get me to hang out outside of class, and I feel bad saying no all the time."

"You shouldn't," Michael said, a sharp edge to his voice. "God, sometimes he makes me so mad! I wish I'd finished with him years ago."

Eva recoiled slightly at his anger, but at the same time, she found it fascinating to see a side of him that wasn't the gentlemanly person who was so calm and helpful. His passion was so alive and fiery. "Why didn't you?" she asked quietly, unsure if she wanted to interrupt his moment.

The fire in his eyes died. "He's practically family, and family's one of the only things you have in this world." For a moment he seemed tired and ancient, his shoulders slumping as if the weight of the world rested on them, but then he straightened and looked at her, eyes bright. "What's this essay on? Same class, right?" He tapped a finger against his chin. "This was the class where you'd have another essay before you made it back to your seat."

"That's the one, though I was sitting when it was assigned." Eva dug out her notebook. "Hierarchy of angels."

"Which one? The classic pseudo-Dionysus one, or an earlier or later one?"

Eva blinked at him. "How long did you study this? It's amazing how much you know."

Michael smiled slightly. "Not actually that long. You've just found me when you happen to be on one of my favorite subjects."

"One of your favorites?" she repeated.

"Angels."

Eva looked up at him. "Really?"

"Why not?" Michael answered. "There's some truly interesting legends relating to them if you look in Jewish rabbinic lore, and I like looking at the differences between Jewish, Christian, and Islamic angels."

"But they're just an add-on stolen from surrounding polytheistic religions," protested Eva.

Michael shrugged. "So little of any modern religion is unique. A lot of Christianity and Judaism was taken from other, older religions. Even the idea of there being an evil being to work against God was not originally included in the Jewish religion but was slowly adapted from Zoroastrianism." He eyed her. "Not for you, huh?"

She remembered Sam asking her the same question a few weeks previously. "Do you believe in angels, then?"

"I don't know if I necessarily believe in angels from a physical point of view, but I think that many of us have the ability to be one if we so choose, though perhaps not in the way that some people think." He smiled at her, then stood up, leading the way to the card catalog. He apparently preferred the card version over the digital.

Michael opened the card catalog and began to flip through the cards. Eva watched him closely, admiring the way his eyes moved quickly over each card before moving on to the next one. Maybe dating wouldn't be so bad—if he was interested, that was. She wanted to reach out and wrap his hair around her fingers to see if it was as soft as it looked. To distract herself she focused on the bookcases.

There weren't many people in the basement, but she did recognize some of her classmates. Best to get to the good books before they did.

"We never did decide on what exactly your topic was," said Michael. He paused on a card and stared at it for a moment before moving on to the next. "Angel hierarchy is kind of a broad topic. Are we comparing different ones, exploring one specifically, attempting to pigeonhole certain angels somewhere in a specific hierarchy?"

"What?" asked Eva, still more focused on him than anything else.

"Take the Archangels, for example," said Michael, turning to look at her. "Most hierarchies include an archangel choir, yet at the same time scholars still try to take one of the Archangels—Gabriel, let's say—and put him in a different, higher choir. It's like we can't accept that the angels that would interact with us might not be all that important."

"That way lies trouble," said Eva. "It sounds entirely too free-thinking and controversial for Professor Axelrad. We'd better stick to something less likely to cause any rumblings in the cores of his beliefs."

Michael smiled. "I always feel like people need a little more of that, but it's probably best to leave your professor alone. I was in a lecture once years go—though I don't remember what it was about—and someone asked a question that so shook the professor that he had a nervous breakdown then and there. Admittedly, he was already not the most stable person ever, but it was not pretty."

"Was it you?"

"What?"

"Was it you who asked the question?" clarified Eva.

Shaking his head, Michael said, "No, it wasn't me. I've found it's better not to draw too much attention to myself if it's unnecessary."

Too late, thought Eva. What she said, however, was, "Let's do the comparison. We can make pseudo-Dionysus our main focus." She stopped, aware that she'd just included him, though it was her own assignment. She needed to stop relying on him. One assignment did not a homework partner make. It was great that he wanted to help but maybe he wouldn't always be there. She definitely did not need his help.

"Okay," said Michael with a wide smile that made Eva's resolve melt. What was a little help between friends, really?

Eva obediently followed him to the bookcases and watched anxiously as they slid on their rails out of the way. She was tempted to just let Michael go in and save her from the possibility of death by library shelf squishing, but part of her rebelled. She didn't need him to do things for her; she was a big girl and she had gotten along just fine—well, mostly fine—before he came along. Certainly there were better uses for a handsome man than having him pick out books for essays.

Slightly dismayed at her own train of thought but not as much as she probably should have been, Eva followed him into the aisle, peering suspiciously at the shelves, daring them to move. A moment later she ran straight into Michael's back. He felt so nice and warm and *right* that it took her mind a moment to process what had happened and even longer for her to decide to do something about it, as a good majority of her had decided that perhaps she should just stay there for as long as possible.

By the time she'd finally squashed any rebellious portions of her consciousness, Michael had taken action into his own hands. He turned to look at her, her eyes bright and dark at the same time, and for a while all he did was look, his gaze reaching into hers. She felt almost uncomfortably warm, but she didn't want to look away. In fact, if anything, she wanted him closer, but she couldn't read his expression; she didn't know what he wanted.

The shelf beeped loudly, startling Eva. She yelped and jumped backwards into the other shelf. She'd forgotten about the shelves and now they would take their revenge for her loss of concentration by squishing her.

"Hey, we're in here!" called Michael, who was a beacon of calmness.

"Sorry!" came the response from outside the shelves. After another moment the beeping stopped. Eva let out a breath she didn't know she'd been holding.

Michael smiled at her, his expression back to normal. "They won't move if there's someone in the way, you know."

"Oh," she said, disappointed in the interruption. Everything was as it had been, but Eva found herself wishing they were back a few moments earlier when the fire had been rising. She'd never felt like that before.

"There are motion sensors and proximity sensors," Michael continued, gesturing vaguely at the shelves. "Or something along those lines."

"Excellent. Good idea." Eva shook her head. "Well, books."

"Yes, well," said Michael, turning back to the shelf. "It seems like here would be the general area to look." He indicated the bottom shelves. It figured; books she needed never seemed to be in a convenient location. She hiked up her pants and sat down on the ground, crossing her legs.

Michael remained standing. "I'm afraid I really do need to go," he said. "But this was nice. We should do it again sometime, without the beginning part." He shifted his weight. "Will you be all right?"

Eva forced a smile, her heart sinking at the thought of him leaving. But she was a big girl; she would be okay. "I'll be just fine. Thank you for your help."

Michael nodded and took a step away, then paused, looking like he wanted to say something. Eva watched him expectantly, but after a moment he gave a little shake of his head and turned and walked away.

Chapter Six

MICHAEL responsibly took up residence in the physics
building's computer lab, attempting to work on his
presentation, but it wasn't flowing. Maybe he should
have stayed and helped Eva longer, but there'd been the
moment when she'd *looked* at him with those warm, dark
eyes and it'd been all he could do not to take her in his
arms and...who even knew. It was best not to think
about it. Nothing could happen between them.

It was early evening when he gave up and headed
out. His presentation was nowhere close to being done—
between Eva's eyes and a nagging feeling that he should
be paying more attention to Sam and Lily, he hadn't been
able to concentrate. Michael frowned up at the sky,
which rumbled. When he'd followed Gabe and Rafe here,
he hadn't considered the weather. And he did not like the
rain.

He trudged the three stories up to his apartment and
threw open the door. To his very great surprise, Gabe
and Rafe were already home, both settled on the couch.

They were leaning toward each other, like they'd been talking, but they turned toward him as Michael stepped inside and dropped his bag with a thud onto the floor. He had the unpleasant impression that they'd been talking about him.

"Bad day?" asked Gabe.

"Maybe?" For a second, Michael considered ignoring both of them and hiding in his room for the rest of the evening, especially since he wasn't sure Gabe wouldn't start up his lecture again. But the scene in front of the library was still bothering him, and maybe it would help to talk about it.

"Maybe?" echoed Rafe, looking amused.

Michael forced himself to take a deep breath. "So," he said, deciding that the beginning was an excellent place to start, "Lily waylaid me on campus, and then Eva walked up with Sam, and I got the very distinct impression that they were all spending a fair amount of time together."

His roommates blinked at him. Michael groaned. "Come on, guys, you know Sam and Lily wouldn't take interest in a human without a reason, and I can't imagine it's anything wholesome."

"How long has Lily been in town?" Gabe asked, eyes narrowing.

Michael shook his head. "I'm not sure. A few weeks, at least. I talked to her then too, and she said Sam had asked her to come."

"You talked to Lily weeks ago and you didn't tell us?" said Rafe.

Michael glowered at him. "Can we please focus on the main issue? For once? I know you guys like Eva—you rarely hire anybody—so can we at least pretend to be a little concerned for her well-being?"

Michael could understand their focus on Lily; something had happened around the time that he had lost Eve between Lily and Gabe and Rafe. He didn't know what it was, exactly, but whatever it was had severely pissed Gabe off. And Gabe did not forgive easily.

But that was all beside the point.

"Calm down, Michael," Gabe said. "Of course we care about Eva."

"Maybe they just got bored and decided they wanted better company," Rafe said, though he didn't look like he believed it.

"Sam calls Lily to come visit just so she can play nice with Eva? Really?"

"There might be something else," Gabe said. Michael glanced over at him, but the other man seemed distinctly uncomfortable. He pushed off the couch and began to stalk around the room. Michael perched on the edge of an easy chair simply because otherwise it felt like there was too much energy in the room.

"So," Gabe said after a moment, "you remember our last chat when we brought up the fact that Eva somewhat feels like one of us?"

"I am unlikely to forget that conversation," Michael replied, earning a glare from his redheaded roommate.

"Anyway, it was a large reason why I hired her."

Rafe stared at him. "What? You never told me that."

"I'm surprised you didn't notice." Gabe shrugged. "It was nice to feel someone familiar."

"Rafe can't sense anything," Michael muttered. "Anyway, Gabe."

"I thought, at the time, that maybe she had some Nephilim blood in her, though I thought the bloodlines had died out. But with Sam and Lily so interested, it may be something else." Gabe paused. He dropped back onto the couch next to Rafe, sighing. "I almost hate to bring this up, but...do you remember, oh, a couple thousand years ago or so, when everyone was obsessed with reincarnation?"

"After the whole Osiris thing?" Rafe asked. "Yeah, I do."

Michael did as well. It had caused quite a stir. "You're saying Eva's the reincarnation of someone? I thought we decided the whole Osiris thing was a giant hoax. Plus, Eva's human."

Gabe sighed again. "We did. This is why I hesitate to bring the subject up but, let's face it, there's always been some sort of weird connection between us and the humans. We look just like them, we can have children with them and, when we die, certain incriminating differences disappear immediately. So is it really so farfetched to think that, maybe, if reincarnation is possible, we could come back as humans?"

"Why would her being the reincarnation of someone interest Sam and Lily?" Michael asked.

"I don't know." Gabe shook his head. "It seems to me that even if Eva was once one of us, she's not going to be much use to whatever their plans are now. But it's the only thing I can think of."

"Could someone regain access to their powers?" Michael asked.

Gabe held his hands out. "I honestly have no idea. As far as I know, I've never seen it happen."

Michael felt a headache coming on. So, Eva was possibly the reincarnation of someone—possibly someone he once knew, which was kind of crazy and so he pushed the thought to the back of his mind—and, if so, there was a possibility she might somehow regain her powers, whatever they were, and then Sam and Lily would use them for...what?

"Well," he said slowly, working things out as he went, "we can't just leave her to them. We'll have to offer her protection, or something."

Rafe groaned. "You've got to be kidding. Protection takes time. *Years*, Michael. We'd have to pretend to age." To demonstrate, he aged himself a good twenty years, letting his skin become less elastic, letting wrinkles form on his face and hands.

Aging was hard, and a pain in the ass, Michael had to admit. They all had the ability to make superficial changes to their appearance—change their skin color, their hair color, look older or younger—but Rafe was considerably better at it than most of them, as his natural skin color would have caused some issues at various points in history. Most of them just preferred to move on when people began to ask questions about their age.

"Anyway," Michael said, "protection?"

Shaking his head, Gabe replied, "With the information we have right now, I've got to say no, Michael. Sam and Lily could be up to nothing. Eva could not be the reincarnation of one of us, in which case, even if they were up to something, they'd never get anywhere. Besides, Eva's always struck me as a strong, independent woman who can make her own decisions about things, so she might stop spending time with them on her own."

Rafe frowned. "Unless that's why he called Lily in."

"Oh, God." Michael collapsed fully into the armchair. "I bet that's it. He couldn't get her on his own, so he called in Lily."

"We're still jumping to conclusions," Gabe said. "I still vote no until we have more information. Sorry, Michael."

"Uriel would have said yes," Michael murmured under his breath.

"Yes," Rafe said—and of course, Rafe would be able to hear him—"but he's dead, so his vote doesn't count anymore."

"Well, what's *your* vote, Raphael?" Michael spat.

Rafe guiltily glanced at Gabe, then back at Michael. "No."

Michael groaned, dropping his head into his hands. "Of course it is." He felt a warmth inside that he generally associated with his temper and fought it down. Yelling at Gabe and Rafe never got him anywhere.

Rafe bristled. "What's that supposed to mean?"

"What do you think it means?" Michael snapped, feeling his temper flare anyway. "You *always* go along with what Gabe says." Gabe's face darkened and Rafe looked hurt, but Michael pressed on before either of them could say anything. "Well, if you won't help, I shall do it by myself."

"Michael," said Gabe sharply.

"No, Gabe," Michael replied. "I can't just sit by on this one. I feel some sort of connection with her, and to just let Sam and Lily do...whatever...you know I can't ignore that."

"What are you going to do?" Rafe asked, sounding annoyed. "Last I heard, you're only homework buddies."

"I was thinking maybe I'd offer to go on her trip with her," said Michael.

"Bloody hell!" said Rafe. "You've gone crazy. After all these millennia, it has finally happened."

That was rich, coming from him. Michael stood, scraping the chair on the floor. Gabe winced. "Look, my mind's made up. You can help, or not, but either way, you need to stay out of my way."

"Everyone calm down," Gabe said, also standing. He took a deep breath, stepping forward. Michael immediately took a step away. Sighing, Gabe held up his hands in a placating manner. "I'm not going to do anything, Michael."

"Whatever you say," said Michael, only slightly reassured when Gabe made no further motion toward him.

"I'm not sure it's a good idea if you go on her trip with her," Gabe said. "It sounds like she wants to get away to figure out who she wants to be and where she wants to go with her life, and if you're along distracting her, then I don't think it's going to be terribly beneficial to anyone."

"Greece is a long way away from here, and we—I—won't be able to protect her otherwise." Michael rubbed the back of his neck. "And I could help. She said she wanted to look at some religious sites, and, let's be honest, I know them a lot better than modern scholars do. I could take her to some that modern scholars haven't even found yet."

"She'd spend the whole time staring at you and completely missing the whole point," said Gabe.

"What? She's more logical than that. She seems to focus on schoolwork just fine when I'm around." Well, except for that look. But even so, once the moment had passed, she hadn't seemed to give it another thought.

"Judging from when you were both in the shop last week, I would say she's probably not focusing as well as you think she is."

"I'm not asking for your permission, Gabriel."

"Fine," said Gabe. "But if she says no, you are not to push the matter in any way. Do I make myself clear?"

"Yes," said Michael.

"Good," said Gabe.

"Not good," said Rafe. "Come on, Gabe, can't you see what's happening here?"

Gabe gave Rafe a look. "The matter's closed for now." He turned, disappearing into his room and closing the door behind him.

Michael glared after him, then retrieved his bag, intending to do the same.

"Michael," Rafe said, quietly, as if he was afraid to disturb their redheaded roommate, "seriously, try to stay away from her, at least for now." Michael blinked at him, surprised. "Gabe and I can keep an eye on her while she's at work, and she's in most days. I think it'd be good for you to at least give it a try. You're kind of freaking me out."

Rafe looked so earnest and worried that Michael allowed himself to smile and clap his roommate on the shoulder, already feeling guilty for yelling at him earlier. "Okay," he said, "I'll try. But I guarantee nothing."

He left the living room to Rafe, pulling the door to his room open and heading inside. He would try. It would be good for him. To be honest, he was freaking himself out a little too. The strength of his feelings when she was around, especially since they'd come on so suddenly, just wasn't natural. And it almost felt like a betrayal of Eve. She wouldn't have wanted him to remain alone, but everything was happening too fast, and they'd been together for so long.

Michael shook his head. He *would* try. It just seemed like Eva was everywhere, now. How many times could you run into one person when you didn't mean to?

———

EVA WAS, thankfully, on time to lecture. Professor Axelrad had yet to make his appearance and so she was fairly certain that she would not be called on to defend her opinions in front of the class today. She took a moment to pull out a notebook and a pen, then wasted a few more minutes by scribbling down ideas for her essay in the margin of the page.

When she looked up, she found Sam had taken the seat next to her. He was watching her silently, looking a little hurt, but when she looked up he managed a smile. "Hey, how's it going?"

"Hey," she replied. "Sorry about Monday. I hope you and Lily enjoyed your coffee."

"I've had better," Sam replied. "And what about you? Was Michael," he paused on the name, looking a bit pained, "...helpful?"

"Oh, sure," she replied, unsure what to say. "He seems to really know what he's talking about."

Sam laughed, a hint of bitterness sneaking in. "I'm sure he does."

Eva felt herself flushing. She'd never seen Sam so upset, and it'd never been hard to talk to him before. She found herself wanting to try to put things right between them. "Sam, we don't have to talk about him, you know. I understand you guys have had some arguments in the past, but it doesn't really matter to me."

"How long have you known Michael?" Sam asked sharply.

Eva pursed her lips, not sure what to tell him. "Not too long."

"Well, I've known him forever," Sam replied. He definitely sounded bitter now, and a little angry. It was a side of him she'd never seen before, and Eva wasn't sure she liked it. "He acts like he's God's gift to mankind, but he's no saint, I'll tell you that."

"Oh?" Eva said, mostly because she felt like she had to say something.

"He stole my girlfriend, you know."

Eva raised both eyebrows. "What?"

"Yeah, she was a real sweetheart of a girl too." Sam sighed, leaning back in his chair. "Had the most gorgeous green eyes, but then Michael comes along and smiles that stupid perfect smile of his at her and I didn't stand a chance."

Eva was thoroughly convinced at this point that the entire lot of them must have come from some mysterious place where everyone had green eyes, and if a child was born without them, they were chased out to live their lives in the real world and not allowed to ever return. Still, questions swam in her head. Who was telling the truth? She supposed there could have been multiple girls. Maybe Sam had stolen the first one, and Michael had stolen the second one in revenge, though she couldn't see him doing that. Unless Michael was some evil genius or a very good actor, he seemed like a genuinely nice guy, and she didn't think he'd risk hurting the girl. Besides, she couldn't see Gabe and Rafe putting up with him if he was a jerk. Rafe would be more likely to just belt him in the face, and Gabe would give him that terrible look of disappointment he sometimes gave Rafe. So, then, was Sam lying? She supposed she didn't actually know him very well either. Maybe it was all some sort of misunderstanding.

She opened her mouth to say something, though she wasn't sure what, when Professor Axelrad finally made his entrance, immediately launching into his lecture for the day. Eva had to focus completely on him in order to keep up, and by the time lecture ended, all thoughts of stolen girlfriends and love triangles had slipped away.

She stood to go, stuffing her things back into her bag, but Sam reached out and grabbed her by the wrist. Eva stared at him in surprise.

"I don't want you to see Michael anymore," he said, his voice low and serious.

"What?" Eva asked, shocked. Sure, they'd been classmates for years and sure, they'd had a good time the two times they'd hung out outside of class, and maybe their relationship would have gone somewhere more, but who was he to tell her not to hang out with someone?

"I don't want you to see Michael anymore," he said again, slower, as if she hadn't understood him the first time.

Eva fought down the urge to slap him with her free hand. "You will release my arm," she said.

Sam must have seen something in her face, because he did so immediately. Eva leveled her best, most condescending glare at him before turning on her heel and stalking out of the lecture hall. She could hear him following her, but she didn't give him the satisfaction of acknowledging his presence.

"Eva, please, wait," he called once they were outside.

With a sigh, she turned to face him. "What?"

Sam pulled a flower out of nowhere and offered it to her. "I'm sorry. I don't know what came over me. Okay, well, my feelings about Michael came over me, but I didn't mean to take them out on you. Please, forgive me?"

There was a small whisper in the back of her head that insisted that she listen to him. *Hasn't he been a good friend,* it said, *always considerate and attentive? Hasn't he always shown you the utmost attention?*

But it was sunny out, and standing there in the sunlight made her feel stronger, and she'd had enough friends go through high school and undergrad in abusive relationships, and she couldn't help but feel like she'd seen something worrisome that she needed to take note of. Maybe it was just Michael that brought out the worst in him. But she'd have to see.

"Why don't you want me to see Michael?" Eva asked. "And don't tell me it's just because you don't like him."

Sam shifted his weight. "Well, I don't."

"Sam." Eva put her hands on her hips. "How can I forgive you if you won't be honest with me?"

"Michael has a habit of...taking things I need from me," Sam said. He met her eyes, and there was something fierce burning in his green orbs—anger and hatred and determination. "I will not let him do it again."

"And you need me?"

Sam relaxed, almost as if he'd thought he'd won. "Yes. Yes, I do."

"Well, then," Eva said, stepping forward. She jabbed a finger at his chest. "Remember this, Sam Payne. You are not to tell me who I can see. You are not to tell me what I can do. And if you ever forget either of those two rules, I will never speak to you again."

It was almost worth it just for the shocked look on Sam's face, like no one had ever stood up to him before in his life. Smiling to herself, she turned and headed across the lawn in the direction of the bookstore. Maybe she'd actually be on time for her shift there, too.

She thought she saw a dark look cross Sam's face as he watched her walk away from him, but when she half-turned back, it was gone.

Chapter Seven

WALKING TO the bookstore, Michael tried to convince himself that he was doing this purely because it was necessary. It'd been a few days. He was listening to Rafe's suggestion, really. Okay, it'd been four days since the library and he'd been keeping an eye out for Eva around campus, though he hadn't seen her.

And he tried to tell himself that he was doing it merely for her protection, to give her a way to get away from Sam and Lily, and not because he wanted to see her. Yes. That was why.

He didn't really buy it.

Michael opened the door to the bookstore, making two visits in three weeks, which was some sort of record. When Gabe and Rafe had first opened the store, he'd visited more often, helped where he could, but he found something stifling about being surrounded by books all the time. Maybe it was because they were flammable. Anyway, it was better once he started spending more of his time elsewhere.

The bell on the door chimed. The only person in view was Eva, settled behind the register with a textbook open and her hair hanging in a braid over one shoulder. She looked up as he entered, smiling when she recognized him. Michael took a deep breath and started forward.

There was no call of greeting from Rafe, if he was there, and no one emerged from the office. Gabe, if he was here, should have been able to sense him, so they were probably avoiding him. Michael hadn't been home much since the other day and had only had the most basic of conversations with either of his roommates in that time.

"Hey," Eva said as he reached the register. She closed her textbook and sat up taller, still smiling. "How did your presentation go?"

Michael shifted uncomfortably. "Not well. I'm afraid I couldn't focus on it as much as I would have liked. And your essay?"

Eva gestured at a stack of books further down the counter. As she did so, she brushed her hair behind one ear, and Michael found himself drawn to the motion. Eve had had dark hair as well, and similar warm, butterscotch skin, but she hadn't had Eva's large, inviting brown eyes. She'd had green, just like the rest of them. He tried to remind himself of what he and Eve had had, but somehow, when he was around Eva, it didn't seem to matter as much.

"Michael?" Eva asked.

Michael blinked. She'd obviously answered his question and he hadn't heard a word of it. God, this was worse than he thought. Eva was still looking at him, brow furrowed in worry, and he felt himself flushing. Maybe he should go out and try again later, when his brain was working properly. "Sorry. I got kidnapped by my own train of thought."

She laughed brightly. "I know how that goes." She sobered, staring at her pile of research books. "I talked to my mother this morning."

Michael frowned, unsure why that would upset her. "I'm...sorry?"

"Sorry, sorry, I forget that not everyone lives in my head." Eva sighed. "She thinks I'm wasting my time and money on this degree. The worst thing is, sometimes I think she may be right. She wants me to move home and marry some nice boy and be trapped forever." She paused, running her fingers absently over her braid. "I told her I was an adult and that I thought that I could make my own decisions, and I swear I could feel her icy glare through the telephone. And then she hung up without another word."

Michael's first thought was that her moving away would get her away from Sam and Lily, but it was short-lived. If they wanted her, they would follow her. And Eva wouldn't have him—or Gabe and Rafe—for protection, then. "Ouch."

Eva shook her head. "She can't make me move home, but she's the only family I've got." She stared at the books some more. "I have to prove to her that I know what I'm doing with my life."

"Right, your trip," Michael said, pleased to have a way to bring the topic up naturally. "About that."

"Yes?" Eva asked, raising an eyebrow. "Actually, hold that thought. I told Rafe I'd straighten the cookbooks. Can we walk and talk?"

She came around the counter and headed into the stacks. Michael couldn't help but notice that she was wearing ridiculous bright pink galoshes as he followed her.

The cookbooks were tucked against the wall farthest from the register. They did need straightening; books were everywhere in every possible orientation. Michael started to help as well, just so his hands had something to do.

"Anyway," Eva said, "what about my trip?"

"I was wondering," he started, and then thought maybe he should actually, you know, make eye contact, and turned, but then thought maybe that was too forward and settled for staring at her galoshes. "I was wondering if I could come on your trip with you."

Eva looked up, clearly surprised, one cookbook still in her left hand. She looked away again after a moment, putting the book back into its proper spot. "I didn't know you were interested." She paused, frowning. "Something interesting down there, by the way?"

Michael forced himself to look away from the galoshes and meet her gaze. "Are you like Gabe and his umbrellas, except with galoshes?"

"I inherited these from a distant cousin." Eva narrowed her eyes, examining him. Michael shifted nervously, unsure what to expect her answer to be, and unsure what he would do no matter which way she answered. It felt like ages that they stayed like that, Eva's face guarding whatever she was thinking. Michael thought he might pass out.

She opened her mouth, closed it, and then opened it again and said, "Okay."

"What?" The word slipped out before he could think it. Apparently he hadn't expected her to agree.

"Okay, you can come." She shrugged, turning back to the books. "Probably shouldn't be traveling on my own anyway."

Michael's face hurt, and it was only after a moment that he realized that it was because he was grinning so widely. He needed to tone it down. Luckily, Eva wasn't looking. "Thank you."

"You're welcome," Eva said to the bookshelf.

Michael was tempted to do something—take her hand, kiss her, bear-hug her—but that seemed inappropriate, so he settled for thanking her again and then making a strategic exit.

Eva watched Michael go. She halfheartedly returned to shelving the cookbooks. She had been intending to say no. Michael was...distracting, to say the least. And she seemed to be more aware of it now that Sam had asked her—told her?—not to see him. When he had come in, she'd know almost instinctively that it would be him. So having him along, when she was trying to figure out her life, was probably not the best idea.

But there was something in his eyes that had changed her mind. She couldn't really explain it. Some part of her wanted desperately to spend more time with him, to be able to approach him from an intellectual rather than an emotional direction. Part of her thought that perhaps she should keep him even closer than that. Eva ran her fingers along her lower lip unconsciously, wondering what it would feel like to feel his lips against hers.

"How's it going, darling?" asked Rafe from directly behind her.

She jumped, dropping the book in her hands. "Jesus, Rafe, don't sneak up on people."

"I can't help it if I am stealthy like the ninja," he replied. Bending down, he picked up the book and offered it back to her.

"You just missed Michael," she said, though she suspected he knew. She placed the book in its proper spot.

Rafe wiped his brow, spreading dust across his chocolate skin. "I think we're fighting, so I thought he probably didn't want to talk to me."

"You 'think' you're fighting?" Eva straightened several books which had fallen over and were threatening to escape to the floor.

"Well, we are obviously not *fighting* fighting or there would be fires and tornadoes and a flood the likes of which you have never seen," Rafe said.

Eva raised both eyebrows at him, unsure what he meant by that. Probably nothing. Rafe had a bit of a gift for exaggeration, after all. "Can I ask you something?"

"Sure, sweetheart."

"I was talking to Sam the other day, and he said Michael had stolen his girlfriend, but you said Sam had stolen Michael's girlfriend."

"Ah," Rafe said. "That's a twisted web. Here, leave the cookbooks to their fate and let's go sit." Eva followed Rafe back out of the stacks. He offered her her usual stool behind the register and relocated a stack of books from the spare one against the wall. "If you want clarification, it was the same girl. Sam was with her first, but she was well and done with him before she took up with Michael."

"Was this Eve?"

Rafe looked surprised. "Sam tell you that?"

"No, Michael did."

Rafe went from surprised to flat-out shocked. "Really? Wow, that's...I'm going to have to reevaluate some things." He peered at Eva thoughtfully.

She shifted uncomfortably. "Rafe?"

He shook his head, seemingly coming out of his thoughts. "Sorry. Where was I? Oh, yes. Same girl. Not stolen so much the first time."

"And the second time?"

Rafe looked distinctly uncomfortable. "I'm...not really sure."

"What happened to her, really, Rafe?"

He shook his head. "I'm going to let Michael answer that when he feels the time is right. It's not my place to say."

"Okay." Eva'd have to live with that, she guessed. "You know, Sam and Michael seemed really uncomfortable around each other."

Rafe burst out laughing. "Uncomfortable is putting it lightly, hon. Those two, well, they've never gotten along."

Eva waited expectantly for Rafe to continue. He sneaked a glance toward the office door, then leaned forward conspiratorially. "You see, where we come from, there was a major issue that pretty much everyone was obsessed with. Michael and Sam were on opposite sides and really caught up in it. Eve was one of the few people who managed to stay completely neutral. Sam got so caught up in it that he started ignoring Eve, so she left him. I'll admit that it was pretty obvious early on that Eve and Michael were interested in each other, but Eve didn't trust Michael to not ignore her like Sam had, and Michael was with Lily at the time."

"Michael used to date Lily?" Eva felt an irrational jolt of jealousy. Lily was ridiculously pretty—even she had to acknowledge that—and the way she moved and talked drew attention from both sexes. If Eva was being completely honest, she didn't really feel comfortable around the other girl, no matter how friendly she'd been. Of course Michael would have been drawn in.

But that was in the past, right? She had no reason to worry about it now. Especially since she wasn't going to date anyone.

"This is where it gets especially complicated," Rafe replied, obviously warming to the subject. Eva should have asked earlier; Rafe never could resist a juicy tidbit of gossip. "So…" He trailed off abruptly, sitting up straighter as Gabe opened the door to the office.

Eva sat up straighter herself. Gabe did not look particularly pleased. "Raphael," he said, "can I see you in the office, please?"

Eva mouthed "Raphael?" at Rafe in surprise. She hadn't realized his name was short for something.

Rafe shook his head almost imperceptibly. "Of course," he answered Gabe. "The cookbooks beckon, love." Without another word he stood and followed Gabe into the office, closing the door behind him.

Eva glanced at the stacks, not particularly eager to get back to the cookbooks, but she felt like she should probably do some actual work, since she was getting paid. Standing, she worked her way back. It almost seemed like the books had tried to escape in her absence. With a sigh, she got back to work.

"Oh, by the way," Rafe said, scaring the crap out of Eva.

"Jesus Christ, Rafe!"

He gave her a ghost of a smile. "Sorry. About Sam—back in the day, he resorted to some pretty underhanded stuff when things didn't go his way. I don't want to say you can't like the guy, or not to be his friend or anything, but…be careful, okay?"

Eva wasn't sure what to say to that, so she said, "Gabe let you go free already?"

"Ah, even Gabe cannot resist my charms." Rafe grinned. "Though I think I may be on probation."

Eva glanced in the direction of the office. "You and Gabe have been together a long time, haven't you?"

"We have," Rafe answered, looking in the same direction. "Though I have managed to get into some thoroughly ridiculous situations all on my own." He was quiet for a moment. "But I like to think that we balance each other out. Gabe keeps me from killing myself in silly ways, and I make sure he has some excitement every once in a while." He turned back to Eva. "Well, I'm heading back into the trenches. If you can't find me in an hour, the history textbooks will have finally got me. Send a rescue party. If the rescue party doesn't return, run for it." He patted her on the shoulder and disappeared around the side of the bookcase.

Eva waited for a moment to see if he was going to come back—in an effort to protect her poor nerves—but when he didn't reappear after a moment, she turned back to the cookbooks and set about digesting this new information.

Chapter Eight

IN THE DREAM desert, Eva could see both gardens, but no one was there to point her toward one or the other. She looked down at herself; she was wearing the same flowy garment she'd noticed the others wearing. She waited a moment, to see if either Sam or Michael would show up, but neither did.

In the end, she decided to head toward the original garden, the one Sam and Lily had stopped her from entering. As soon as she stepped foot onto the lush grass, she could tell this one was different. It felt more...real, more solid. The grass was soft under her feet, and several types of trees, many of which shouldn't have been growing in the middle of the desert, waved in the breeze.

At first Eva thought the place was deserted, but then she caught a glimpse of Lily, just a glimpse, like the other woman was a shade moving through the landscape. Eva turned to follow her, trailing her hand along the tree trunks as she went. The landscape seemed to shimmer, and there was a change in the air, though Eva wasn't sure what was different.

Then she heard voices. She moved closer, slowly, to discover Lily and Michael standing close together, both dressed in the desert garb and looking younger—not physically, but emotionally. Michael's hair was long and tied back at the base of his neck. He had his arms around Lily's waist and their heads were bent together.

"I have to go," he said. "I will see you tonight."

"It will seem like forever," Lily murmured.

Michael kissed her on the cheek before he turned to go, disappearing into the trees. Lily watched him go, her smile transforming into a smirk as he was lost from view. She waited a moment, then turned and headed in the opposite direction. Eva looked after Michael, but decided to follow Lily instead.

Lily moved quickly through the garden. As they went, Eva saw there was more than just the grass and the trees. There were large patches of flowers, a stream, and the occasional well. But there was no one else that Eva could see.

Lily finally entered a clearing. She looked around carefully. A moment later, Sam entered. He smiled as he saw her, immediately crossing to her and pulling her into a deep kiss.

Eva raised both eyebrows.

After a long moment they pulled apart, Lily smiling seductively up at Sam.

"Lilith," he said. "What have you learned?"

Her smile faltered. "I am beginning to think Michael suspects where my true loyalties lie. He is not as open as he once was." Lily ran her hand down Sam's chest, twisting her fingers in the thin material of his shirt. "And what about your Eve? Does she...suspect?"

Sam snorted. "Eve? No. But let's not talk about her. We only have limited time before the meeting. Eve will be there when I need her. Otherwise, she is unimportant."

He leaned in for another kiss, which Lily eagerly provided. Eva pulled back into the trees, feeling distinctly uncomfortable. This was another new twist on the dream, if that was what this was.

"Eva," said Michael from beside her. She looked at him, knowing instinctively that this was her dream Michael.

"Michael," she said, "I don't understand what's happening."

"You are returning to yourself," he said. "Though this memory...it is not yours." He looked in the direction of the clearing, but the voices were gone. "Some sort of foreign influence."

"What is this place?" Eva asked.

Michael took her hand, leading her through the garden. "This is where it all began. Where we congregated. Where we met. Where things fell apart."

"What was that back there?"

"Eva," he said, looking down at her. "I am a figment of your subconscious. I cannot know what you do not. Since the memory is not yours, I do not know its intention or purpose any better than you." He paused, cocking his head. "Still, we should probably get rid of the foreign presence."

There was that strange shimmer again, and Lily's wraith moved through the garden just ahead of them.

"That's it," Michael said. "You must tell it to go."

The wraith paused expectantly, smiling at Eva with that strange, seductive grin Lily seemed to wear most of the time. Eva took a hesitant step forward, releasing Michael's hand. "Lily, you need to go."

"Ah," said the wraith, its voice barely a whisper, "so quickly you have found me, Eva. I told him you might. We were always incompatible, after all." The wraith leaned forward, trailing a ghostly hand down Eva's cheek. She shivered. "Did you enjoy your present? Eve never knew, not even after she was already gone."

"Knew what?" Eva asked, though she suspected. Sam had cheated on Eve with Lily. "Did Michael know?"

"Oh, eventually, yes." The wraith twirled around Eva, barely visible in the bright sunlight. "Michael may not be the most observant of people, but he has friends who notice much. I am not sure he ever forgave me that." There was just a touch of sadness to the wraith's voice. "I will go. You have been rejecting me since I started, after all."

And just like that, she was gone.

Eva turned back to find Michael had gone as well. In fact, there was a new, unpleasant feel to the garden. The hair on the back of Eva's neck stood on end. Clouds blew in, blocking the sunlight, and the wind grew strong and cold, whipping Eva's hair around painfully. Eva folded her arms across her chest.

When she turned back around to where Lily had been, she found someone new.

It was another woman, similar in coloring to Eva, but taller, with a proud, strong bearing. Her green eyes flashed dangerously, and Eva knew without a doubt that this was Eve.

Eva wasn't sure what she'd been expecting. From Rafe's description, perhaps someone less confident, more timid. Someone who wouldn't notice Sam's deception. Eve was none of these things.

"He is mine," said Eve in a low voice, watching Eva closely.

Eva wished dream Michael hadn't gone. What was this supposed to be? A memory, a twisted part of her subconscious? Another foreign presence? "You're gone."

Eve took a step forward. Eva forced herself to stand her ground—it was her dream, after all—and Eve stopped less than a foot away. "How can you be so sure?"

"Michael has been lost for years without you. If you were still here, why wouldn't you have come back? You are out of the picture."

"Hm," Eve replied. She had a deep, throaty voice that reminded Eva of a jazz singer. She looked Eva up and down one more time, then suddenly struck out with her hand, grabbing Eva by the collar and hauling her close. "You know nothing," she hissed. Eve held up her free hand, and a strange, glowing ball of light began to form, floating slightly above her palm. "You are lost. I will change that."

She drove the ball of light toward Eva's chest.

Eva let out a squeak, sat up suddenly, and fell out of bed. Az went with her, turning the whole mess into a hissing, extremely sharp tangle of linens. It took several minutes for Eva to free both herself and the cat, and Az sulked off to the corner and glared at her, swishing his tail.

Eva sat on the edge of her bed, feeling out of sorts with the unexpected turn the dream had taken. "What the hell is my brain trying to tell me?" she groaned, flopping backwards. Was it some sort of not-so-subtle hint that Michael wasn't over Eve, so she should back off? Except, she was surprised to find, she didn't want to. There was something about him that made her want him closer.

Why shouldn't she give into that?

And that whole thing with Sam and Lily—only Sam had called Lily Lilith, and there was the whole garden motif that had mixed itself in—did it mean anything, or was her brain just stuffing her coursework in on top of everything else?

Slightly shaken, she got up and went in search of breakfast and clean clothes.

A FEW HOURS later, she headed out for class. Her hat was still missing—she definitely suspected Az now, but couldn't find where he'd stashed it—but it was unseasonably warm and it turned out that her jacket was overkill as well. It was a beautiful day, not a cloud in sight, and Eva rubbed her forearm as she went. Az had gotten her with his claws during their scuffle earlier, and she had several scratches. They itched.

If he hadn't already, he'd probably eat her hat now for revenge.

She tried to focus on planning out the rest of her essay, but her thoughts kept straying back to what she could remember of her dream. Is that really what Eve had looked like, and if so, where had Eva conjured her image from? She supposed she could ask Rafe or even Michael for a description, but how would she explain why she wanted to know?

She missed the dreams that just been her and Michael and the desert. At least those were fairly obvious in their meaning.

She wasn't paying attention and walked straight into someone. Jesus, she needed to get her act together. Looking up, intending to apologize, she paused, mouth half-open.

"We've got to stop meeting like this," Michael said, though he was obviously joking. "Are you sure you didn't just walk out in front of that car?"

Embarrassed, she covered that fact up by punching him in the shoulder. Apparently she had the emotional maturity of an elementary school student. Flushing, she said, "Shut up. I was thinking."

Michael grinned. "I'm not saying I mind. You can run into me as many times as you like." He offered her his arm. "Where are you off to?"

"That class with the obsession with angel essays." Eva took the offered arm. Michael's skin was warm beneath her hand. He was wearing a blue t-shirt, and she could see one of Gabe's brightly-colored umbrellas sticking precariously out of one of his back pockets. "And you?"

"Lunch. Thought I might try the cafeteria at the UMC and see if the choices had improved since the last time I tried." He gave her a brilliant smile, and she almost tripped.

Michael steadied her, frowning down at the scratches on her arm. "What happened here?"

"Az and I had a disagreement. He took offense to getting smooshed, though it's his own fault for sleeping so close."

"Did you put something on these? They look pretty bad."

Eva waved the comment off. "I'm not worried. The sun helps."

Michael froze. "I beg your pardon?"

"Being out in the sun always makes me feel better, whether it's a headache or a scratch or what-have-you." Eva turned her face up to the sky, closing her eyes. When she opened them again, she found Michael staring at her, mouth open. "What?" she asked.

"I...uh..." Michael closed his mouth, swallowing hard. "Nothing."

It was obviously not nothing. She frowned, debating whether or not she should push him on the matter.

Michael shook his head absently, then smiled at her again. "How many essay topics do you think one professor can get out of the angel topic?"

He was trying to distract her. She sighed, but let him win, for now. "Oh, probably a few more. I bet you he makes it through the entire semester."

"I'm okay with that." Michael replaced her hand on his arm and they started back across campus. "I am happy to help, if you want me to. Give me an excuse to see you more. Plus, angels are—"

"Your favorite, I know." Eva smiled at him. He seemed to be in a good mood today, which was nice, and a bit contagious. She could feel the last vestiges of strangeness from her dream wearing off. "Let me guess. Your favorite angel is Michael."

Michael laughed. "How did you know? What can I say? Something resonates there."

"You know he was stolen from the Chaldeans, right?"

"Hey, the Chaldeans were cool," Michael said. "I liked them rather a lot."

Eva raised an eyebrow. "Liked them?"

Michael rubbed the back of his neck. "Let's just say that religious studies wasn't my first rodeo either."

"Man, how long have you been in school?"

"I told you I was a chronic student."

Eva laughed, reveling in the warm weather and the company. It was over too soon. Her building loomed up across the grass. She should probably hurry so she wouldn't be late, but she couldn't bring herself to care.

Michael moved her hand from his arm to his hand. Eva turned to look at him, gazing up into his eyes. They seemed even brighter in the sunlight. "Eva," he said, "I was serious when I said I wanted to see you more."

Something caught in her throat. "I'd like that too," she said, though it came out more as a whisper. He was so close. Eva found herself leaning closer, her gaze drifting toward his lips, but he caught sight of something over her shoulder and his eyes instantly hardened.

Eva pulled back, knowing what she was going to see before she turned. Sam was leaning on the wall next to the door to the building. His stance was practiced ease, but the dark look on his look said otherwise. When he realized they were looking at him, his face cleared, all emotion disappearing.

"I'd better go," she murmured.

Michael's gaze was still on Sam. After a moment he shifted his gaze to her, and then back to Sam. "Okay. I'll see you later?"

"Of course." She straightened her backpack on her shoulder, making her way toward the entrance of the building. Michael stayed where he was, tucking his hands into his pockets. Eva forced a smile as she got closer, waving at Sam. "Good afternoon! How was your weekend?"

"Not as productive as I had hoped," he replied. He seemed content to play along with the charade that everything was okay between them, at least for now. "Lily was helping me with a project, but she's been running into issues. I'll probably have to rethink my entire execution."

"Was it a school project?"

"No, just something I've been wanting to do." He reached forward, pulling the door open for her. Eva risked a glance over her shoulder; Michael was still there, watching them, his shoulders stiff.

She noticed Sam was looking the same direction. "Smug bastard," he murmured under his breath.

"Hmm?" Eva said, though she had heard him just fine.

"Nothing," Sam said. He placed a hand on her back as she passed him, following her inside. "How about you? Are you sleeping okay?"

Eva paused mid-step. "Why do you ask?"

"You look tired, that's all."

"I'm fine."

Sam's hand finally dropped from her back as they entered the classroom, just barely making it in time. Professor Axelrad was already at the lectern, organizing his notes. He still used paper notes, though many of the other professors had switched to tablets and laptops.

As Professor Axelrad began his lecture, Eva let her mind wander. She glanced at Sam, sitting next to her, one foot up on the seat in front of him and an arm draped loosely around the back of her seat. He looked over after a moment, smiled at her, and turned back to the front of the classroom. What was going on there? Eva absently scribbled down whatever the professor had written on the board. Sam was obviously threatened by

Michael, but almost to a point that seemed past what she would have expected based on what Rafe had told her about their history. And she couldn't figure out if he was really interested in her or not. He'd kissed her cheek, but that'd been over a week ago, and he hadn't made a similar move since, aside from unwanted possessiveness.

And now that things were heating up with Michael, she didn't think she wanted him to, no matter how pretty his hair was.

Professor Axelrad began calling on people to answer questions, so Eva was forced to switch her attention back to the subject at hand and didn't have another chance to drift off before class was over.

Sam gathered up his supplies, still staying almost uncomfortably close to her, like he felt he had some sort of claim. "Off to work, I suppose."

"As always," Eva replied, sliding her bag back over her shoulder. "I don't mind, though. My bosses let me work on homework when things are slow." She moved into the flow of students leaving, forcing a bit of distance between her and Sam. If he noticed, he didn't seem to care.

Eva moved straight out into the sun, but now clouds were starting to roll in. Of course it'd been too good to last.

Lily was standing where Michael had been, wearing tight jeans and a thin sweater. She smiled and started toward Eva. She leaned in close as she reached her, her hair tickling the side of Eva's neck. "Did you enjoy your present?" she murmured, so low Eva almost couldn't hear her.

Lily's words seemed oddly familiar, and for a moment Eva got a glimpse of her dream from the night before, but the details wouldn't solidify. She blinked at Lily, wondering if she should ask for clarification, but she suspected she wouldn't get any.

"Lily," said Sam brightly from beside them. Lily pulled away, straightening. For a moment, she just looked at Sam, but then her usual smile slid back into place.

"Ah, what can I do for you, my dear cousin?"

"I find my project has more and more issues every time I look at it."

"I warned you," Lily said. "By the very nature of said project, there's an aversion to cold and dark. I told you I might not be able to help, if that was the case. Actually, the fact that the aversion exists should help prove your hypothesis."

"I'd better get to work," Eva said. She turned to go, but Lily reached out and grabbed her by the wrist.

"Stay for a moment, Eva," Lily said. Her green eyes met Eva's, and for a second, just a second, Eva felt impelled to listen to her. But she shook her head, and the feeling fell away. Lily looked at Sam. "You see?"

Sam frowned. "It used to be more effective. What happened?"

"Opposing influences," Lily said, releasing Eva's wrist. "Others are stronger."

Eva had no idea what they were talking about, but she knew she didn't like it. "What the hell was that? What are you talking about?"

This time Sam reached forward to grab her hand. "You'll come to the meeting on Thursday, right? I'm doing Rocky Road this time."

It took Eva a second to realize what he meant. While the last one had been fun, she was beginning to realize she didn't really feel comfortable being alone with both of them in the same room. Or with Lily at all, honestly. Eva didn't think the other woman necessarily intended anything bad, but there was something there that made her skin crawl.

"Opposing elements," Lily said, giving her a sympathetic smile. "Can't be helped."

"What?" asked Eva.

Sam squeezed her hand. "The meeting?"

Eva sighed. She pulled her hand back, and Sam let her, thankfully. "No, I don't think so." She was tempted to tell him—them—that she didn't want to spend time with them at all, especially not after...whatever that just was. "I just...it's not for me, Sam."

The smile faded off Sam's face. "Really?"

"Yeah. Look, I really need to go. I can't be late. I'll see you later. Bye, Lily." Without waiting for a reply, she turned to go. She had goosebumps on her arms. As she went, she rubbed them, freezing in the motion when she reached the scratches from that morning. She looked down in surprise. They had scabbed over and looked several days old.

That—that was new.

Chapter Nine

MICHAEL KEPT meaning to take Rafe's advice and try to stay away from Eva, but it just didn't seem to be working out. Even if he didn't go looking for her, it seemed like she was everywhere now. And he guessed he could have moved out of her way the other day—she'd been so deep in her thoughts, she probably wouldn't have noticed him—but he couldn't bring himself to do it.

But he was really trying now. Yes. Giving them both time apart before the trip would be good for them. Even though he'd told Eva he wanted to spend more time with her. And he did. But it wasn't the best idea. Gabe's warning echoed in his head.

He'd made a mental list of places that were off-limits. He couldn't stop by the shop, though to be honest, before Eva he hadn't really bothered, but now, not knowing what Eva's hours were—and Rafe and Gabe didn't seem to know either—it was too great of a risk. Much of campus also became off limits as well, as he didn't know her schedule at all and the religious studies department had an annoying habit of sticking their classes wherever they pleased. And the library—his heart still raced at the memory—was definitely off limits.

That left him the physics building. It was an okay building, as far as they went, being relatively new. They'd even thought to put in some areas with windows and a sufficient amount of light. That didn't change the fact that it wasn't very big and something on the third floor smelled a little like rotten fish, and Michael wasn't quite sure what it was. He suspected that if he were forced to spend any more time in there, he might go insane. So he let himself go outside into the rain.

To be honest, he wasn't sure trying to keep away was helping at all. When he actually focused on trying, it just gave him more of an excuse to think about her and where she might be. So, if he ran into Eva, maybe it was meant to be. She haunted his dreams as it was. The end of the semester was coming up soon, and that meant her trip was as well, if she was still going.

He'd done a lot of thinking, and despite Gabe's worries, he was still convinced about accompanying Eva on her trip. And she had said he could come along. If nothing else, he wanted to make sure she stayed safe. He'd make sure she focused on what she was supposed to be doing. Or so he told himself.

Michael walked around campus, letting the rain wash over him. He still had Gabe's umbrella with him, but he found a good rain cleansing. A thorough circuit of the school grounds didn't reveal any sign of Eva, though he hadn't realized he'd been looking until he went by the place where he'd first seen her. He smiled faintly.

Maybe he'd been silly to coop himself up in the physics building, he decided after a second circuit of campus still didn't turn her up. After all, they must have been going to school here for years overlapping and he hadn't ever run into her before, so the likelihood of it being a regular occurrence now wasn't that high, never mind that it had happened twice in as many weeks. He would have remembered her if he'd seen her earlier, he was sure of that.

Desperation was beginning to set in. How long did a guy have to wander in the rain before he found who he was looking for?

Someone was approaching out of the downpour, and as they got closer, Michael was supremely displeased to find that it was Sam.

"Sammael," he greeted.

"Michael," said Sam. He didn't seem that happy to see Michael either.

Michael debated just moving on, his temper flaring just by standing next to the other man. There was too much bad blood there, and there was nothing that Sam could say that could help him out.

"You need to back off," said Sam.

"What?" Michael looked at the other man. Sam's green eyes nearly burned with loathing, his black hair plastered down on his forehead, partially hiding them.

"I saw her first. You can't just waltz in and take her from me again," Sam said.

Again? What does that mean? Michael felt his temper rising. "She's her own person—it's up to her who she chooses."

"I'm warning you." Sam thrust his shoulders back. "You back off."

"Fuck off," said Michael. "I'm going to do whatever I want, and you just try to stop me."

Sam growled low in his throat. His eyes flashed. "I'm so sick of you. I should have gotten rid of your sorry ass millennia ago."

"Are we really going to do this right here, in the middle of campus?" Michael asked calmly, though part of him hoped that Sam would push it, would give him a reason to fight. It had been so long since he'd been able to fully release. As civilization pushed on, it became more and more a necessity to attempt to live as a normal person.

"No one can see through this rain," replied Sam. "It won't take that long anyway. I know you and Gabriel and Raphael haven't been keeping up with your powers, with your stupid policy of non-interference. Don't you think it's about time to stir things up anyway? Humans have become so defiant, so sure their gods have left them."

"We've fought about that in the past," said Michael. "We decided to leave them alone, to their own fates. They don't need us doing any more damage than they can do to themselves."

"We could save them," insisted Sam, taking a step closer. "Tell them what to do, have them worship us."

"We tried that. It didn't work four thousand years ago, and I see no reason why it would work now. You'd never get everyone to work together, never get everyone to agree to a single course of action. We saw how it affected people when their gods fought amongst themselves."

Sam shook his head before a slow smile that Michael did not like at all spread across his face. "You're right, of course. But if there were less of us, then there would be fewer differences in opinions, which brings me back to my original purpose."

"Ah," said Michael, thinking that this was entirely too civilized to be a fight, but then Sam released his wings and Michael was forced to change his opinion. Sam's wings were impressive and large, probably twelve feet in wingspan, covered completely with black feathers. Sam's laughter reached Michael through the rain, and he glanced around quickly, making sure there was no one present. The rain was still coming down hard, keeping all but the most determined people inside, and though Michael hadn't really been paying attention, Sam had chosen a spot out behind the engineering building, where it was mostly just empty field. Michael could hardly see the building himself, so even if there were people peering out into the rain, they probably wouldn't be able to see this far.

"Just going to sit there and take it?" asked Sam, looking positively gleeful.

The ground beneath Michael rumbled and he took a few involuntarily steps backwards. It'd been so long since he released that it was no longer instinct to when confronted with a threat, and he couldn't help wishing that Gabe was here to do something about the rain.

Sam advanced, grinning maniacally. "Come on, Michael, at least make it interesting. It's no fun if I can get rid of you because you just sit there."

Michael debated not releasing, just because it would annoy the hell out of Sam, but the ground beneath him shifted again, and moments later large pieces of earth lifted themselves. For a second, they just hung in the air unnaturally, but then they were flying through the air towards Michael at a deadly speed.

Instinct finally kicked in and Michael let his wings out. It felt almost euphoric to have them extend to their full size, their golden feathers beating back the rain. He reached out with his flame, burning the bits of earth to a crisp. They dropped back down to the ground, and Michael watched them fall, wondering what the groundskeeper would think when he found them. Belatedly, he wondered why they couldn't just throw punches like normal people. At least it didn't do property damage.

Sam let out a whoop and picked up a larger bit of earth. It left a large hole behind, and as Sam carefully aimed it, Michael considered his options. Water was bad—it tended to make wielding fire more tiring. He couldn't do anything about that, so it would be best to take out Sam as quickly as possible, which was going to be difficult with him flinging dirt about. It would be worse if he found some rocks instead.

Sam let the wad of earth fly and Michael dodged to the side. There was nothing that would burn for more than a few seconds in this rain. Cursing, he ran towards the other man, intending to get up close and do...something, but Sam stepped backwards as the ground beneath Michael shot up sharply, throwing him several feet into the air. He opened his wings, but by the time he'd steadied himself, a new barrage had started, one that he wasn't ready for. He threw up his hands to block his face as the dirt—more mud than anything else—slammed into him. One clod hit him in the stomach, forcing the air out of his lungs. He coughed, but moments later more mud slammed into him, and he couldn't see what was happening at all through the rain.

He folded his wings and dropped back to the ground as he was hit again. Something hard bounced off his left wing, and he cried out in pain. Damnit, Sam had found the rocks. Michael hunkered down near the ground, curling his wings around his body, trying to think. If he couldn't get close to Sam, and he couldn't get anything to burn, then there wasn't much he could do. Sam didn't have much ammunition in an empty field either, but Michael had to admit that he would tire out first, and then it was only a matter of time.

Thunder rumbled overhead, and that was all that was needed to turn the tide of battle. Michael straightened, aware that he was probably grinning like a madman. He could barely see Sam through the rain, but he was scowling, looking up at the sky. No doubt he knew what it meant too—they'd fought enough times, after all.

Lightning flashed, and Michael reached out, directing the flow of the lightning towards his adversary. Sam dodged, but part of his wing was scorched. Michael could hear his stream of cursing.

Now that the playing field was leveled, Michael was tempted to follow through with his thoughts from earlier—Sam had been a pain in his ass for as long as he could remember, and life would be much easier if he took him out, like the other man had been intending to do to him. There was another flash of lightning, which Michael again steered toward Sam. The other man dodged faster this time, but he was obviously favoring one wing. Sam picked up an enormous section of dirt and flung it at Michael, hardly bothering to aim, expecting sheer mass to be worth more than accuracy.

Michael threw up his wings to protect himself, gritting his teeth as the mud and rocks bounced off of them. Thunder rumbled again, but when he opened his wings Sam was nowhere to be found.

Michael sighed in relief, tilting his head up and letting the rain run down over his face. He waited a few minutes before regretfully reabsorbing his wings, just in case, but it seemed like Sam wasn't going to come back. He took off his jacket and ran his fingers along the back of it—damn, his wings had ripped it. Gabe would fix it, but he wouldn't be happy about it. His shirt was probably torn as well.

Sliding his jacket back on, Michael took off through the middle of campus, doing a better job of peering through the rain to see if anyone was coming. It had been a long time since Sam had confronted him, and he was right, Michael hadn't been keeping up with his powers. They seemed like an unnecessary attention-getter when one was surrounded by humans.

The rain began lightening as he left campus. He'd been so intent on his surroundings that he hadn't been paying attention to where he was going, so it took him a moment to realize that he was apparently headed for the bookstore. Well, that was probably for the best—the sooner Gabe and Rafe were aware of things, the better.

Rafe was in the front of the store as Michael pulled the door open, straightening the books in the window display. He glanced at Michael as he walked in, then went back to his work for a moment before dropping the book he was holding and turning back. "What the hell happened to you?"

"That bad?" Michael tentatively prodded at his face. It hurt. Damn.

"That bad, the man says." Rafe rolled his eyes. "It looks like you ran into a pole, and then ran into it a couple of more times for good measure. Now, what happened?"

"Well, I ran into Sam," started Michael, then paused as Rafe cocked his head in an urgent manner towards the register. Michael turned to see Eva sitting behind the register, her eyes wide. Oh, hell. It must look like Sam had done a number on him, and he had never stopped being competitive. "Anyway, you should see him."

"Good man," said Rafe. "Let us go see Gabriel and see what he thinks about you fighting." He clapped Michael on the back, then purposefully steered him around the counter toward the office. "It will give him a much-needed break from his solitaire game. It is terrible, somebody," he said, shooting a look at Eva, "found him a new variety on the internet."

"You can glare at me all you want," said Eva, "but I know who is in charge of the Christmas bonuses." Despite the joviality in her voice, her eyes showed her uneasiness, and Michael could feel his cheeks heating up as they followed his path through the store.

"Well played," said Rafe, opening the door and stuffing Michael in the office. He stepped in after him and shut the door.

Gabe looked up from his computer, which really was a solitaire game for once, frowning as he noticed Michael's face. Michael was tempted to go find a mirror so he could see how bad it really was. "What on earth have you been up to?"

"You're not going to be happy," said Michael. He crossed the room, sliding his jacket off as he went. He heard Rafe's sharp intake of breath as he offered the jacket to Gabe.

"Wings?" asked Rafe. He glanced at the door, then moved closer to the other two, lowering his voice. "Are you *crazy*?"

"He started it." Michael frowned at his roommate. "I had to defend myself."

"Of course you did," said Gabe, sticking his hand through one of the holes in the jacket. "We all know how irrational Sam can get at times. Did anyone see you?"

Michael shook his head. "I don't think so." He sighed. "I thought I was dead there for a second. This climate is not helpful."

Gabe frowned. "Maybe we shouldn't have you wandering around by yourself."

"Please don't talk like that," said Michael. "I am much too old for a babysitter."

"Yes, but neither Gabe nor I have issues with a little bit of rain either," said Rafe, crossing his arms.

"Why did Sam start a fight with you now? We've all been living here for a while now." Gabe held the jacket up, pursing his lips at the twin holes. "This is not going to be easy to fix."

Michael glanced at Rafe, then back to Gabe. "I think it has something to do with Eva, honestly, though I am not entirely sure, because there was also rambling about becoming gods and things along those lines. But he did say I couldn't take her from him *again*."

"Why can everyone sense this except me?" asked Rafe.

"Your senses really suck," replied Michael pleasantly. "They always have, and you've never bothered to do anything about it, so there you are."

"I'm not the one trying to start fires in the middle of a downpour," said Rafe. "Why don't you do something about that?"

"Stop that," said Gabe. He set the jacket to the side of his desk and leaned back in his chair, eying his roommates. "This is serious. It's been a couple hundred of years since we've released, hasn't it?" He ran one hand across one shoulder blade absently, as if he was trying to remember the sensation properly.

"Sam also called our policy of trying to blend in stupid, if I'm remembering correctly, and implied that he, at least, was getting plenty of practice." Michael pulled up the chair from Rafe's desk—it had dust all over it—and sat down. "I don't suppose you have any extra shirts lying around, do you? I'll go back out with the holes in the back if I have to, but it's slightly suspicious."

"Yeah, Rafe keeps a stash because he gets dust all over the place," replied Gabe, gesturing off to one of the back corners. "So, are you saying that Sam is thinking about declaring himself a god again?"

Michael debated staying where he was, but the dust on the chair was starting to make his nose tickle. He rose, heading towards the haphazard stack of clothing in the corner. It wasn't an ideal solution, since Rafe was considerably broader than he was, but it would have to do. If nothing else, it'd be nice to put on something dry. "I don't know if he was serious or if he was just letting off steam." He peeled off his wet t-shirt and dropped it in a wad on Rafe's desk. Rafe made a small murmur of protest, but Michael ignored him as he extracted a blue t-shirt from the pile.

There was a knock on the door and all three of them froze. Eva pushed the door open. "I'm sorry to interrupt, but there's someone here who had a book..." Her voice trailed off as she caught sight of Michael half-naked in the back of the office. Her eyes slowly made their way up to his, and Michael found himself falling into those eyes, unable to look away, and not sure he wanted to.

"Michael. Michael!" Michael blinked, surprised to find Rafe practically up his nose. "God, what's the matter with you? Put your shirt on. This is a respectable outfit Gabe and I are running here. We don't need you seducing employees and customers." Rafe had placed himself between Michael and the door, and if Eva was still in the door, he couldn't see her around Rafe's bulk. "Besides, I think if you blushed any harder you might set something on fire, and there is a lot of flammable material around here, so we would prefer you didn't."

Michael glared at Rafe, sliding the shirt over his head.

"Now!" said Rafe. "What were you saying, Eva?"

So she must still be there. Michael sighed—what was he going to have to do to stop acting like an idiot around her? He sat down heavily on the floor and laid his head back against the cool metal of Rafe's desk.

Eva's voice sounded a little funny. "I said there's someone here who thought they had a book they ordered come in."

Rafe nodded. "Okay, let's look them up in the computer." He strode across the room, closing the door behind him. Michael could hear him talking to the customer through the door, though he couldn't make out what was being said.

Gabe's head appeared over the side of the desk. "How are you feeling?"

"I am going crazy. Rafe was right. It was only a matter of time." Michael stretched his legs out. "I am going to live in this corner and never leave it."

Frowning, Gabe crouched next to him. "You must be exhausted."

He hadn't been, until Gabe had said anything about it, but now an overwhelming urge to sleep crept over him. It'd been a long day, with too many emotional extremes. A good long rest would be fantastic.

"Why don't you take a nap?" Gabe was saying. "You won't have to worry about anything here in the store, and we'll wake you up when we close for the night and we can all go and have a nice dinner. And we can worry about Sam then."

Michael nodded slightly, his eyelids drooping. From somewhere Gabe produced a pillow and a blanket, which Michael took gratefully, if a bit sleepily, and curled up with, still in the corner. *What a terrible day*, he thought to himself as he dropped off to sleep.

THE CUSTOMER, satisfied with his purchase, was just leaving when Gabe came out of the office, closing the door gently behind him.

"Where's Michael?" Eva asked before she could think better of it. She could still see him as clearly as if he were standing right in front of her, his body hard and tight, but covered with terrible bruises the like of which she'd never seen.

"Sleeping," answered Gabe. "He's worn out."

Rafe shot Gabe a suspicious look, but for the life of her Eva couldn't figure out why. She'd want to sleep too if she'd been hurt like that.

"Will he be all right?" she asked, taking a peek at the door to the office.

Gabe gave her a reassuring smile. "Don't worry about him. He's a fast healer."

Eva rubbed her forearm at the comment. Though it'd only been a few days, her scratches were gone. She knew she was being obnoxious, but panic fluttered uncomfortably about her stomach. "But what happened?"

"Sounds like Sam jumped him in the rain," said Rafe, lounging against the counter. "I'm sure Sam looks just as bad."

Gabe glared at Rafe.

"What?" said Rafe. "Sam probably looks worse, only less bruised and more..." He trailed off as Gabe elbowed him in the stomach.

"Anyway," said Gabe, ignoring the look Rafe was making at the back of his head, "Don't worry about it. We'll make sure he's okay." He glanced at Rafe, who opened his eyes wide and nodded, then back to Eva, sighing. "You can come out to dinner with us after we close the shop if you'd like."

Eva looked away, watching the people pass by outside under their umbrellas. Why was she so worried about him, anyway? Gabe would react appropriately, she told herself, if he was seriously hurt. So things would probably be okay. She glanced at the counter, where she had the materials for her essay spread out. She was mostly done. "Okay," she said. Why not? She hadn't spent time with her employers outside of work before, but she enjoyed their company in general, and she'd been feeling a little lonely lately, so it certainly wouldn't hurt. "I won't get much work done after dark anyway."

Gabe gave Rafe another look, then disappeared back into the office.

Rafe sighed. "Gabe is mean when he feels like it," he said, rubbing his side. "Still working on essays? I keep putting aside mysteries for you, and they are languishing."

Eva smiled slightly. "Languishing?"

"A book without a reader," said Rafe seriously, "is no book at all." Leaving her to ponder that gem, he turned and returned to the window to straighten the books. Eva watched him go, telling herself to stop worrying about Michael. In fact, if he hadn't been so beaten up, the image of him shirtless would have been very nice. He had a good body, so he obviously spent time making sure he stayed in shape. She bet it felt nice too, smooth and soft and warm. Blushing, she forced herself to go back to writing.

It slowly got dark outside, the sun disappearing behind the buildings and then the horizon. Eva felt her concentration slipping. She dug a mystery out of the pile Rafe had made for her under the counter and began reading.

The door opened behind her, and Eva spun on her stool so quickly she almost fell off, but it was just Gabe. He raised an eyebrow at her as he shut the door behind him. She'd needed to stop acting crazy around Michael. Hell, he wasn't even in the room, and she was all on edge.

"Let's close up," said Gabe. "I'm getting hungry."

Rafe had long since abandoned the window display to return to the stacks. He emerged now, carrying a large stack of books in his hands. "Turns out we do have a couple copies of that book you were looking for," he said to Gabe. He went around the counter, smiling at Eva as he noticed she was reading one of the books he'd picked out, and disappeared into the office.

Gabe nodded absently as he crossed to the door and flipped the sign to closed. Eva jumped up to help, shutting off lights throughout the building. She personally thought the store was a little creepy in the dark, and didn't like to enter the stacks after the lights were off. Luckily, Rafe was normally more than willing to venture back into the dark, so usually she could foist any last-minute errands off on him. Sometimes it seemed like she could hear a breeze sweeping through the books, though one would think they would be less dusty if that were true.

Rafe reemerged from the office followed by Michael, who was rubbing one eye sleepily. Eva's heart skipped a beat. He was already looking much better than he had earlier; much of the swelling in his face had gone down, and the bruises had faded. Gabe hadn't been kidding when he said he was a fast healer. "How are you feeling?" she asked.

He gave her a small smile. "I'm a bit sore," he said, rubbing at his left shoulder. It looked like he was favoring that arm a little, and Eva wondered if he'd broken it, and why no one had done anything if he had.

"Out we go," said Gabe, holding the door open. "Otherwise you get to spend the night in the store."

Glancing around at the darkened stacks, Eva thought that sounded terrible. She hurriedly slid on her coat and pulled her bag over one shoulder.

She watched out of the corner of her eye as Michael slid on his jacket. He winced a little as he pulled the sleeve up his left arm, but the arm seemed to have full movement.

The four of them left the shop, Gabe pausing to lock the door. It had stopped raining, and the sky had cleared. Eva looked up at the stars twinkling overhead. It was such a rare sight this time of year, and she delighted in it. Each twinkle seemed to be a star saying hello. The night didn't seem so dark.

It was cold, but none of her companions seemed to have noticed. She had a scarf in her bag, and now she pulled it out, wrapping it around her neck and watching her breath create a bit of steam in front of her mouth.

There was apparently an unspoken agreement about where they were going, because her companions headed up the street without saying a word. Eva trailed along behind them, not minding the silence. The world seemed peaceful and still, and she could feel tension she hadn't even known she been harboring slowly leaving her body.

Ahead, Gabe hovered almost protectively by Michael's side while Rafe flitted back and forth. Eva watched them, wondering again how the three of them had ended up together. Maybe she'd ask, some day.

They reached the same restaurant Michael had taken her to that first day they'd met. *It must be a favorite for all three of them,* Eva thought as Gabe held the door open for her. Michael navigated around the tables, choosing a booth by the window. He slid in on one side and, before Eva could follow, Rafe had slid in after him. Gabe slid in first on the other side, leaving her on the aisle, about as far away from Michael as she could get at a four-person table. She felt a wave of irritation rise, but she was sure they hadn't done it on purpose, and it would only cause problems if she made a fuss about it. These were her bosses, after all. With a sigh of resignation, she slid onto the bench next to Gabe.

Rafe grinned at her. "I see you were reading one of the mysteries." He paused, his smile fading. "You never read anymore. Is something wrong?"

For a moment, she thought about pointing out that she couldn't think in the dark, but something else came to mind instead. "Yeah, maybe," she replied, hazarding a glance at Michael. He had his head buried in a menu, though Eva suspected that he came here often enough that he had the thing memorized. "I had a very strange...encounter with Sam and Lily the other day."

She was distinctly aware of their attention being sharply focused on her. She shifted uncomfortably. "It seemed like Lily tried to...I don't know, mind-control me or something." Great, now she sounded crazy. She probably should have just kept the whole thing to herself. "And she said something about a present, but I have no idea what she was talking about."

"Did it work? The mind control, I mean," asked Rafe. He glanced at Gabe, who eyed Michael out of the corner of his eye. Michael's menu slipped a little lower, and she could see him looking over the top of it.

"No, and I got the impression she didn't think it would anyway," she replied, unsure whether or not Rafe was messing with her.

"Well, excellent," said Rafe.

"Is Sam bothering you?" Gabe asked suddenly. Eva noticed Michael raise an eyebrow at him over his menu. "I mean, if you want help getting rid of him, just let us know."

"Sam?" Eva shook her head. "No, I can handle Sam. I'm more worried about Lily, but even then, I don't think she means anything bad. But I don't think I'll be spending as much time with them anymore."

"Are you sure?" Gabe asked.

Eva nodded, staring purposefully down at her menu and hoping Gabe would drop the subject.

Pat came by, smiling widely at everyone. Eva felt her mood lift slightly. "Well, if it isn't my favorite group of people," she said, pulling a notepad out of her apron. "Drinks for you tonight?"

Eva ordered a hot chocolate again. Michael got his tea, Rafe ordered a beer, and Gabe just wanted water.

"So, Eva," said Rafe when Pat had wandered off to get their drinks, "any plans for the holidays? Are you going to go home and see your parents?"

"I haven't decided yet." She leaned back against the padded back of the booth. Michael had put the menu away, but he was settled back in his seat now, head resting against the booth, eyes closed. Maybe he was still tired. "I still want to go on that trip I was telling you about, but I should probably go see my mother for a little bit too. She worries that I'm not doing so well on my own."

"Where are you thinking of going on your trip?" asked Gabe, looking at her intently.

Eva felt herself flush a little, unused to having so many people focused on her at once. Didn't they have anything else they wanted to talk about, or their own plans to make? "Greece, hopefully—it may depend on what I can afford." She didn't want to answer questions all night. "What about you guys?"

"What about us?" said Rafe. He leant his head on one hand, giving her a one-sided smile.

"You know," she said, gesturing vaguely. "Holiday plans."

"I don't know about everyone else, but I plan to fly over mangers announcing the birth of the Messiah," replied Rafe. Gabe shifted in his seat, and a moment later Rafe grimaced and rubbed his leg under the table.

"I don't think we've really thought about it," said Gabe calmly.

"You're not going to see your families?" asked Eva, surprised. She always tried to make it home, at least for a little bit, even though things had been weird ever since she left to come to school here.

There was a moment of silence while her companions exchanged glances. "Not this year," Gabe said finally.

Pat saved them by delivering their drinks. Suspecting hers was too hot to drink straight out, Eva cupped her hands around it, intent on gathering what warmth she could. Everything was still quiet around the table, and Eva found herself wondering how they could get along so well at work just to sit in awkward silence outside of it.

Sighing, she took a sip of her cocoa which turned out to be mostly whipped cream.

Rafe took a few sips of his beer and started in on a story about a man he'd known once who had always insisted on wearing two shoes that didn't match. It was an odd story, but Rafe had a natural way of storytelling and it got everyone laughing, even Michael, who seemed to relax as the story went on. The tension diffused, the evening went better. The food was as good as the previous time, and the company became more animated as the night went on. For the most part, Eva sat back and listened, comfortable in the presence of three friends who obviously cared for each other. As the evening went on, she even forgot to worry about Michael.

After the meal was concluded and the bill paid, they stood and wandered outside. It was still bright and clear, though the temperature had dropped several more degrees. As she wrapped her scarf around her head as a makeshift head warmer, Eva decided that perhaps a new hat would be a good thing to ask for for Christmas.

Her companions waved their goodbyes and started down the street in the opposite direction of her apartment. She watched them go for a moment, wondering again at how they didn't seem to be cold. None of them had any hats or gloves, yet they stood up straight, their backs unbending under the cold. Still they made an odd group, Gabe tall and skinny with his long red hair, Rafe shorter and broader and darker, the light glistening off his shaved head, and Michael, still somewhat favoring his left arm, somewhere in between the other two.

Despite the cold, it was still a nice night. The stars were still out, and the streetlights created halos of brightness against the dark. She should have brought the mystery novel with her; she'd get no more work done tonight, but that was okay, because she felt relaxed and in control, more sure of herself than she'd been in some time, though she had no idea why.

Turning, she began to make her way up the street when there was the sound of running footsteps behind her. She froze, but she couldn't find a sense of urgency to cause her to panic. There were plenty of other people on the street, and the stars were watching over her.

"Eva," said Michael from behind her.

She turned, raising an eyebrow. He seemed flushed and somewhat out of breath, but his coloring was definitely getting better.

"I just realized we should plan that trip," he said. "I mean, unless you have it all ready to go, in which case, I'll just be on my way."

Eva laughed. "Oh, if you only knew me better. Of course it's not planned out."

"Okay, then," replied Michael, smiling. "My original statement stands. Friday sound good?"

The semester was almost over; if she didn't plan this trip soon, it wasn't going to happen, and she wouldn't have anything to use as ammunition against her mother. "I think I can fit you in," she said.

"Glad to hear it." Michael took one of her hands, giving it a squeeze. "Thank you again for letting me come with you." He glanced up the block, where Gabe and Rafe were just barely visible underneath a streetlight. "To be honest, I think I need to get away too."

"Hey, is something wrong? Rafe said something about you guys fighting."

Michael sighed, wrapping his fingers around hers. His skin felt much warmer than it should have, judging by the chill of the night, but, then, he always seemed to be hot. "I don't know that we're fighting, per se," he said, "but we do have a definite disagreement going." He shook his head. "I can't fault them their position on the matter, I just can't seem to do anything about mine."

Without really thinking about it, Eva reached one hand up and gently ran it down his cheek. His breathing hitched. He looked down at her, green eyes bright against the night, looking a little lost, confused, and scared. But the emotions were gone in another second, like he'd made some sort of decision. He bent his head down toward her and she found herself standing up straighter, tilting her head toward his.

Then his lips were on hers, and it was as if her lips had caught fire. The heat spread through her body, filling every bit of her essence. It was unlike anything she'd ever felt before, and she never wanted it to end, never wanted to lose his warmth. His arms slid across her back, pulling her closer. Reaching up, she twisted her fingers in his hair. It was as soft as she had hoped.

The kiss lasted only a moment. Michael pulled back first, taking his warmth with him. "I'd better go," he murmured, inclining his head toward Gabe and Rafe. "But I will see you Friday." He leaned forward again, pressing a quick kiss against her forehead, then gave her hand a squeeze before he dropped it. He turned and headed down the street toward where her bosses were still waiting.

Her forehead tingled. She absently rubbed where he'd kissed her as she watched him disappear into the night.

Chapter Ten

Two mornings later, Eva slid into a seat near the back of Professor Axelrad's classroom. Her dreams had changed again—the second garden was gone, and while she got hints of people and conversations in the remaining garden, they were nowhere near as complete as the previous ones, and she hadn't been able to remember any of them for long. But at least she was less confused when she woke up.

She'd already dropped her essay off at the front of the room and was mulling possible angel-related essay questions when Sam slid into the seat next to her. She looked up, images of Michael's injuries still fresh in her mind, but any sort of statement she was going to make died on her lips. Part of his hair was singed, and the right side of his face was a deep, angry red, like he'd been sunburned. To top it all off, his right arm was bandaged and in a sling.

"What happened to you?" she asked without thinking. Could his injuries really have come from a fight with Michael? Michael was covered in bruises; Sam looked more like he'd stuck his head in a fire. That didn't make any sense at all. She peered at him closely, trying not to be too obvious about it, but she couldn't make out any bruises.

He looked up at her and smiled, but the expression looked painful and Eva grimaced involuntarily. "Had a bad day on Wednesday," he said.

"Yes, I can see that," she replied, hoping he'd go more into it.

Sam was making a valiant attempt to get his supplies out of his bag with only one arm. Slightly wary but unwilling to just sit there, Eva bent over to help him. Her mind whirled, trying to figure things out. Rafe had said that Sam had started a fight with Michael, but she hadn't heard Michael say it himself, though it was obvious enough that the two didn't get along that well.

"Thank you," said Sam when his notebook and pen were out. He took the pen in his left hand and neatly dated the top of his page. He looked at Eva out of the corner of his eye, as if considering something, then sat up. "I was hit by lightning."

"You were hit by lightning?" repeated Eva, her voice higher pitched than usual. A few people in the surrounding rows turned to look at her. Coloring, she slid down in her seat.

Sam nodded. "Yes, I was out in that downpour we had the other day, taking a walk." He smiled at her, but she couldn't find anything reassuring in it when it pulled at his burned skin. "It's nice to walk in the rain—it's like the whole world belongs to you. And while I was over by that field by the engineering center, I was apparently the tallest thing there." He shook his head. "I should know better by now. I've got burns down the entire right side of my body, but the doctor said they should heal without too much scarring."

Rafe must have been confused as to what happened. Either that, or Sam had somehow found time to fight with Michael and then get hit by lightning, though that seemed unlikely. Still, some thought in the back of her mind was trying to tell her that everything made perfect sense. Eva pushed it down. "Did it hurt?" she asked, generally curious. "I hear that sometimes people's hearts stop when they get hit by lightning."

"Yeah, it hurt," said Sam. "Like burning yourself on the oven but a thousand times worse." He cocked his head at her. "You know what would be nice? Some ice cream."

She'd never known someone quite so obsessed with ice cream. "Right now?" asked Eva.

"Let's go after class," said Sam. "I'll treat."

Eva didn't get a chance to respond, as Professor Axelrad decided to make his entrance and launched immediately into a presentation. Sam dutifully began to take notes with his left hand, but Eva felt a bit steamrolled. No matter how she turned events over, she couldn't figure out how one came out bruised and the other came out burned. And it really felt like she should be able to.

After class, Eva helped Sam with gathering his supplies again. "It's a good thing you're left-handed," she said as she held his bag open for him.

"I'm not," he answered.

Eva raised an eyebrow. She'd peeked over at his notes a few times, and his handwriting had been concise and easy to read. "Really?"

"Just thought I'd teach myself to write with my left hand for fun," replied Sam with a shrug. He smiled again, but the expression didn't look as painful this time—Eva could have sworn his face was less red now than it had been at the beginning of class. "Didn't know I'd need that skill, but apparently it's a good one to have."

"Guess so," said Eva, gathering up her own supplies. She slid her bag on over her coat.

"I know a nice little ice cream parlor just south of campus," Sam said, picking up his own bag and slinging it over his unbandaged left shoulder.

Eva hesitated, unsure of whether she wanted to go with him or not. It would probably be okay if Lily wasn't there, but she couldn't condone what he'd done to Michael, and she didn't think Michael was lying about what happened. After all, when he'd started to tell Rafe, he hadn't even known Eva was there. And Rafe had warned her about him, and she generally trusted Rafe too.

But she couldn't help but be curious, and maybe he'd explain more if she went along. Besides, it seemed terrible to deny him ice cream when he'd been struck by lightning. It was a freakish accident, and while she knew it happened, she had honestly thought she'd go through life without ever being hit by lightning or knowing anyone who was. "I can't stay for too long," she said.

Sam led the way out of the building and across campus, Eva trailing a few steps behind him. Lily was nowhere in sight, Eva noted. It was overcast but not raining, which was nice, though Eva was wearing her galoshes. But she suspected she was coming down with a cold, and until she got a hat or an umbrella—she hadn't been able to bring herself to borrow another one from Gabe—she wanted to be out in the rain as little as possible.

"Come up here with me," said Sam. He stopped, wrapping his good arm around one of hers. Eva stiffened, but there was no spark, no warmth, and while he actually smelled a little charred from this close, she supposed it didn't mean anything.

The ice cream shop was just off campus, though Eva didn't normally come this way and had been unaware of its existence. Sam insisted on paying for hers, and pushed her into getting multiple scoops, though she felt a little bad about imposing on him.

Curiosity still was buzzing around in her head. "Did you see Michael on Wednesday?" she asked.

A dark cloud descended onto Sam's face for a moment before lifting. "Michael?" he repeated, forcing a smile onto his face. "No, I didn't. Why, are you looking for him? He owe you money or something?"

"No," she said, pretending to innocently lick at her ice cream cone, though her nerves were twitching. "But he came into the shop. It looked like someone had beat him up." She peered at him out of the corner of her eye.

Sam frowned for a moment then let out a laugh. "Michael's a bit of a klutz," he said. "I bet he fell down a flight of stairs or something like that."

"Hmm," said Eva noncommittally.

"Hey, listen," said Sam, leaning in close, "don't think too much about him. He's a bit of a jerk, you know. Always in other people's business, telling them what to do and what to think." He shook his head. "He thinks he's so great. Don't bother with him."

Eva nodded and found herself wondering what exactly had happened, and how long ago, to drive such hatred into these two—well, four, if you counted Rafe and Gabe as well—men. Sam obviously meant what he said, though that hadn't been Eva's experience.

Sam took a large bite of his ice cream. "People today," he said, "are so out of touch with the world. They need some sort of proper direction, don't you think? Need someone to tell them how to act, how to show respect."

"I guess," said Eva, though she didn't really have any idea what he was on about. It seemed to be an odd segue.

His eyes flashed. "I'm thinking about doing something about that."

"Besides the club?" asked Eva, poking her spoon at her ice cream. "Joining a student group, or getting into politics or something like that?"

"Sure, why not," said Sam. "Though I'm thinking something more efficient than that. Government and red tape get us nowhere in this life."

Eva looked up at Sam, but he seemed to have disappeared into his thoughts, that darkness again sitting on his features. To be honest, he was making her a little uncomfortable. His green eyes glowed brightly with some quality she couldn't readily identify, but she didn't think it was a pleasant one.

"Thank you for the ice cream," she said with a smile that she didn't really mean. "I'm afraid I have to go, though, or I will be late for work."

"I'll walk you," said Sam, coming out of his stupor.

"No, no," said Eva, feeling like she needed to get away. Her eyes darted around and fell on his half-eaten ice cream. "You deserve to have your ice cream in a nice and relaxing manner, and I would feel terrible dragging you from it. I insist you sit here and finish it."

He seemed displeased, but he didn't raise any objections.

"See you at lecture," she said before fleeing the shop.

WHEN EVA arrived home later that evening, she discovered Az had spread himself across the front entrance of the apartment, and she tripped over him on her way in. The cat hissed and, with as much dignity as he could muster, sauntered over to the lone chair and launched himself on top of it. It wasn't as impressive a maneuver as the cat probably hoped it was, since his girth made the landing more of a scramble than a clean movement.

"Sorry, Az," Eva said, dropping her bag next to the door, though she wasn't sure she was. It was the cat's own fault for sleeping someplace where he knew he was going to be in the way.

She stared around her apartment, unsure what to do. She'd been so distracted by Michael and the kiss that she hadn't noticed they hadn't agreed on any specifics on when they'd meet. She'd swung by the library on the way to the bookstore, just in case, and when she hadn't found him there, she'd thought maybe he was just planning on coming by the store and that's why specifics had not come up. But by the time Gabe and Rafe declared it to be closing time, there'd still been no sign of him.

She felt oddly betrayed.

Shaking her head, she forced herself to focus. They would have to talk about the trip at some point, and if she had an idea of what she wanted before they started, that would help. She wanted to be able to soak in the ancientness of Greece, to see if anything felt right, if there was anything she could use toward her thesis. Mostly she just wanted a sign that she was anywhere near being on the right path. But, with Michael tagging along, would she even be able to tell?

If she was to be honest with herself, she knew she wouldn't get the answers she needed from a two-week trip, not even if she found the most holy, inspirational sight in the entire world. That was simply not enough time. With a sigh, she dumped her coat on the chair, half covering Az, though the cat didn't seem to mind terribly, then bent over to pull off her galoshes.

She found her slippers by the refrigerator and slid them on, padding about the kitchen in search of dinner. She'd expected to be at the store until much later, but Rafe had decided to close at about 5 o'clock, despite the proximity of final papers and exams. Things had been a bit strained at the shop recently, though Eva couldn't put her finger on why. There was a tightness in the way Rafe interacted with her, though his words were friendly enough, and at times it was like he forgot what was bothering him and acted normally, though it never lasted. She hadn't seen Gabe hardly at all, and he hadn't spoken to her. Admittedly she rarely saw Gabe, since he was generally holed up in the back office with his solitaire and the occasional book ordering, but this was something different.

A thorough search of the freezer revealed some sort of boxed chicken meal which Eva plopped in the microwave with a sigh. She really needed to eat better. Maybe if she put some fruits and vegetables in the refrigerator, she'd be tempted to eat them.

Leaving the meal to cook, she crossed into her room and turned on her computer. It had seen better days, but it still worked well enough for what she used it for, which was mostly essay writing and the occasional trip to Wikipedia. Az had been chewing on the mouse cord again, she noticed with some irritation. Some day he would chew through something that would shock him and it would serve him right. Sitting down, she pulled up an internet browser window. She'd just check her email and then she'd do some searching for good travel deals. Maybe she'd just stumble across one that was so spectacular she'd have no trouble making a decision.

Halfway through her email—mostly random spam interspersed with official school notices, like that tuition was due for next semester—there was a knock on the door. Eva paused mid-mouse scroll, cocking her head. She didn't think she was expecting anybody. She hadn't ordered any take-out, though maybe she should have, when the chicken monstrosity in the microwave was the best she could come up with, and she had paid her rent on time, so the landlord shouldn't have any reason to bother her.

Maybe someone had finally come to fix the radiator. Cheered by that thought, she half-skipped to the door, undid the chain, and pulled it open.

Michael stood on her doorstep, his hands in his pockets and his face looking completely healed. He gave her a small smile then ducked his head. "Sorry," he said. "I realized I forgot to, you know, set a time and a location." His cheeks colored slightly, and Eva found herself wanting to reach out and run her fingers over those cheeks.

"How do you know where I live?" she asked instead.

He shrugged. "Gabe told me."

Eva tilted her head, considering. Her apartment was a mess, and she didn't even have two chairs to her name, unless you considered the atrocity that she used at her desk. Plus there was the chicken whatsit in the microwave. On the other hand, she did need to plan this trip. Airfare was probably already going to be ridiculous as it was, and it wasn't going to get better the longer she waited. Having Michael at her door made the idea more real, and for a minute, she had a rush of anxiousness. What was she doing, traipsing about the world? But Michael would be there, and that was some comfort.

"Oh, and I brought your Christmas bonus," said Michael, pulling a check out of his pocket.

"Well, in that case, come right in," said Eva, stepping out of the way. She snatched the offered check as Michael stepped through the door, peering at it. Gabe had been very generous. She must find him more solitaire, and maybe bake him cookies, as a thank you.

"Lovely place you have here," said Michael as he peered at the messy dining room. There were papers strewn everywhere, and Eva suspected there was some old pizza hanging out on the counter. "Very nice." Eva could tell that he was lying, but at least he was trying. He sniffed. "Making dinner?"

"You could call it that," she said. "Have you eaten?"

"Depends," he said, grinning lopsidedly at her.

Eva shut the door behind him, wondering where Az had gotten to. He wasn't particularly friendly, so he was probably under the bed or in a closet somewhere. "We could order take-out," she suggested hopefully. She was more than willing to send the chicken back from whence it came.

"Then no, I haven't eaten," he said. He took off his coat but seemed unsure where to place it.

It'd been so long since Eva had had a visitor—if, indeed, she'd ever had one—that she didn't know what to do. She finally took Michael's coat from him and hung it on a hook on the back of the front door, then set about digging through the papers on the table in search of take-out menus. "Would you like something to drink?" she offered even as she went over the inventory of her fridge in her head. There was some slightly decayed milk, and maybe a can of Dr. Pepper that had been in there for years.

"Water would be fine," said Michael. His eyes followed her movements as she went into the kitchen and retrieved a clean glass—one of very few—from the cabinet. Filling it with water, she handed it to him and went back to the mess on the table. There should be a couple of Chinese places, maybe some Thai, or even some Mexican, but of course, now that she wanted them, they were nowhere to be found. Az had probably stashed them behind the toilet or someplace odd, along with her hat.

Michael took a few sips of water before going into the kitchen himself. He looked about with his hands on his hips, then began to wash her dishes.

Eva blinked at him. "Are you honestly cleaning my apartment for me?"

"Hey, I know how busy you are," he said, giving her a brilliant smile. For that smile, she'd let him get away with just about anything. "And I'm the one imposing on you. Besides, I kind of like it. Easy to get some thinking done."

Eva left him to it and returned to the table, clearing it off and taking care of some trash that had been hanging around for longer than she'd like to think about. After that, she peeked at Michael, his shirt sleeves rolled up to his elbows, methodically going about the dishes. The longer she cleaned, the longer she could put off working on the trip. It was pretty bad when the chores seemed like the lesser of two evils.

With the dining room mostly clean, she moved on to the clothing on the floor of her room. Might as well stuff everything in the hamper and do laundry the next day. Why not? School was almost out, free time was almost upon her.

It wasn't until she was in the middle of making her bed that she realized Michael was in the doorway, watching her, a small smile playing across his handsome features. Eva finished what she was doing, blushing a little bit. Well, at least the apartment looked somewhat presentable now, even though her desk was still covered with God knew what. Maybe he'd just want to plan at the dining room table, but somehow she doubted it.

"Did you find those take-out menus?" he asked.

"Oh." She'd completely forgotten about dinner. Hell, the microwave had dinged a while before, signaling that her chicken was done, and she hadn't even noticed. It was probably stinking up the kitchen. "Yes, right."

She walked up to him and he backed slightly out of the way so she could get out of the door, but not enough so that she didn't have to slide past him, her back against the door frame to avoid touching him. Her breath caught in her throat, and she thought perhaps he'd reacted similarly, but then she was free. She picked up the stack of menus off the table. "What do you feel like?"

"You pick," he said. He turned so he was facing the dining room, but he didn't leave the doorway.

Eva selected a Thai menu—she hadn't had that in a while—and offered it to him. The chicken had to be dealt with. She moved around the counter into the kitchen to retrieve it and force it back into the freezer, but stopped short. Her kitchen sparkled.

"How did you...?" she started. "I don't even own this many cleaning supplies."

Michael shrugged, his face in the menu. "You were really into your cleaning, and I didn't want to bother you."

Had it really been that long? A glance at the clock revealed it had been over an hour since she'd gotten home. Geez. She should clean more often so when she did it wasn't an all-evening affair.

Michael offered her the menu. "Do you know what you want?"

The food was ordered, and with that, Eva realized she had nothing else to procrastinate on until it actually arrived. She would have to face the trip.

"So, Greece," said Michael.

"Greece," Eva echoed. Michael seemed to be waiting for her to provide something else, but nothing came to mind.

"Any particular sites you want to look at? You're doing something about relating the Greek pantheon back to Christianity, right?"

Okay, good. This was familiar territory. "Yes, more or less."

Michael leaned against her sole chair. "If at any point I am annoying you, feel free to tell me to shut up. I don't want to push you into anything. But it seems like there's really two ways to approach it—either from the Ancient Greek side or the Christianity side." He paused, watching her. "We can go wherever you want. But I have been thinking about it, just a little. I mean we could do both, too. The Acropolis, Delphi, all that jazz. And there's tons of old Eastern Orthodox churches, and some monasteries too."

He'd obviously looked more into this than she had. Well, at least one of them was on top of things. He pulled the chair out for her, so, giving up for the moment, she sank into it. "I don't know where to start." She began braiding her hair to give her hands something to do. "To be honest, I'm not terribly far on my thesis. I'm still trying to figure out what sections I'm going to include." And her advisor was not the most help, but he did have several students he was working with.

"Just as well," said Michael. He moved around to her side, half sitting on the table. "If we've got a variety of things to look at, then maybe we'll be more likely to run into whatever you're searching for."

"Mmm," she said.

"We could even climb Mount Olympus, if you want. I don't know if you're much of a hiker, but the view is pretty nice from up there."

Eva looked at him sharply. "You've been there before."

"Yes," said Michael. "A couple of times, actually. Though it's been years at this point."

Eva blinked at him. Sometimes he felt a little too perfect. What were the odds that he'd be so familiar with her chosen destination? "I need to look some things up on the internet," she said, getting slightly overwhelmed. There was such a thing as too much research, though part of it was her fault for not having any preconceived ideas about what she wanted to do. Standing, she pushed past Michael into her bedroom. Her computer was still on from earlier, though it had gone into standby. Her desk really was a mess. How had she let it get so bad?

She heard Michael come in behind her and sit on the bed, but he didn't say anything as she opened Wikipedia and looked up some of his suggestions. He stayed quiet through the whole process, and Eva soon forgot he was there. Wikipedia had a wealth of links for her to follow, and after a while she began to think that maybe it would be nice to look at both the ancient stuff and the stuff that came after. Maybe there would be some sort of obvious progression that would help her figure out her thesis. Surely having an organized plan of attack there would make everything else look less dire.

"What have you decided?" asked Michael.

Eva jumped. Somehow he'd managed to sneak up on her, standing right behind her left shoulder. She hadn't even heard the usual telltale creaking from the bed when he'd gotten up. "I think I'd like to do a little of both," she said.

He smiled. "There's plenty to see. We can start in Athens and work our way out," he said.

"You know, I've never even left the state," said Eva, turning back to the computer. "We didn't travel much when I was growing up."

"Really?" Michael's brow furrowed. "Well, we'll get you out into the world now."

Eva turned to look at him, brushing her hands against his on the back of the chair. There was that telltale spark again and Michael actually gasped. Eva, heart beating hard in her chest, purposefully laid her hands over his, looking up into his eyes.

"You drive me crazy," he said, his voice quiet yet urgent at the same time.

"I know," she heard herself say before Michael pushed her up against the desk, his lips hungrily seeking hers. The corner of the desk poked into the back of her leg, but she found she didn't care. His hands found her hips, fingers looping through her belt loops, pulling her closer. Eva gasped, a heat she hadn't known could exist surging through her body. She clung to Michael's shoulders, eagerly exploring his mouth with her own. Michael broke the kiss to bring his lips to her neck, sucking gently on her skin. It felt amazing, and Eva thought she might burst. She hissed through her teeth, sliding her hands up under his shirt. He was so warm; Eva wanted that warmth all to herself.

Michael moaned into her neck, coming up to kiss her again. Eva slid backwards on the desk, paper and God knew what else tumbling to the floor. Michael followed her, his hands supporting his weight against the wall. She wrapped her legs around the back of his, groaning into the kiss.

The doorbell rang. Michael jerked back, blinking at Eva. He was flushed and his hair was completely out of place, but somehow that just made him more attractive. She sighed in frustration. "It's probably dinner." She hoped it was dinner. If not, there was entirely too many people visiting tonight, and she already had the one she wanted here.

"Right," said Michael. He slowly disentangled himself from her, looking displeased about the whole process. "I can get it."

Eva was tempted to tell him to forget the food, but the moment had been broken, and so after he'd gone into the other room she slowly slid off the desk, surveying the damage. Some of the papers were probably school related and should be organized at some point, but Eva couldn't bring herself to care about that at the moment. The computer had been pushed to the side, the URL bar in the internet browser filled with a variety of gibberish, no doubt left when someone's hand had accidentally run into the keyboard.

Leaving the desk to itself, Eva slid her slipper back on—one had fallen off—and padded back into the dining room. Michael had paid the delivery person and was in the process of setting up the food on the table. He got two plates and forks from the cabinets and brought them over. Eva couldn't remember the last time she'd had a sit-down meal at home, actually using her dishes how they were meant to be used.

She went back to the bedroom to retrieve the computer chair and brought it to the table, setting it across from the dining-room chair. Now that the food was here, she discovered she was hungry and eagerly dug into the portion that Michael placed on her plate. It was much better than whatever that chicken meal would have been.

Michael sat down and half-heartedly attempted to brush his hair back into place with his hands. "Sorry," he said.

"For what?" asked Eva around a bite of pad thai, trying not to think about how nice his warmth had been.

He gestured vaguely towards the bedroom. "You know," he elaborated unhelpfully.

"I don't think you have anything to be sorry for," she said, adding *except stopping* in her head.

"Mmm," he said in response, but he seemed to relax a bit.

"You know," Eva said, "I still haven't told my mother about this trip." She sighed. "I don't know what to say. She won't like it. It conflicts with her deadline, and she'll see it as a waste of money."

Michael lowered his fork, scratching behind one ear. "Look, if this is something you feel you need to do, you need to do it. Or else you'll wonder for the rest of your life what would have happened if you had. Your mother will either understand, or she'll forgive you for it later."

He was right, of course. She sighed and stabbed at her food.

After dinner, they returned to the computer, but Michael's mind seemed to be on business now. They looked at a variety of different vacation packages before choosing one and booking it. Michael paid for it on his credit card with the idea that Eva would pay him back once she cashed in her Christmas bonus. Gabe would definitely be getting cookies.

Another opportunity never presented itself, and after they were done making plans, Michael said his goodnight, giving her a small peck on the cheek. Then he was gone, leaving Eva rubbing her cheek and feeling a profound sense of loss.

Chapter Eleven

THE SEMESTER ended without much more excitement. She got a few emails from Michael confirming plans, but she didn't actually see him, though she did spend a few hours staking out the physics building and the library in the hopes of running into him. Her finals went smoothly enough, though she'd taken to sitting in odd places in the classrooms, hoping that Sam wouldn't be able to easily find her. She was still a little weirded out by the conversation they'd had earlier, and she still couldn't figure out what had happened between him and Michael, but now when he was near he made her nervous, and she thought it was probably best to trust her nerves.

After she turned in her last final for the semester and was finally free, at least for a few weeks, she strolled leisurely across campus. The air was crisp and chilly and she could see her breath, but the sky was clear and the air was filled with the sounds of happy students, discussing holiday plans with friends. Eva watched them a bit jealously. She'd finally gotten up the nerve to call her mother earlier that morning.

"Eva!" her mother had said. "Have you made your decision?"

"About that," Eva had replied, twisting the phone cord around her fingers, "there's still one more thing I need to do."

"Will it happen before break?"

"No, it will happen during break. I couldn't do it during school."

Her mother had made a noncommittal noise in the back of her throat. Eva winced. "I do not like it when you disregard my instructions, *chica*."

"This is important, Mother."

"Fine, what is it?"

Eva braced herself. "I'm taking a trip. To Greece."

"What? Are you crazy? The country is falling apart! You'll be attacked by rioters!"

"Mother," Eva said, knowing that, if left to her own devices, her mother would be able to come up with unpleasant possibilities for hours, "I'm going. But I'm not going alone."

It was silent on the other end for so long that Eva had started to wonder if she'd given her mother a heart attack. "Well, that's something, at least," she finally said. "I do not like it, though. Just come home, where it's safe—"

"I'm going on this trip, no matter what."

"Do not interrupt your mother." There was a pause. "I will see you in a week." And she had hung up.

Eva had been too nervous to call back and ask whether or not her mother expected her for good at that point. Oh, well, she'd just have to stand her ground if it came to that. And Michael was coming to pick her up, so she had a built-in escape route.

As she walked now, garlands had been hung across campus and on the surrounding streets, and as she walked toward the shop, she could see someone putting up some last-minute wreaths on a wire stretching over the road. She hummed to herself, taking delight in the cheer that suddenly seemed to permeate everywhere and trying to forget her worries.

When she reached the bookstore, Christmas carols were blaring over the speakers. Eva had begun to suspect that the only reason the store had a sound system at all was for the Christmas carols, as she'd never heard it be used up until the last few weeks, and apparently the only reason for the Christmas carols was to drive Gabe mad. He was holed up in the office and she hadn't seen him since the music started. Rafe, on the other hand, was clearly having a good time of it. He sang along with every song, sometimes loudly and off-tune just for the hell of it.

She paused for a moment outside, bracing herself. Something still felt off between her and Gabe and Rafe, and if they were going to spend several hours being awkward at each other, it was best to be prepared.

Eva dropped her bag off behind the counter, grabbing a foil-wrapped package out of it. She knocked on the door to the office, but seeing how she couldn't hear anything over Rafe warbling "O Holy Night" she just waited a second and then let herself in.

The difference in volume level between the office and the rest of the store was huge. Eva closed the door behind her and instantly the Christmas insanity faded to a low rumble. "Oh, thank God," she said.

"I don't know how you've been putting up with it," said Gabe. He was at his computer, busy scribbling something off the screen onto a sheet of paper. "Michael came by for an hour or so yesterday and was threatening to set the entire history section ablaze by the end of it." He shook his head.

"That would be bad," said Eva, disappointed that she'd missed him. "Those books would burn really easily." She set the package down next to Gabe's elbow. "Merry Christmas!"

"Hm, what's this?" Gabe pulled the foil open to reveal a variety of Christmas cookies.

"I baked them myself," supplied Eva. "Well, I made them out of premixed dough, but I did use my own cookie cutters." She'd had grand plans for icing and sprinkles, but it had turned out that she was barely up to the cookie cutters, so she'd had to scale back her expectations.

Gabe pulled out a cookie shaped like an angel, grinning. "Thank you, Eva. This is very thoughtful of you."

The door flew open, letting the Christmas carols in with it. Gabe and Eva groaned.

"What's this now?" asked Rafe, leaving the door open as he strode across the office. "Making secret plans without me?"

"You see this?" said Gabe, indicating the angel cookie. "I am pretending this is you." With that, Gabe bit off its head.

Rafe ignored him. "Cookies! How come I don't get any?"

"Because you are trying to kill everyone with Christmas carols," said Gabe. "It is only a matter of time before some passerby blows the store up to put everyone out of their misery." He took another bite, making a show of enjoying the cookie.

"Don't be such a Scrooge," said Rafe. He darted in, snagging a cookie, then retreated to a safe distance out of Gabe's reach. "I am merely trying to spread some Christmas cheer."

"Some people find bonfires cheery," replied Gabe. He wrapped the rest of the cookies back in their foil and hid them in a drawer.

"Anyway, no one's complaining but you two." Rafe cocked his head, looking thoughtful. "And Michael, but he has no sense of fun anyway, so he doesn't count." He took a bite of his stolen cookie.

"No one's complaining because no one's dared to set foot in the store in weeks," said Eva, earning a snort from Gabe.

"Sadly true," he said. "You want a cookie too?"

"No thank you," replied Eva. She paused, considering, but she'd already gotten one unpleasant conversation over for the day, so she might as well keep going. "Can I ask you guys something?"

"Anything," said Gabe. He closed the document on his computer, turning to face her. "What's on your mind?"

She'd first noticed this right around Sam and Michael's fight, but it hadn't gotten better in the following weeks. "Did I do something wrong?"

Rafe choked on his cookie.

"Wrong?" Gabe leaned back, rubbing his hand down the back of his head and ignoring Rafe. "Why would you say that?" He stood, beginning to pace the office.

"You guys have been a bit...distant. Like I did something wrong and you don't want to tell me."

Gabe stopped his pacing, exchanging a look with Rafe. He seemed distinctly uncomfortable and, if Eva didn't know better, a little guilty. "Well," he said, "this seems like a good conversation for you and Rafe to have."

Rafe pointed the remains of his cookie at Gabe. "Oh, no you don't, Gabriel. You're not pinning this on me."

Gabe ignored him. "I'm sure he'll explain everything in a satisfactory manner." He edged for the door.

Rafe noticed him going. "Gabriel! I am serious, if you set foot out of this room, I am going to..." But the threat went unsaid, as Gabe was already out the door, shutting it behind him.

Eva's stomach felt queasy. What was so bad that Gabe would rather weather the carols than talk to her?

Rafe banged on the closed door. "You're supposed to be the mature one, you know!" He grumbled something else uncomplimentary under his breath before turning back to Eva. He groaned, rubbing a hand over his bald head. "Okay, that looked really bad, but if anything it was a compliment."

Eva raised both eyebrows.

Rafe perched on the edge of his desk. "It means Gabe really likes you and he'd rather I screw things up than him. I don't normally get to do the serious talks because Gabe says, and I quote, that I 'reveal too much information.' Also, it's possible that he thinks that I am easier to get along with, which is probably true." He smiled, but it looked forced.

"Rafe," Eva said.

"Okay, okay. Look, it's not you, necessarily. It's more Michael." Rafe paused, scratching his chin. "It's really more the way Michael looks at you."

"What's wrong with the way Michael looks at me?"

"Nothing," said Rafe a little too quickly. "It's just...um."

"Wait a minute," Eva said, "are you saying you guys don't think I'm good enough for Michael?" For a second, she was a little appalled at herself for even asking, but it would explain the awkwardness, and it would explain why Gabe had run for it. She wasn't sure whether she should get mad or cry.

"No!" Rafe said. "It's more..."

"Well, you can't possibly tell me that you think your dear friend Michael isn't good enough for me." She could hear her hurt seeping into her voice.

"That's not..."

"I mean, goddamnit, Rafe, you were implying you wanted us to date when I first met him! And now—"

"Eva, will you *shut up* for a second so I can get a word in edgewise?" snapped Rafe.

Eva's tirade died off in surprise.

"Let's all just calm down," Rafe said. He pulled out Gabe's chair. "Here, sit." He waited until she did so before returning to his perch. "Look, there is nothing wrong with you, and there is nothing wrong with Michael. There is *potentially* something wrong with the two of you being together, but quite frankly we're not sure about that and so everything is a bit awkward with everyone."

Eva forced herself to take a deep breath. "Okay," she said. "What is this potentially wrong thing?"

Rafe looked pained. "Augh, Gabriel, why," he muttered to himself. "Okay, um, where we come from, there's rules about who we can, um, be intimate with— oh my god, this is the worst conversation ever."

Eva agreed. She felt herself getting warm in the face. "So, uh, you're saying if Michael and I were to..."—and, holy hell, she was talking to her *boss*—"...there'd be...consequences?"

Rafe seemed relieved. "Yes! Yes, that."

She was beginning to suspect her theory about anyone without green eyes being kicked out was true. "Is it because I'm Hispanic?" she joked lamely.

For once, Rafe didn't catch it. "Honey, in case you haven't noticed, I am a black man. That definitely doesn't have anything to do with it."

Not only that, but the only thing all three of them—all five, if you counted Sam and Lily, and she probably should—had in common were their eyes. "What if I had green eyes? Would things still be a problem?"

"It...depends." Eva waited for Rafe to elaborate, but he didn't.

Eva groaned, sliding down in the chair. "What am I supposed to do with this, Rafe? What am I supposed to make of 'it's not you, it's us, and I can't tell you specifically why'? It all sounds like a lame excuse to not tell me what you really think."

"I'm sorry," Rafe said. And he honestly looked like he was, which really only made Eva want to punch him.

She pushed herself upright, suddenly feeling too full of energy. "I suppose this is the source of your disagreement with Michael." She sounded bitter, but she couldn't seem to help it. She felt betrayed. She'd never had a connection with anyone like she had with Michael, and Rafe was essentially saying she couldn't act on it. That was crap. Standing, she began to pace, crossing her arms over her chest.

Gabe tentatively pushed the door open, letting the carols back in. He had a stack of chocolate Advent calendars under one arm. "How are we doing in here?" he asked, looking even guiltier than he had earlier. Rafe leveled a cold glare at him.

"I think we're done," Eva said shortly. She stalked past Gabe into the store beyond and sat down on her stool, arms still crossed over her chest.

Gabe apparently thought he'd manage better with Rafe than her because he stepped fully into the office and closed the door behind him. After a few moments, she could hear the muffled sounds of an argument, barely audible at all over the carols. She forced herself to take a few deep breaths, pushing her emotions down.

It hurt, but ultimately what was between her and Michael was between her and Michael. And screw what anyone else thought about the matter.

MICHAEL WAS feeling pretty pleased with himself. School was over for the semester, but that wasn't really an issue for him. After all these millennia he had a pretty good feel for things, and he liked to go to school for a few years every few decades to keep up with new scientific developments and societal changes. It was something to do, and it gave him the feeling of actually accomplishing something, though on some level it didn't feel like much. Despite his dislike of Sam and their disagreements on how to handle things, Michael did at times miss older days, when he'd actually tried to change the direction of human civilization.

But these were new days, and humans in this time tended to like to do things for themselves.

He could hear the music blasting from the shop a full block before he reached it. The people on the street, huddled together and full of good cheer, didn't really seem to mind. Well, maybe if Rafe hadn't been doing it every year since the mid-'60s, Michael would be slightly more open-minded about the whole thing.

He thought maybe he might look at the travel books, see how Greece had changed over the last few hundred years. Or he might just set the history books on fire to see what Rafe would do, except he'd probably just get Gabe to put it out, and that would be no fun at all.

"God Rest Ye Merry Gentlemen" assaulted him as he pulled open the door. Maybe he'd just set a lot of little fires throughout the shop to make them more difficult to put out. Clamping his hands over his ears, he sighed. What was he thinking? He should go to one of those big-box bookstores, though Gabe would be mad at him for weeks. At least he would be able to hear his own thoughts over the Christmas music there.

"Advent calendar!" said Rafe, appearing from the stacks to his right, thrusting one into his hands. "I got them on sale! Buy one, give the chocolate to your lady friend before she kills us all."

"What the hell." But Rafe had already disappeared.

"I can never wait on those," said a voice off to his left. His heart skipped a beat and he turned to find Eva standing beside him, hands clasped behind her back and looking so sweet and innocent that Michael thought perhaps his breath would never return to him. "I always decide I can skip a couple of days ahead, and from there it's a downhill slope. At home, we never got the chocolate kind. We have a little popup one with doors with pictures of animals behind them."

"Isn't that less fun?" he asked, a little dizzy from her proximity. He really needed to see her more often—it was worse each time he spent some time away from her. He imagined that if he had gone off for a few years, he wouldn't have had any control around her at all when he ran into her again.

"You'd be surprised," she said, smiling softly. "Even though I knew that there was a cat behind December 14, I still looked forward to opening it every year, with no candy or presents involved at all."

"How much is he selling these things for anyway?" asked Michael, holding up the Advent calendar.

"They're not in the computer system, so for now they're free," Eva replied with a wink. "And you can share with your lady friend, who is seriously debating arson as a response to the endless Christmas carols. I hear that other people are thinking along the same lines. The chocolate may placate me into submission for another hour."

"Well, then," said Michael, following her over to the register. He was drawn to the movement of her body, the way her hips swayed from side to side as she walked. *I must keep my hands to myself*, he told himself. Gabe would not approve of him seducing his employees. "For the good of the books, then. Fortunately for you, we are already a ways into December and so you may eat several days guilt-free."

"Good man," she said, sliding on to her stool. "I knew I liked you for a reason."

She said it jokingly, but even so, Michael felt his pulse quicken. Restraint. He must show some restraint. What was wrong with him recently? "Well, if I'd known the way to your heart was through chocolate, I would have tried that instead of saving you from that car," he said, leaning over the counter towards her.

"Mmmm, well, now you know," she said, settling her elbows on the counter just inches away from his own. "For future reference." Eva's eyes strayed to something over his shoulder and she sat up quickly, eyes widening.

Damn. Michael straightened and turned, already knowing he wasn't going to like what he was going to see. Sam and, to Michael's great surprise, Lily stood in the doorframe. Sam was focused on the scene at the register, while Lily glanced about with thinly disguised amusement.

"Oh, hell," Michael found himself saying. "What are they doing here?" Lily, as far as he knew, had made it a habit for the last few centuries to stay as far away from Gabe as possible. And, as far as he knew, Sam had never set foot inside the bookstore before in all the years that he'd been here.

Sam stalked toward him, his face still slightly burned, Michael noticed with some amusement. He must have hit Sam more squarely than he thought that first time. Lily trailed behind him, hands tucked into her pockets. "I should have known you would work here," Sam said to Eva, practically radiating displeasure. He frowned, eyes flickering from Michael to Eva and back again. "I thought I told you to back off."

"And I thought I told you to fuck off," replied Michael, squaring his shoulders. The never-ending Christmas music continued in the background, adding a bizarre element to the entire situation. Michael had to fight to keep a smile off his face. "What the hell are you two doing here?"

"Such language, Michael," said Lily. She laid a hand on Sam's shoulder. "Maybe we are in need of books. Besides, I haven't alienated anyone recently, so why am I unwelcome?"

"You're unwelcome by association," Michael replied.

"Advent calendar!" said Rafe, popping out of a completely different set of shelves and forcing one on Sam. "Probably not poisoned!"

Sam glowered at Rafe. "This doesn't concern you."

Michael crossed his arms. "Does it concern how you ran away in the middle of a fight last time?" Sam flinched, his eyes burning. "And what, is Lily your back-up?"

"No fighting in my store," said Gabe. Michael hadn't even heard him come out of the office. He walked around the counter, placing himself next to Michael. Lily looked away as Gabe made eye contact with her, suddenly becoming very interested in Rafe's Advent calendar display. "I'd prefer there be no fighting in general. Now, what can we help you with?" Gabe was considerably taller than anyone else and all the more imposing for his calmness. Michael had many times over the years been glad that—generally—they were on the same side.

"He cheated," Sam said, pointing an accusing finger at Michael.

Michael frowned. "If anybody cheated it was you."

"Who cares," said Rafe, rolling his eyes. "Now, my good friend Gabriel here has asked you if you need anything, and if you don't I suggest you find somewhere else to spend your afternoon. We don't take kindly to loiterers here. In fact, we feed them to the books."

"Do you really?" asked Lily brightly, running her eyes down Rafe. "I'd like to see that."

Gabe glowered at her.

"Well, not that it involves anyone here," said Sam, brushing his hair out of his eyes, "but I came to talk to Eva."

Michael felt, more than saw, Eva stiffen behind him. A protective instinct that he hadn't felt in years raised up, and he was tempted to go for Sam's throat, to eliminate any threat to Eva, imagined or not. Gabe laid a hand on his shoulder, and the feeling faded a bit. He took a deep breath.

"It's all right," Eva said.

"Fine," said Gabe. "We'll all go." He looked pointedly at Lily, and after a moment she shrugged and sashayed away as if it had been her idea to do so all along.

His hand still on Michael's shoulder, Gabe purposefully steered him away from the counter and into the books. It was very tempting to break Gabe's hold and go after Sam anyway, but Gabe had always had a bit of a weird power over him. Michael suspected it had to do with their ruling elements; water, after all, could often prove to be stronger than fire.

Gabe led him behind a bookcase not that far from the counter where they could still see what was going on without being seen themselves. Rafe joined them a moment later, and all three of them peered around the shelf at Sam and Eva. Eva looked extremely uncomfortable, almost leaning away from Sam, and Michael twisted under Gabe's hand, but the other man tightened his grip, his fingers digging into Michael's shoulder.

Over the music in the store, it was impossible to hear what was being said. Michael still found it disconcerting after all these years to watch Sam go from showing his own feelings to becoming a charismatic charmer, and he was good at it. He smiled at Eva, leaning forward over the counter, while Eva backed up a step, eying him warily.

"Hey, baby," narrated Rafe, using a low voice for Sam. "What say you and me blow this joint and I'll show you a good time." He sounded like a '70s porn star. Michael punched him in the arm.

"I don't understand why he brought Lily along," Michael murmured.

"I don't understand why she came along," said Gabe.

"Leave me alone, you creep!" said Rafe in a higher-pitched voice that was meant to be Eva. "I don't want anything to do with you!"

"I don't understand why we're letting Sam talk to her at all," said Michael, ignoring Rafe. "We don't owe him anything, and Eva obviously doesn't want to talk to him."

"I want the store to live through the day," replied Gabe. "It's bad enough that you're probably going to set it on fire any time now, and we've pissed Eva off so she'll probably help, but I would prefer that it just be some burning instead of a mixture of problems, and I'm not sure how I would explain an earthquake that affected just my shop to the insurance company. Relax. We're right here if he tries anything, and Eva doesn't need you to fight her fights for her. She said she could handle Sam."

Michael didn't necessarily agree on the last two points—especially since Eva didn't understand what Sam was—but Gabe's fingers were starting to bruise his shoulder and he hoped that if he was calm his roommate would release him.

Eva had her hands up in front of her and she was shaking her head. Sam straightened, his expression darkening. He said something else to Eva then turned on his heel, stalking out of the store. After a moment, he and Lily went past the window, and then they were gone.

"Fuck, Gabe," said Michael. "You're hurting me."

Gabe quickly released him. "Sorry."

Michael rubbed his shoulder, wincing. "I'm going to feel that for a while." He used the bookshelf to push himself back into a standing position. Now he felt a bit like a voyeur. How would it look when he, Rafe, and Gabe all reappeared from the same place?

He shouldn't have worried. Rafe and Gabe were already gone.

Still rubbing his shoulder, he walked back out of the shelves. Eva was leaning against the wall, looking a bit pale. A mess of emotions welled up—concern and anger and, for some strange reason, fear. "Hey," he said. "You okay?"

Eva looked up at him, her eyes tinged with red. Shoulder forgotten, he closed the distance between them, wrapping his arms around her. She buried her face in his chest. For a moment, she didn't move, but then she twisted her face to one side. "He kind of scares me," she whispered.

"Yeah," Michael said, "Me too."

AN HOUR LATER, Eva had left to go home. Michael had asked, but she wouldn't tell him what Sam had said. They'd discussed airport plans a bit, arranging for him to meet her at her mother's, and then she had gone by herself, though Michael had offered to go with her. She'd said she had some things she needed to think about, given him a quick kiss on the cheek, and left without saying anything to either Gabe or Rafe.

Now Michael was perched on Eva's usual stool behind the register. Rafe had, thankfully, turned down the Christmas music. The area still vaguely felt like Eva, even though she had gone. That in itself was a bit strange—normally he couldn't sense individual humans. He'd pulled out some books about Greece, but he couldn't focus. Something wasn't quite adding up, and that bothered him.

"Can we talk?" he said out loud, knowing that Rafe would hear him no matter where he'd disappeared to. Having air as his ruling element, Rafe could do some pretty strange things with sound.

Sure enough, Rafe appeared out of the back left corner of the store. Unusually, he wasn't covered in dust, so he must not have been trying to organize. "What's up?"

Without answering, Michael stood, knocking on the office door. "Gabe," he called.

A moment later, Gabe pulled the door open and stepped out. "We have been needing to talk," he said. "I think we've all been avoiding it."

Michael certainly had. "Can we all agree that what just happened is out of the norm?" he asked. "I mean, Sam's been here for decades but never come anywhere near the store, and I don't think Lily's been in the same room as you, Gabe, since right after we lost Eve."

Rafe gestured at Gabe. "See how this is a good thing? We can talk about Eve again like she was a normal person."

"That doesn't change the fact that there are consequences, Rafe, which Michael knows all too well," Gabe said.

"Come on, Gabe. Michael knows better than to have little Nephilim running around. I bet you our kind does it all the time, these days, and nobody's the wiser because we're all spread out and never check up on each other." Rafe folded his arms over his chest. "I don't think it's fair to say we have to be lonely if we can't find another of our kind to spend our time with. It's old-fashioned."

Michael looked at Rafe in surprise. "How long have you been on my side?"

"I'm not technically on your side," Rafe said, "because I know you agree with Gabe about consequences and whatnot and are beating yourself up about the whole thing. I am actually more on your side than you are."

"Anyway," said Michael. "Can we agree that this behavior is out of the ordinary and perhaps a bit worrisome?"

"Yes," said Gabe. He frowned, rubbing his chin. "That Sam would come here does speak of some sort of urgency. I don't like it, and I wish I knew why."

"I think I might know why, at least partially," Michael said. "Eva was—is—a Light, I'm pretty sure."

Gabe nodded. "I suspect that as well, since she can't work well once the sun is gone."

"It's more than that, Gabe. She can heal herself using the sun too. I mean, she can't actively control it or anything, but the ability is there."

Rafe whistled. "Lights are rare, so I can see why Sam would want one, but I admit I can't think of any reason why he would want one that doesn't make my skin crawl."

"Michael," Gabe said. He rubbed the back of his head, looking uncomfortable. "If she is a Light, and she is the reincarnation of someone, there's only a few people she could be."

Rafe blinked at Gabe, apparently picking up his train of thought. "Oh, God."

Michael shook his head, holding up his hands. "We can't think like that, guys. Whoever she once was, she's Eva now. And whatever Sam's planning, he thinks he needs a Light, which means he's expecting to need healing and some way to judge if people are lying. If he's willing to come here to try and get Eva on his side, he might be willing to go after her at her mother's house too."

Gabe was already shaking his head. "You're going to freak her out if you insist on going everywhere with her. I'm still not sure how you got her to let you go on the trip. If you really care for her, Michael, you need to let her maintain some sense of normalcy in her life."

"But—"

"Hold on a minute. Just because I'm not going to let you follow her around doesn't mean we can't keep an eye on Sam. He's easier to track, after all, and then we'd know if he went after Eva without freaking her out in the meantime."

"I don't like this, Gabe," Michael said, folding his arms across his chest. "I don't like not knowing what he's up to or what he's planning, and I don't like that he wants Eva. I think we should go after him now."

"He hasn't done anything yet," Gabe replied. "I don't think we can act on just suspicions and bad blood."

Michael groaned, resisting the urge to pull on his hair. "Maybe Sam's right and we have gone soft."

Gabe gave him a look. "If we're watching him, we'll know if he's going to start anything. That's the best I can offer you right now."

Michael closed his eyes, taking a deep breath and forcing his temper down. What Gabe said made sense. They'd be able to sense Sam because he was one of them, and if they just kept track of his whereabouts, then they'd generally know what he was up to. "Okay."

"I'll do it," Rafe said. He closed his eyes. After a moment, a breeze swirled up around him, displacing dust and a few smaller books, but then there was a swish of movement and it was gone. Rafe opened his eyes again. "There. I'll keep an eye on it and let you know about anything worrisome I find."

"Thanks, Rafe." Michael was curious about what the other man had done, but he'd tried to have Rafe explain his air tricks a few times, and Michael couldn't seem to make any sense of them.

"Let's close up and go home," Gabe said. "I'm exhausted." He laid a hand on Michael's shoulder. It was a comforting gesture, and Michael felt like he could tell that Gabe understood his worries about Sam, even if he wasn't willing to act.

Michael helped them get the store ready, feeling slightly better. He was still worried about what Sam was up to, and what he would try, but at least Gabe and Rafe were willing to stand by him.

Chapter Twelve

EVA'S MOTHER had moved to a smaller house when Eva left for college. In some ways, she missed her childhood home, but on the other hand, this new house didn't hold lingering memories of loved ones who had passed on.

Christmas had been good to her. She had both a new alarm clock and a new hat, and she and her mother had gone shopping the day after Christmas for some new clothes for her to take on her trip. She was mostly packed now, her bag lying open on her bed. She suspected she was over-packing, but never having been on any sort of real trip before, she wanted to make sure she was prepared.

Things had been less awkward than she had predicted, though there had been a surprise visit with Mrs. Wong and her son, who looked about as amused about the whole situation as Eva felt. And there was a strange undercurrent to all her interactions with her mother, like neither was quite sure where they stood and didn't know how to fix it.

Eva was supposed to be at the airport in a few hours. She thought she might explode from a mix of excitement and fear. Now that this was happening—really, truly happening—she didn't know what to expect. It had been silly to think she should go by herself. And she'd managed to put to rest at least half her mother's fears based on the fact that Michael was coming and that he'd been there before.

Eva hadn't actually told her that she was traveling with a guy yet, though she wasn't sure her mother would care. Her mother probably hoped that she would settle down soon and give her grandchildren.

She tucked in a few additional pairs of socks and called herself done. Zipping the bag, she heaved it off the bed and lugged it downstairs, wincing as it thunked against each and every step on the way down.

Her mother had been a bundle of nervous energy all day. She'd vacuumed the entire house, including the tile in the bathrooms and the kitchen, and then had managed to scrub the shower into shining, which Eva hadn't thought the plastic was capable of. Now she seemed to be going through her office. Several large trash bags filled with papers and Heaven knew what else were sitting outside in the hallway.

"I'm going to be just fine, Mom," she said, leaning up against the doorframe.

"I know, *chica*," her mother replied, not looking up from her paper shredding. "The house has just been such a mess lately. Will you take those bags out to the trashcan, please?'

Eva suspected that all that mess wouldn't fit in a single week's load, but seeing how she had nothing to do but let her nerves stand on edge until it was time to leave for the airport, there didn't seem to be any reason not to help out. Maybe after the garbage, she could go shine the glasses in the kitchen cabinets or something.

The bags of paper were surprisingly heavy, and one ripped before she'd managed to even get it out the back door. Eva managed to wrestle it into a second bag for stability before retrieving her coat. It had lightly snowed the day before, and the temperature was still sitting down near freezing. She slid on her new hat and borrowed a pair of her mother's gloves before flinging open the back door and dragging the bag out.

Her breath misted against the cold. The trashcans were kept in the yard near the garage, which sat near the rear of her mother's property. The house might be smaller, but Eva suspected the yard was bigger, which seemed a waste when there were no children or dogs or other animals to enjoy it.

There was a layer of ice on the walk which helped the bags glide along towards the cans, though Eva found it harder to get any sort of leverage. She managed to get two of the bags to the trashcan, but the thought of trying to pick them up and stuff them inside didn't seem very appealing, so she left them where they were and went to retrieve the final bag.

The entire trip was much easier with a single bag, and feeling charitable, she was even willing to try to stuff it inside the trashcan, but as she lifted the bag up she lost her footing and slid onto the ground, the bag falling to the wayside.

"Need a hand?" asked a familiar voice.

Eva looked up in surprise to find Lily in the alley, leaning against her mother's fence. She actually seemed to glow against the gloom of the weather, her fiery hair pulled back into an effortlessly attractive ponytail. She had no hat or gloves, but she didn't seem to mind. "What are you doing here?" Eva asked, pushing herself back onto her feet.

"I thought I'd come and pay you a visit," replied Lily. She unlatched the gate and stepped into the yard. "We left things off on such a bad note."

Eva retreated instinctively before the other girl's advance, unsure why she felt so uneasy. "How did you know where I live?" Not even Gabe knew her mother's address, though she doubted he would give it to Lily even if he did.

"Phonebook," answered Lily, as if that sufficiently answered the question. Eva didn't think it did. She stepped closer to Eva, the ice not seeming to hinder her progress. "Now, Eva, my dear, let me help with that and we can have a chat."

"No, seriously, why are you here?" repeated Eva.

Lily ignored her, stepping closer. She placed one nearly white hand on Eva's cheek, and Eva noticed with a start that Lily's breath was invisible, though she could still see her own.

Then darkness had closed over her. The world faded from view, and all she could feel was black and cold and agony. She couldn't cry out, she couldn't move, and she was dimly aware of fading into nothingness.

She wasn't sure how long she remained in the darkness, but all of a sudden the world came rushing back into view. Eva gasped, sinking to her knees. Lily was several feet away, sprawled in the snow, and Michael was standing over her, his breathing ragged, his face flushed. His attention was on Lily, and a dangerous look Eva had never seen before glowed in his eyes.

Eva tried to say his name, but her mouth didn't seem up to working quite yet. Michael's eyes softened as they switched to her and he kneeled next to her in the snow, taking her in his arms. Within moments, she felt warmth begin to return to her body. He was murmuring things in her ear, but she couldn't quite seem to make them out.

Lily pulled herself out of the snow, eyes flashing. Michael released Eva slowly before standing and placing himself between Eva and the other girl. For a moment, neither of them moved, their matching green eyes locked on one another. Then Lily looked away, and without another word she turned and walked out of the yard, closing the gate behind her.

Michael was at her side again as soon as Lily was out of sight. "Are you okay?" he asked. "I'm so sorry; I didn't even think about the fact that she might come after you." He shook his head, looking miserable, and Eva wanted to wrap her arms around him and tell him everything would be all right. "God, sometimes I can be so stupid."

She felt like all she wanted was something warm to drink. "Help me up," she said, pleased when her voice actually worked. Michael did so, peering at her with concern. "I'm okay, I'm feeling all right now. What happened?"

He looked away from her, rubbing his hand down the back of his neck. "I'm not sure. I know Lily has some pretty strange interests, like the occult and things along those lines, but when I came up it looked like she had in you in some sort of weird pressure-point hold."

Something didn't ring right about his explanation, but Eva felt too out of sorts to pursue it. She looked over at him, suddenly very glad that he was there. She leaned up against his side, basking in his warmth. "You're early," she said.

"Good thing," he answered.

"Well, come inside and meet my mother." Eva pulled away from him regretfully, casting a glance over her shoulder at the alley. Lily was nowhere in sight, but she shivered anyway. "Although I don't know why everyone's coming in the back today."

"I'll go around if you want," offered Michael. "I parked out front."

Eva was tempted to ask him why he'd come around the back, then, but decided she didn't really care. "You really are some sort of guardian angel," she said, thinking back to Pat's words the first time they'd gone to the restaurant.

Michael's cheeks flushed bright pink. "I'll go ring the doorbell like a normal person," he said, and before Eva could say anything else, he was gone. She blinked, then shook her head. Damn Lily; it was going to take a while before she was going to be able to think straight again.

Eva slid the back door open and let herself in just as the doorbell rang.

"I'll get it," said her mother, who had apparently moved from the office to the dining room while Eva had been outside. She bustled to the front door and pulled it open as Eva came up behind her, thoroughly aware that her shoes were dripping water all over the hallway, but at least it would give her mother something real to clean.

Michael stood in the doorframe, looking considerably calmer than he had in the back yard. Somewhere he'd found time to straighten his hair as well. He smiled down at Eva's mother, who was considerably shorter than her daughter and only came up to the middle of Michael's chest. "*Buenas días, Señora Martinez,*" he said with a very passable Spanish accent. "I'm Michael." Eva stared at him in surprise.

Her mother laughed. "You must be Eva's friend. Come in, make yourself comfortable, and call me Maria." She held the door open for Michael and winked at Eva behind his back as he came inside. Eva blushed.

"You have a lovely home," said Michael. Unlike Eva, he wiped his feet on the doormat.

"Let me take your coat, and then go have a seat in the living room. You have some time before you have to leave for the airport, yes?" Eva's mother took his coat, frowning at Eva as she noticed the water down the hallway. "Can I get you something to drink?"

Michael gave her one of his brilliant smiles. "No, thank you," he said.

"Well, Eva's all packed, so you just go sit down, and we'll be there in a moment. I'm afraid I've had Eva doing odd chores for me all morning." Michael obediently turned and wandered into the living room. After a moment, she turned to Eva. "Nice-looking young man," she said.

Eva slid her hat and gloves off. "Yes," she agreed, suspecting she wasn't going to like where this was going. Her mother opened her mouth again, but before she could say anything, Eva added, "We're just friends, if that's what you're going to ask."

Her mother pursed her lips. "You could certainly do worse than that," she said. She took Eva's coat from her as she shrugged it off and hung both hers and Michael's on a hook by the door. "A lot worse."

Eva agreed, but she suspected this visit would be awkward enough without giving her mother any encouragement.

Giving her a little push, her mother followed her into the living room. Michael had chosen to sit on one half of the sofa, leaving the armchair or the other half of the sofa for Eva. She felt like she had to sit next to him, or else her mother would, and that just seemed like it might be odd.

"So," said her mother, as she sank into the armchair. "You said your name was Michael? Eva didn't do a good job of informing me of things."

Eva sighed and sank back into the couch cushions.

Michael gave her a small smile. "Yes, I'm Michael—Michael Lohrengel," he said, and Eva couldn't help thinking that she wouldn't have done a good job anyway. She didn't know his favorite color, or his favorite movie, or anything basic, really. And yet, she knew that she trusted him, and that he made her heart race and made her feel more amazing that she had thought possible. "I'm a doctorate student in physics. I'm twenty-nine years old, and I live with my roommates, who just happen to own the bookstore Eva works at."

"Is that how you met her?" asked Eva's mother, looking pleased.

"We met at school, actually," answered Eva, feeling like she should take part in the conversation so she could have some control over it, otherwise it would probably descend into her mother telling Michael embarrassing stories about her childhood, like how she'd had a teddy bear that she called '*El Diablo.*' "And he's been helping me with some of my schoolwork." She didn't elaborate.

"It's been my pleasure." Michael smiled at her.

Her mother eyed both of them intently. "My Eva is a very smart girl, you know. She won a poetry contest in high school, and she went to the state Geography Bee. Her good looks come from my side of the family."

"I can tell," agreed Michael amiably.

"She always has had a lot of boys after her," continued her mother. Eva tried to sink further into the couch. "Who can blame them? But my Eva only accepts the best."

"Mother, I don't think Michael needs to know that," said Eva, trying to keep her exasperation out of her voice. This was already getting into uncomfortable territory, and they'd only been there for ten minutes.

Her mother ignored her, focusing on Michael. "A man would be very lucky if she accepted him."

Michael was beginning to flush, his cheeks just slightly pink. "Mmm," he said in response.

"So, Michael," her mother continued, "do you have a girlfriend?"

This conversation needed a change in course before her mother offered Eva's hand in marriage. "I'm so excited about this trip!" she said, sitting up and turning to Michael.

"Let's see how you feel after the plane trip," he said with a grin. "Plus we'll probably be jetlagged when we get there, but maybe you'll be one of the few people who can sleep comfortably on a plane and be all rested when we arrive."

Eva's mother made a disapproving noise in her throat. "This trip," she grumbled. "It seems like an excuse. An unnecessary delay."

Michael raised an eyebrow, glancing at Eva. She shook her head slightly. They'd had this fight at least once a day since Eva had come home, and her mother was trying to fit it into every conversation she had with anyone. Eva didn't understand why she had to make a decision now, and she didn't understand why her mother was pushing her so hard. Eva wanted so badly to be able to prove that she was an adult, that she could take care of herself, and the thought of revealing any sort of weakness to her mother made her blood run cold. What sort of person in their twenties didn't know where they were going in life, what they wanted to do? That's what her mother would say.

"This is something I need to do," she said.

Her mother shook her head and humphed.

"Well, it was very nice to meet you, Señora Martinez," said Michael, "but I'm afraid we should probably go. The recommended time to be at the airport for an international trip is considerably longer than a domestic flight, unfortunately." He rose, offering a hand to Eva, which she gladly took and let herself be pulled up. "Don't worry; I'll take good care of her."

"Already?" Her mother looked a bit pale. She came over to Eva, taking her daughter's face in her hands and kissing her on both cheeks. "Come home safe," she whispered.

Eva took her mother's hands in her own. "I will," she answered, giving her hands a squeeze. She gave her mother a tight hug, then headed out into the hallway, Michael trailing behind her. As she took her coat back off the hook and looked at her bags, piled at the end of the entryway, uncertainty welled up inside of her. What was she doing? There were so many things that could go wrong. It would be safer to stay home with her mother.

"Go ahead and go out to the car," said Michael. "I left it unlocked. I'll get your bags."

Eva took a deep breath. There was no need for last-minute worries. She needed to be strong for her mother.

Her mother stood in the entrance to the living room, looking frail and sad. Eva went to her, again hugging her. "Everything will be okay, I promise," Eva whispered. "Michael will be there too, and he'll protect me."

Eva's mother's eyes slid over to Michael, who returned her gaze calmly. He stood in the middle of the hallway, back straight and strong, and for a moment Eva had a picture of him with giant wings and Romanesque armor with a sword. She blinked in surprise, and the image was gone.

"He'd better," her mother whispered, but when Eva pulled away, she looked calmer and less pale. "Have a good trip."

"Thanks, Mom," said Eva, smiling. Before she lost her nerve, Eva turned and walked out the front door into the cold beyond. There was a yellow convertible of some sort on the driveway and she stopped, staring at it.

"Problem?" asked Michael, coming out of the house behind her, his arms laden with her bags.

"This is your car?" she asked.

"Well, it belongs to Rafe," said Michael. "We don't need to drive very often, living in a college town, you know, so Gabe and I never bothered to get our own."

Eva trailed behind Michael as they made their way to the car and he opened the trunk. Eva peeked in. Michael's bag was considerably smaller than hers was, but he didn't comment on that fact as he heaved her bag in next to his and then slid her carry-on on top. Slamming the trunk, he blinked at her. "Everything okay?"

"Just a little nervous," she admitted.

He reached out as if to touch her face, but then glanced back at the house and apparently thought better of it, dropping his hand back to his side. "We're going to have a great time," he said firmly. "It will be very interesting, and we'll see all sorts of nice things." He followed her around to the passenger side of the car, opening the door for her.

The inside of the car was black leather, and it smelled nice and clean. Eva slid inside, rubbing her hands along the seat. How had Rafe been able to afford this from the proceeds the store generated? It didn't seem like there were a lot of people that came in, but she didn't really know much on the business end of things. She knew Gabe spent some time looking for rare books people ordered specifically, so maybe that helped.

Michael closed the door behind her and moved over to the driver's side of the car. He slid in, starting the ignition. "Here we go," he said, giving her a smile. Eva's pulse quickened. Here they were, alone together, about to go off on a trip for a few weeks. Despite the happenings of the last month, she was still surprised to find herself here. Things seemed to have moved entirely too fast, and yet, she wasn't sure she minded. Looking at Michael out of the corner of her eye as he pulled out of the driveway and started down the road, she had to admit to herself that things would have been different if she hadn't run into him, and she pitied that other Eva.

Michael glanced over at her, his green eyes bright, and Eva suddenly remembered Lily and the backyard and felt a chill go down her spine. "Michael," she said, "what was that, really, with Lily? What was she trying to do?"

His hand tightened on the steering wheel. "I'm not really sure."

Eva frowned, but he didn't seem to be lying. She let the matter drop, for now at least. "Sorry about my mother," she said.

He laughed. "Don't worry about it."

"What about your family?" she asked, stretching her feet out in front of her. "Are they worried about you going on this trip and being thoroughly nosy about whom you're going with?"

The smile faded off of Michael's face. He was quiet for a moment before answering, a myriad of emotions flashing quickly across his face faster than Eva could identify them. "I don't have any family, really," he answered finally.

"No family?" echoed Eva before she could stop herself. What did that mean? Was he an orphan? She couldn't bring herself to pry.

He shrugged, trying to sound nonchalant. "I consider Gabe and Rafe to be my family. We've been together for a long time. But to answer your question, no, they weren't nosy because they probably know more about you than I do, and yes, I suspect they are worried about this trip."

"Why?" asked Eva, trying to imagine her bosses sitting Michael down and warning him about the dangers of the world.

"While change might be constant," answered Michael, his eyes on the road ahead of him, "it doesn't mean that people like it."

To Michael's relief, Eva didn't bring up Lily again. They reached the airport without issue, easily caught their plane, and experienced no issues during the flight, though Eva slept most of the way, obviously feeling the residue of Lily's attack. Michael was exhausted himself, but the hum of the engines jostled his nerves and kept him awake. He hadn't been expecting to have to deal with Lily. Her power was draining, even without her wings released, and the only reason things had probably gone as well as they had was because he'd surprised her and she hadn't had a chance to move her attack over to him. He'd never directly experienced one of Lily's attacks, but he'd seen the aftermath enough times. Luckily he'd gotten there before Lily had really had a chance to get going.

He should have paid more attention to Lily. His only thought had been to protect Eva from Sam, but the last report from Rafe on Sam's activities hadn't turned up anything unusual. Michael really was an idiot. How could he have forgotten that Sam had specifically called Lily there to help?

Michael glanced over at Eva, sleeping beside him. Maybe he should tell her something, just enough so that she'd know what she was dealing with and—what? What would she be able to do with that information? She couldn't control her powers, and whatever lingering ones she had from whomever she was previously wouldn't be enough to stand up to either Sam or Lily individually, let alone both of them.

Besides, there were rules. Michael sighed and went back to staring out the window at the empty expanse of ocean beneath them.

They had a layover in London; Eva woke up just long enough to shuffle between planes. She didn't wake up again until the plane touched down on the runway at their destination. She blinked several times before she seemed to get her bearings. "Where are we?" she asked, rubbing on eye sleepily.

"Welcome to Greece," said Michael.

"Are we really there?" She sat up, peering out the window. "I can't believe it. I slept the whole way?"

"It's better that way," replied Michael. "You'll be less jetlagged." He folded his hands in his lap, wondering how much the country had changed in the last few hundred years. Hopefully he would be able to find enough familiar landmarks to figure out where he was.

"Did you get any sleep?" Eva asked.

He gave her a wry smile. "I'm afraid not, but don't worry about me."

They didn't have any issues with Customs, and their bags came through in a relatively short time period. It was midday, and Michael wondered how coherent he'd be by the time they went to sleep later that night. He'd certainly gone much longer time periods without sleep, but it had been a while.

They caught a cab from the airport to a neighborhood just south of the Acropolis where they'd be staying while in Athens. Michael watched the city go by the window of the car. It had gotten so much bigger and more modern, as he had suspected it might, but there was a still a feel in the air that was distinctly Athens. Millennia hadn't changed that. He would need to get up higher to get his bearing, though.

"How are you feeling?" he asked Eva, who'd been staring out the other side of the car with equal intentness, her eyes opened wide. If she was tired, then he certainly wouldn't mind a good nap, but if not, maybe they could head for higher ground. The Acropolis was the highest thing around, and Eva would probably want to see it anyway. "Up to some sightseeing?"

She smiled at him, her eyes bright with excitement. "That would be nice," she said.

After leaving the bags at the hotel, they caught a bus to the Acropolis. It was crawling with tourists, but Michael wouldn't be doing anything that would call too much attention to himself. Michael offered Eva his arm, unable to suppress a shiver as she laid her hand in the crux of his elbow. He steered her through the crowds, their voices a symphony of different languages. It was one of the things he liked best about the present. Back even a few hundred years before, it was a huge ordeal even to travel to the country next door. Depending on where one was going, the trip could take weeks, months, even years. Now the other side of the world was never more than a day away.

The Acropolis looked much like it had the last time he'd seen it. It still sat high above the majority of the city on its rocky plateau, though the different buildings were dirtier and in more pieces than he remembered. It never failed to amaze him what the human mind and human body were capable of producing. Here was a place that had withstood the passage of time when so many others had disappeared into time. The landscape had changed, it was true, but aside from the colorful throngs of tourists from all nationalities, he could believe that it was two thousand years ago.

Eva seemed very excited. She twisted this way and that, staring at the buildings. She squeezed Michael's arm. "Let's go to the top," she said, beaming. Michael felt his breath catch in that smile.

The top would suit his needs. The crowds thinned a little as they proceeded. It was a long way to the top, and by the time they reached it, Michael was feeling extremely worn out. It had been a much longer day than he had thought it was going to be. He led Eva to a spot to sit and took a deep breath, closing his eyes for a moment. He was never going to make it all the way to tonight.

"Athens was named in honor of Athena, Greek Goddess of Wisdom," he told Eva. "This was a temple to her. There used to be a large statue of her in the center."

"What happened to it?" asked Eva.

Michael wasn't actually sure. "I think it got looted somewhere along the way by invaders or something," he said. "Do you want to get a closer look at the temple?"

Eva nodded and Michael was pleased with her enthusiasm. He sort of felt like he had pushed her on some aspects of this trip, so it was nice to see that she didn't mind. He led her over, glancing around. This seemed to be as good a spot as any.

"Go on ahead," he told her. "I need to do something."

She didn't need any further encouragement. Within seconds she had disappeared into the crowd and Michael felt a sudden panic, but he forced it down. There were entirely too many people around for anything to happen to her. He needed to figure out where he was and where they needed to go.

Closing his eyes, he breathed in deeply, clearing his mind. He gave a gentle push with his mind, feeling it spread out over the surrounding area. He began to pick up residues of others like him. He pushed out farther. There was the occasional acknowledgement from others, but from this distance he couldn't tell who they were. Hopefully they wouldn't take unkindly to being scanned. It used to be a very common practice, an indication when someone new moved into a territory, but it had been a long time since Michael had felt the telltale tickle himself. He didn't know if it was because there were so many less of them now, or if it was because those who were left didn't move around as much anymore. They wouldn't be able to tell who he was from this distance either, but everyone was more suspicious these days. The world had become too small, too fast.

There was a lot of residue left over from thousands of years previously. Michael wasn't terribly surprised.

There'd been a lot of them here in Greece, and though Michael had spent his time farther south in what was today considered the Middle East, he had occasionally come up this way. It was essential in those days to travel occasionally, or else one wouldn't know what was going on in the world.

There was no one especially close to where they were, which made Michael feel a little better. Not that Sam or Lily could have gotten here to Greece before them, if they even knew about the trip—which Michael doubted—but it never hurt to be safe.

Satisfied that he had the information he needed, Michael pulled himself completely into his body.

"Michael," said Eva.

He opened his eyes slowly, looking down at her.

"Oh, thank goodness," she said, relief evident across her pretty features. "Are you feeling all right? You've been standing there forever."

"Sorry," he answered. "Guess I'm just a bit tired."

"Do we need to go?" asked Eva, biting her lip. Michael could almost hear her thoughts: she would go if he needed to, but she was having a good time and would like to stay. And Michael was going to do nothing to ruin her enjoyment this trip. He was there to guide and help, and nothing else. *Nothing else.* He had a feeling he would be reminding himself of that often enough as time went on.

"No, I'm fine now," he said, accenting his words with a bright smile. Eva looked a little dazed before her own smile answered. "Did you have something you wanted to show me?"

She wrapped her slight arm tightly around his and his heart lurched, but she seemed to be oblivious to the effect she had on him. He definitely needed to keep his hands to himself. He would be in trouble with Gabe for years if he messed this up for Eva.

Eva led him around the temple before they moved on to other parts of the monument. Michael had to smile at some of the informational placards; interesting how the buildings could withstand the years but the information had not. Maybe when he got bored with physics he'd go into history for a while, try to get some of the truth back into modern theories. He noted a couple of particularly interesting interpretations to tell Rafe about later. Eva was particularly attentive, asking questions often as if she thought he was an expert on Ancient Greek culture— he supposed in some ways he was, since he'd been there—and commenting on everything that caught her interest. He was happy just to let her go on, listening to the harmonies of her voice. He could listen to it for eternity.

Unfortunately, since they'd gotten a late start, they weren't able to see everything there was to see before it was time to go. Michael didn't really mind. The longer they stayed, the more he noticed things that were different—pieces of art that were missing, areas of buildings that were damaged. There was something very wrong about walking through a place that he could remember so clearly as being full of life and purpose now being treated as a ruin. Absently, he wondered what had happened to Athena herself. He'd liked her. There'd been so many of them here—where had they all gone? Interesting that as humans became more advanced they'd had to disappear further into the background until no one knew where anyone else was anymore.

Eva seemed pleased with the day's events. She continued to chatter pleasantly as they walked back down into the surrounding neighborhoods, searching for a place for dinner. Michael focused on the conversations circling around them, trying to reconcile modern Greek with the language he was more familiar with. Unfortunately, the neighborhood right outside the Acropolis was full of tourist shops and many people were speaking English. It took him several minutes before he was confident that he had picked up enough. Maybe he needed to travel more than he did. It was always a little disarming to arrive back someplace a few hundred years later and realize the language had changed enough to be nigh incomprehensible.

"Michael," Eva said suddenly. "What did you mean earlier?"

Michael blinked down at her. "When?"

"When you said you should have thought about Lily coming after me. Why would she? And why should you expect something like that?"

"Oh," said Michael, mostly to stall. Hell, what did he tell her? "Well, to be honest, I thought it would be Sam if anyone."

Eva's eyes widened, and Michael mentally kicked himself. He was going to freak her out, and then she was going to worry the whole trip, which wouldn't do.

"I don't understand," Eva said. "I thought Lily liked me. Though she did say something weird the last time I really spent time with her—something about opposing elements and incompatibility." She shook her head. "Why would Sam come after me? What's happening, Michael?"

"What's happening is that we're on a lovely trip, and we don't have to worry about Sam because Rafe is dealing with him." He patted Eva's hand in what hopefully was a comforting manner. "Put them out of your mind; they've no bearing on the purpose of us being here."

"But how—"

"I don't have anything to tell you, Eva."

Eva pursed her lips, but she let the matter drop.

They found a little restaurant outside the tourist quarter. Luckily they spoke enough English that Michael didn't have to use his newfound language. He didn't want to have to explain to Eva why he knew the language. He would have had to make something up, and he tried to lie as little as possible. Afterwards, they strolled back to their hotel, enjoying the view of the Acropolis at night. Though Athens was typically chilly at this time of year, the night was warm enough that it was still comfortable out.

Michael had made sure to get a room with separate beds. He didn't honestly know if Eva would care, but he wasn't sure he trusted himself and it seemed best to go ahead with it without asking her about it. Less awkward that way. Unlike at most American hotels, however, these were twin beds. That was fine. More incentive to keep his hands to himself.

He let her have her pick of the beds and then waited until she had disappeared into the bathroom to change into his pajamas. He had never been more happy to see a bed in his life. He crawled in, and was asleep before Eva re-emerged.

Chapter Thirteen

EVA AWOKE the next morning to the sun shining in through the window right into her face. She didn't terribly mind; after all, the sooner they got up, the sooner they could get going for the day.

The Acropolis had been a wonderful way to start the trip. She'd seen pictures of it before, but it was so much more impressive in person. How amazing to think that it was still standing after all these years. She had liked moving along between the buildings, trying to picture what life would have been like so long ago. Michael had been the perfect companion. She almost felt like she had learned more from him than she had from the placards and other displays in the monument itself. She had to admit she was glad he had come along. She wasn't sure she would have gone through with it in the end if she'd been alone. Plus it gave her a chance to have him all to herself.

No, she chastised herself. Best to stick to what they were here to do.

Michael was still asleep, his back turned to her. His covers had slipped halfway down his chest, revealing two ugly scars on his back near his shoulder blades. They were red and raised, like they were recent.

Throwing off her covers, she quietly padded over to his bed, bending over to get a better look. They were mirror images of each other, one a couple inches on either side of his spine, running vertically several inches. She frowned, reaching one hand slowly forward. As she ran a finger lightly down one, Michael shifted in his sleep. Eva froze.

"Eve," he whispered, "I'm sorry."

Eva pulled her hand back, straightening. What was he sorry for? She turned away, heading for her bag to pick out clothes for the day. She felt a little jealous, which was ridiculous, because she knew Eve was out of the picture, and she and Michael had obviously been together for a long time, so he could dream about her all he wanted.

That didn't really make her feel any better, though. And she could still remember Eve in her dream—she hadn't gotten up the courage to ask anybody to actually describe Eve, because she was afraid of what it would mean if her dream had Eve right—and how Eve had claimed Michael as hers.

Eva shook her head. It was no use dwelling on it. She went into the bathroom to get changed.

Michael was sitting on the edge of his bed when she emerged, rubbing sleepily at his eyes. He was only wearing a pair of plaid flannel pants, and Eva caught herself staring at his chest and wondering how it would feel under her hands. She forced herself to look away, focusing on his face, though that wasn't much better, as his hair was attractively mussed from sleeping.

"Where did you get those scars on your back?" she asked, wincing as her voice came out more accusatory than she would have liked.

Michael blinked at her sleepily. "What?"

"The scars. On your back," repeated Eva.

Confusion played across his features. He stood, pushing past her into the bathroom, turning in an attempt to see his own back in the mirror. "Oh, hell," he said.

"You didn't know about them?" Eva asked disbelievingly. "They're six inches long. I can't imagine that didn't hurt."

"Not as much as you'd think," Michael said. He stretched, which distracted Eva for a moment. Michael came back out into the bedroom, digging through his bag.

"Michael," Eva said. "I feel like you're keeping things from me."

He found a blue t-shirt and slid it on over his head. "What do you mean?"

"First there's the thing with Lily, and now with your back—why can't you just tell me what's going on?"

Michael stared down at his bag, rubbing the side of his neck. "It's best if you don't get involved."

She was already involved. Lily had come after her, after all. Eva huffed and headed toward her own bag to get some shoes and socks out. Michael seemed relieved, retrieving a pair of jeans and heading toward the bathroom.

"What happened to Eve, Michael?"

He stopped short, slowly turning to face her. "I don't..."

"You were talking in your sleep," she said. "You guys are always beating around the bush—what actually happened to her?"

For a second Michael looked lost, and Eva's heart melted a bit. But then some sort of determination settled in his face. "She died," he said.

Eva almost dropped her socks.

Michael looked down at his pants. "And I think Sam killed her." With that, he entered the bathroom, shutting the door firmly behind him.

Wow. Eva sat down on the bed, still clutching her socks. That would explain a lot. It would certainly explain why they didn't get along. What did you say to someone you suspected killed the person you loved?

Michael took much longer in the bathroom than could possibly have been necessary. She should really apologize, but she couldn't shake the feeling that he wasn't being completely honest with her. He knew more about what Lily was trying, she was sure of it. So why wouldn't he tell her? Especially since it directly affected her well-being?

By the time he emerged, Eva was feeling grumpier. "Breakfast?" he asked. He sounded like he was trying to be cheery, and failing miserably.

"Yeah, sure," said Eva.

After breakfast, they wandered around Athens a bit. Most of the major tourist areas were within walking distance of the Acropolis, which continued to loom overhead, protected by its limestone cliffs. They started the furthest back in time, looking at leftover Greek and Roman ruins, then toured through the National Archeological Museum and finished the day with a couple of medieval Byzantine churches, including one set into an otherwise modern pedestrian mall. Everything was fascinating, but Eva felt her concentration slipping. She kept focusing on Michael and what he was hiding instead of the archeological marvels in front of her.

She suspected he noticed a few times, because he'd trail off in the middle of whatever he was saying and give her a nervous glance.

Sometimes, though, she could swear she saw the ruins whole and complete, as they would have been in their prime.

Eva took a lot of pictures as they went, thinking she'd be able to use them later for her thesis, but the main goal of the trip—the one where she figured out what the heck she was doing with her life—didn't seem to be going so well yet. Admittedly, it was hard to focus on when she was so distracted, but she kept hoping she'd look at something and she'd have a sudden epiphany.

"Eva," Michael said, as they left their final church for the day, "are you okay?"

"Just fine," she said shortly.

Michael caught her hand. "Hold up a minute. You've been weird since this morning."

"It's nothing."

He gave her a look that clearly said that he thought she was full of it, which was somewhat infuriating, all things considered.

"Look, Michael, I don't know why you can't just be honest with me. How is this," she gestured between the two of them, "ever going to work if you can't tell me the truth?"

Michael looked pained. He closed his eyes for a second, taking a deep breath, then opened them again. "Okay. The scars on my back."

"Yes?"

"They're from the fight with Sam."

Eva stared at him. "What? What'd he do, come at you with a knife?"

"I don't remember any knives," Michael said, "but there were rocks involved."

She blinked. It was hard to match a violent, potentially murderous Sam up with the same guy she'd sat next to in class for years, even though he had been getting weirdly possessive there at the end of the semester.

"Eva," Michael said, drawing her attention back to him, "I want to apologize."

"For what?"

"I'm not trying to keep things from you, I promise. I'm being as open as I can. There's just...some things I'm not in a position to share."

Of course. "Tell me the truth—you all escaped from some cult somewhere, didn't you?"

Michael laughed. "Maybe we did," he replied, though from his smile, it was clear he didn't mean it. After a moment, he sobered. He took her other hand as well, intertwining his fingers with hers. "Listen, Eve was...very special to me. And when she was taken from me, I felt the pain would never fade. Until recently, I didn't think I'd ever feel anything for anyone ever again." He looked up, meeting her eyes. "But, Eva, now that I've met you, that pain's grown fainter. I feel complete in a way that I haven't felt in a very long time."

Eva could feel her pulse quicken. She wanted to say something, anything, but nothing seemed willing to come out.

"And I know why we're on this trip, and I promise that I won't do anything to get in the way of that," he continued, looking down at their entwined hands. "But I wanted you to know." He was quiet for a moment, but then he looked up and smiled at her. "I'm hungry. Let's find something to eat."

He let go of one of her hands and led her down the street. Emotions swirled through Eva's head and she found it hard to concentrate on where they were going. How did she feel? It seemed like such an honest confession should receive one in return, and she did like him. Maybe even more than that, though she was loath to admit it. But there was something so right about the world when she was with him.

He led her to a fancier restaurant than she would have chosen, not listening to her protests. "It's on me," he said, still smiling. He seemed calmer now than he had earlier, and so she relented.

Michael insisted on buying them a bottle of wine as well. Eva didn't drink very often, and she suspected Michael didn't either, as they were both laughing halfway through their first glasses.

A little while later, after the entire bottle of wine, dinner, and something sweet, they wandered back out onto the street. It was still a pleasant temperature outside despite the fact that the sun had disappeared some time before. They walked back to the hotel still laughing between themselves, and let themselves back into their room.

The next morning Eva awoke to find them both on Michael's bed, fully clothed. Michael was pressed up against her back, one arm draped possessively over her body, his breath warm on the back of her neck. She snuggled back against him. He felt so perfect where he was, like he had been made just for her.

He shifted slightly, nuzzling her neck with his chin. It both tickled and sent shivers down her spine. "Morning," he murmured before drifting back off to sleep.

Eva rolled over, peering at him. She'd heard people say that some people—children—were like angels when they slept, but the phrase fit Michael. The sun shone in through the window, bathing his hair in gold and looking not unlike a halo. A little hesitantly she reached out, cupping her hand against his cheek. His skin was soft and warm—he was always so very warm, no matter the weather.

It was five days later when Eva figured out that they were being followed. At first she had thought it was her imagination playing tricks on her—one too many horror story of the things that happened to people in foreign countries—but the longer time went on, the more sure she became. She felt better here in Greece, where the sun was out every day, like she was sharper and stronger than usual. She couldn't make out who it was as she just caught glimpses around corners and from within the shadows, but she had been able to discover one thing—their stalker had eyes like Michael's, brilliant and green and completely noticeable even from across the street or down the block.

"I had a question about your eyes," she said to him as they wandered down a street. They'd moved on from Athens, visiting ruins and other landmarks as they made their way north. Their goal for the afternoon was an 11th-century church near the center of town.

He looked down at her, raising an eyebrow. His hands were tucked in his pockets, and he'd been somewhat distant since they'd spent the night in the same bed. He was friendly and entertaining, but he was also keeping his hands to himself. Eva found that distracting. As time went on, as she got to know him better, she found that she had certain cravings that had begun to develop and become stronger. Sometimes she could hardly focus on what he was telling her because she was trying to keep herself from doing anything rash. "What do you mean?"

"You have a very unique color of green," she said, "and I noticed that it's not just you—Gabe, Rafe, Sam, even Lily—you all have the same eye color. Are you all from the same area?"

Michael smiled wryly. "Noticed that, did you?" He looked up at the sky for a moment before answering. "Yes, we came from the same place."

Part of her wanted to break off and follow that train of thought, ask about his childhood, how he grew up, but she needed to focus. "Did everyone have the same eyes?"

He stopped, brow knitting. "Where are you going with this?"

She stepped closer to him, lowering her voice. "Someone's following us. Someone with eyes like yours."

Michael stiffened and for a moment his eyes seemed to go blank, almost like his soul had wandered off somewhere. Then he rolled his shoulders and took off back in the direction they'd come.

Eva let out a half-formed cry and followed after him. What was he up to?

He turned the corner and headed across the street, heading for an alcove between two buildings. Eva followed, her heart beating in her throat. Surely this wasn't safe. Michael was normally smarter than this, but what should she do? Even if he was likely to get them assaulted she would rather stay by his side than wait on the street for him to come out. She hurried to catch up with him.

It managed to be extremely dark in the alcove for it being just slightly after noon. Michael strode purposefully down toward a pile of boxes near the rear. Eva followed him closely, but her breath began to quicken and she glanced over her shoulder, fearing attack from behind. That was the only way in or out except for a door chained shut off on their left.

Michael stopped and Eva almost ran into him. "What are you up to?" he asked the alley, crossing his arms.

Their shadow practically melted out of the wall off on the right. Eva gave a little shriek and stumbled backwards, but Michael held his ground. The shadow was wearing a dark cloak; all that was visible were the eyes, brilliant and glowing in the dark. "My apologies," it said.

Shaking his head, Michael took a step towards the figure. Eva shrank back, unsure what to do. The figure moved to meet Michael, and for a moment the two stood, a mere foot apart, their eyes studying one another.

Then a wide smile broke across Michael's face and a laugh issued from the hood of the cloak, and then the two were shaking hands. "Gave me a fright," Michael said. "How long have you been following us?"

The figure pulled off his hood, revealing a man probably about the same age as Michael, though slightly taller, his hair blond and curly. "Since the Acropolis. You should know better than that, in this day and age."

"It's still the best way to get information," replied Michael, though he looked slightly embarrassed.

Eva frowned, trying to figure out what they were talking about.

Michael caught her look. "Eva, this is Thor. He's an old friend."

She tentatively stepped forward, offering her hand to Thor. He took it, pressing the back of her hand to his lips. "Pleasure's mine," he said. He looked to Michael. "Is she...?"

Michael shrugged. Eva frowned, irritation growing inside her. What on earth was going on?

"Why have you been following us?" Michael was asking, his hands back in his pockets. "Surely you must have better things to do."

Thor laughed. "Not really. And how can I say no when good old Gabriel calls and asks me to keep an eye on you? Though I should warn you that you haven't been the only one in the last couple of days."

One what? Michael seemed surprised by the news, whatever it meant. "Who else?" he asked. "I didn't feel anything."

Thor shook his head. "Whoever it was didn't want to be noticed. Some of us are simply more sensitive than others. It was shortly after you arrived, though, and then you didn't come to visit, so I thought I'd come see what you were up to." He glanced at Eva, pursing his lips. "Thought you might be running from something."

"I don't think I am," said Michael, though he seemed troubled. "Gabe didn't tell me he'd called you. I'm a little insulted that he thought I needed a babysitter. And I didn't realize you were here now. Last I'd heard you'd gone back to Scandinavia."

"It is cold and lonely in the frozen north," replied Thor. "I thought I'd come down and get some sun, maybe get a nice tan, though you know that never happens. Still, be on your guard, will you?"

Eva wanted to scream with frustration. She had absolutely no idea what on earth they were going on about, and it seemed like they'd forgotten she was there. She had a sudden, strong urge to kick Michael in the shin, but she fought it down.

"I heard about Eve," Thor said, rocking on his heels. "I'm sorry. She was a strong woman; I liked her quite a bit."

Michael nodded, looking at the ground. Eva frowned at Thor, a little annoyed that he'd brought Eve up. After Michael's confession the other day, there'd been no mention of her, and Eva thought the trip had been going better now that they had an understanding.

"Any idea how?" Thor was asking.

"No," said Michael, though his voice caught on the word. He took a deep breath. "Sam had something to do with it, I *know*, but I don't know what happened."

Thor shook his head in disbelief. "She should have known better than to go off with Sammael. Kid's been off his rocker for a while."

Eva was beginning to feel like she was eavesdropping on a private conversation. Just when she thought maybe she was starting to figure Michael out, she'd learn a little more that would turn him into a complete enigma again.

A wave of anger and sadness washed over her, and she moved back toward the street, unsure if the men even noticed her leave. She was starting to hate Eve, which was a terrible thing, really. What harm could a dead woman do to her, nightmares aside? But Eve was blocking her from Michael, from the only thing that had really felt right lately. How could Michael love her when he was still in love with someone else?

Did she really care? She found a crate just outside the entrance to the alcove and sat on it. Did she really care how Michael felt about her? Did she care if he wouldn't be hers?

The answer, she was only mildly shocked to discover, was yes. When had her feelings become so strong? Sighing, she leaned her head back against the building. So much for finding herself; all she'd found was frustration.

It didn't make any sense; she didn't really know Michael, and though he was smart and a gentleman and undeniably attractive, was that really enough to explain her feelings? Logically, no, but that didn't change anything. Even this far into the trip, spending every waking moment together, her breath still caught when he smiled at her, her skin still tingled when his hand accidentally brushed hers, and her pulse raced when he was close. She dropped her head into her hands. She was so very screwed.

"Eva." She looked up to find Michael standing over her, Thor just behind him. Thor was looking at her curiously. "Are you okay?"

"Fine," she lied, forcing herself to smile. Judging by the look that passed over Michael's face, she didn't do a terribly good job of it. "I just didn't want to interrupt you two."

"We're done now," said Thor. "Terribly sorry to have interrupted your trip." He smiled slightly. "Haven't seen Michael in a long time, couldn't miss him while he was in town. He's all yours again now." He clapped Michael on the shoulder. "Be careful. I'll see you around."

Michael held up a hand in farewell as Thor pulled his hood back up and disappeared into the crowd.

"What was that all about?" she asked when he was gone.

Michael shook his head. "I'm not really sure, to be honest." There were lines in his face where there hadn't been earlier; he was worried and he wasn't telling her why. Eva wanted to punch him to relieve some of her frustration. "Do you want to go to the church still?"

"Michael," Eva said warningly.

He sighed. "I guess Gabe called him and asked him to keep an eye on us, and he thought we knew, so then he was worried when we didn't check in with him when we got here."

There was more to it, Eva was sure of that, but Michael didn't seem like he was going to volunteer any additional information. She was beginning to see that that was typical. With a sigh, she stood. "Let's go."

The church was very pretty, with all sorts of frescoes on the walls that would have been very interesting had she had any ability to focus on them. Michael seemed just as distracted as she did, trailing off halfway through comments and occasionally staring off into the distance, his brow furrowed.

Eva had enough. She kicked him in the shin. The sound echoed through the small space but there was no one in the church but them to hear it.

He grimaced. "Okay, what the fuck?" he said, sounding annoyed.

"You're driving me crazy," she hissed under her breath, knowing he heard every word. "I am sick of you! You declare your...love, or your like, at least, and then you practically act like I'm a leper."

To her great surprise and joy, he returned her anger. "It's not like that at all," he said, trying to keep his voice from echoing.

"Then what?" asked Eva. "Am I not good enough for you? Not as good as your precious Eve?" She regretted the words as soon as they left her mouth, but not enough to apologize.

Michael straightened, fury dancing in his eyes. "You don't understand," he said, his voice deadly calm.

"Then make me understand," she challenged.

Then his lips were against hers, their fire spilling across her features. He pressed her against the cold stone wall of the church, his hand protecting the back of her head. His body was so warm this close, radiating heat into her entire body. She gasped around his kiss, her anger melting as quickly as it came.

He pulled away, stalking away a few feet, running his hands urgently through his hair. Eva halfway slid down the wall in shock. "You don't understand at all," he said again, his cheeks flushed bright with color. "It's all I can do to keep myself from touching you all the time, and that's just not normal." He moved jerkily, seeming unsure as to whether he was going or staying. "You make my heart race, you take my breath away, I think about you all the time. It's not healthy. I am going insane."

Eva watched this display, still feeling his lips on hers. She had to do something. Do something to make sense of the madness. "Michael," she said.

He paused, his eyes wild. For a short moment she was afraid he would run away. "What?" he asked.

She stepped forward, taking one of his hands in hers. He shivered, but made no attempt to pull away. She ran her fingers up along the inside of his wrist, moving closer to him. His breathing was ragged and she felt a strange sense of power, being able to affect him in this manner. She stood on her toes, pulling his head down towards hers. His breathing hitched as her breath caught his neck. "Is that really such a bad thing?" she whispered.

He jerked back. "We can't—not here," he said.

"Fine," she said, "Not here."

It took him a few minutes of steady, deep breathing to calm himself down to the point where his complexion returned to normal. "Okay," he said, sounding much more like himself. "Okay. Are you finished here?"

Eva glanced around the church. There was no way she'd be able to concentrate on anything. "Yes, I think so. I'm sorry, I'm just very distracted."

Michael chuckled. "Yes, well. Could we...not touch until we get back to the hotel, please? I think it will be for the best." He accented that statement by pressing his hands back into his pockets. Eva watched him. Was this what he'd been doing the whole time? Trying to keep his hands to himself as much as she'd been?

She nodded her assent and they left the church, heading up the street they'd come by as quickly as they could manage without drawing too much attention. Eva peeked at Michael out of the corner of his eye, but he'd managed to smooth over his features, the urgent need he'd been babbling about not visible on his face. Eva doubted she looked so collected.

They'd arrived at this particular hotel only that morning. They were only supposed to be here for the night, and move on to new ruins and landmarks the next day. They wouldn't get a chance to get back to the little church, though Eva couldn't bring herself to care that much. Hopefully Thor had really moved on and was no longer following them, though she was still confused why he'd bothered in the first place if he knew and was friends with Michael. Why not just walk up to him on the street and tell him what he wanted?

The man at the desk looked up as they entered, apparently not used to guests reappearing in the early afternoon. Michael just gave him one of his charming smiles as they passed to get to the staircase to get to their room on the second floor. As they got closer to the room, Eva's heart began to beat faster, and she could hear the unevenness of Michael's breath as he fumbled with the room key and finally got the door open.

He held the door open for her and then followed her inside, locking the door behind him. Almost immediately he was pressing his lips up against hers again, gripping her upper arms. Eva let out a low moan, wrapping her arms around the back of his neck.

After a minute or so, he pulled back. Eva groaned in frustration.

His emerald eyes sought hers. "Is this what you want?" he asked, concern echoing in his voice and his gaze. "I mean, I don't want to do anything you don't want to, and this is supposed to be a trip for you, for you to discover what you want in life and good God if I mess it up Gabe will kill me."

In response she pressed her lips up against his. He responded immediately, one arm sliding around the small of her back and pulling her close, the other cupping the back of her head. She was on fire; she needed release. An echo of what he'd just said remained—was this what she wanted? As Michael moved from her lips to her neck, she had to admit that yes, yes, it really was, and fuck Gabe and whoever else got in their way.

She slid her hands under the front of his shirt, making her way up his chest. It was as warm and hard as she had always thought it would be. Michael pulled away from her for a second to pull off his shirt, and then he was back, gripping her hips tightly. She pressed against him, her breath escaping from her body.

Michael picked her up, biting her shoulder lightly as he carried her across the room, dropping her onto one of the beds. He climbed on top of her, kissing up her collarbone back to her lips.

Eva arched her body against his, moaning into his kisses. She grabbed at his upper arms, pulling herself further up into his lips. With a small growl, Michael slipped his hands under her shirt, pulling away momentarily so he could be rid of the offending fabric between Eva and himself.

She shivered as the cold air found her bare skin, but only momentarily before Michael was pressing her down into the mattress. His chest was as warm as the rest of him, warmer even perhaps. Eva slid her fingers into his waistband, grinning slightly to herself as he moaned into her ear.

Eva left one hand where it was and ran the other up Michael's side. She pulled his bottom lip into her mouth, running her tongue along the ridge of his lip. He shivered, his breath catching again. She took the opportunity to press up, rolling him over onto his back. She seated herself across his hips, reaching behind her to unhook her bra. Michael's breathing continued unevenly beneath her, his hands sliding up her sides.

Dropping her bra off the side of the bed, she suddenly found herself underneath Michael again, unsure how exactly he'd moved so quickly. His eyes were darker than usual, though the fire burned brighter in them, and his breathing was rough. Michael pulled insistently at her pants, and she found herself lifting her hips so he could slide them and her underwear off easier. When he was done with hers, he pulled off his jeans, throwing them across the room, leaving them both completely naked.

Then his full weight was on her, his lips sucking lightly at her skin. Eva moaned, writhing beneath him. She'd never felt this way with anyone before, this feeling of being truly wanted and worshipped.

"Are you sure?" he whispered again.

"God, yes," she breathed.

Michael pulled back for a moment and Eva groaned, but he only fished a condom out of the drawer next to the bed and slid it on. "Best to be prepared," he murmured.

Eva wanted to ask him why he'd packed any at all when he was trying to keep his hands—and other parts—to himself, but then he was inside her and it was even better than she'd imagined it. She arched into him, gasping loudly.

He grunted, leaning down to run his teeth along the side of her neck. She wrapped her arms around his back, aware that she was digging her nails in, but he didn't seem to mind. He hissed against her neck, the action sending shivers down her spine.

"Eva," he murmured into her neck, and it was like something sparked inside her at the sound of his voice whispering her name. *Her* name, not anyone else's.

"Michael," she answered, her voice low.

He half-whimpered, his hips pushing insistently against hers. She moaned again, rising to meet his thrusts. He shuddered against her and in the same moment something inside her gave, a flood of emotion and feeling rushing forward. She cried out even as Michael pulled her closer, whispering her name repeatedly.

They lay there for a while afterwards until their breathing slowed to normal. Michael eventually pulled himself off of Eva and rolled over onto his back. It was much cooler with him gone. Eva shivered and cuddled up next to him. He wrapped an arm around her, rubbing her back lightly.

"Was that okay?" he asked after a long time. His eyes had faded to their normal color, and he seemed to be studying the ceiling intently, though his head rested against hers.

Eva propped herself up on one elbow, using her free hand to tilt Michael's face toward hers. "Michael," she said, "Grow a backbone."

He chuckled. "Mm, you're authoritative today. I think I like it." He leaned up, pressing his lips against hers, and all thought fled.

Chapter Fourteen

THINGS WERE definitely going better, if Michael had to be honest. Something had been relieved, and it was no longer quite so painful to have to hold his urges in. And it had felt so right, too, and the world hadn't fallen apart, so maybe Rafe had been right and he was being too hard on himself. And she was practically one of them anyway, right? So surely there should be some sort of moratorium on potential punishment in that case. It was a shame about the church, though. He'd always thought it was pretty. They'd moved on now, and it was too late.

He had a special treat for Eva today, a temple nearby that apparently hadn't been re-discovered by modern archeology yet. Smiling, he half-listened to her latest theory on the Ancient Greeks and their relationship to the so-called Western religions.

Something caught his attention out of the corner of his eye, and he paused. Eva continued on a few steps before she noticed. "Michael? What's wrong?"

"What are you two doing here?" he asked the men sitting at the café table next to him.

"I don't know what you mean," said Rafe, lowering the newspaper he'd been unsuccessfully hiding behind. Eva blinked at him in surprise. Michael couldn't blame her; she'd been so into what she'd been talking about, and they had been trying to be inconspicuous. "Lovely weather this time of year, isn't it?"

Gabe rolled his eyes. "We're not really here," he supplied.

"You look like you're here," pointed out Eva, a slight edge to her voice. "Who's minding the store?"

Gabe and Rafe shrugged and went back to their pastries.

It took Michael a moment to realize that he was annoyed. He'd been in such a good mood lately that the emotion was foreign, but seriously, what were they doing here? Had they been following them this whole time? Did they not trust him to keep an eye on things? Wasn't Thor enough? "It seems to be a rather large coincidence," he said. "You know, I didn't give you our itinerary so you could tag along. It was meant as more of an emergency sort of thing."

"Listen, Michael," Rafe said, setting his mug of something—knowing Rafe, there was probably chocolate in it—down. He steepled his fingers and looked up at his roommate. "Gabe and I got to talking, and we decided that it had been entirely too long since we'd gone on vacation, and that Greece had sounded so nice when you and Eva had been talking about it, so we thought we'd take a few days off and have some fun." He leaned back in his chair, throwing one arm over the back. "Having a much more limited time frame than you two, we had to condense things a bit, and it just worked out that we'd be here the same time you were. That's all there is to it."

Michael doubted that, but there didn't seem to be a good way to broach the subject while Eva was standing right there. Though, judging by the look on her face, she didn't much buy it either.

Gabe looked between him and Eva. "What about you?" the redhead asked. "Have you been behaving?"

"I don't know what you mean," Michael replied.

Gabe pursed his lips, but he didn't pursue the topic.

"Here," Rafe said. He reached down into a bag leaning against his chair and pulled out a book, offering it to Eva. "I bring mysteries for amends."

Eva's face lit up as she accepted the book. "Well," she said, "I am partially mollified."

"Traitor," said Michael.

She gave him a half-smile. "Don't be too hard on him, Michael. After all, now he is going to have to put up with me forever." She slipped her arm through his.

Michael flushed, carefully avoiding looking at his roommates. "It's going to be his pleasure. Anyway, off we go. I hope the store doesn't suffer any earthquakes while it's unwatched."

"I'm not terribly worried," said Gabe. "Local seismic disruptions have ceased."

Michael whipped his head around so quickly it hurt his neck. "What?"

Gabe's eyes met his, and the redhead discreetly shook his head. "Don't worry about it. I believe you two were on your way to see something...?" He took a sip of his own drink.

Eva's arm tightened around his. "Yes, let's go. We can see these old ruins any time." She stuck out her tongue at her employers and dragged Michael off down the street in the direction they'd been going.

Rafe's call of "These old ruins know where you live!" followed them down the sidewalk.

"That was weird," Eva said as they turned a corner. The buildings began to thin out here, and Michael could see a wide meadow up ahead starting to be overtaken by forest. "I would have thought they'd have waited for us to come back before they left themselves."

"You never can tell what those two are up to," Michael replied, trying to sound happier than he felt. Truth be told, his roommates' presence made him anxious. It was true that Gabe and Rafe would occasionally decide to up and leave whatever they were currently doing for different pastures, but the timing was just too coincidental. And there was Gabe's cryptic message—what did he mean? Had they lost track of Sam? And if Sam had left, where had he gone?

Michael glanced over at Eva. The warm sun gave her hair a sort of glow. She caught him staring at her and smiled up at him. "Let's not worry about it. They can do whatever they want, and we can do whatever we want. So, where are you taking me?"

The sidewalk abruptly ended. A few intrepid souls had continued out into the meadow, over time forming a definite dirt path. Michael took Eva's hand and led her along it, taking a deep breath to calm his nerves. Maybe Sam and Lily had simply decided to move on. It would be odd after all this time, yes, but it was not unprecedented. Even if they were coming after him and Eva, they probably didn't know about this trip. So he needed to relax. The last thing he wanted to do was worry Eva about something that was probably nothing, and if it wasn't, well, then there was no need to worry her over something she could do nothing about.

"Michael?" Eva prompted.

"It's a surprise," he answered. He rolled his shoulders. Right. Having a good time.

If he remembered correctly, the temple would be somewhere up ahead. It had been massive at one point in time, but he hadn't seen it in several thousand years and apparently, neither had anyone else, since he hadn't been able to find any mention of ruins in this area in any of the books he'd consulted, aside from the odd column lying in the middle of a field. There'd been a little settlement here as well, but there was no sign of that either.

They continued along the path, with nothing but meadow and trees in all directions. Michael began to worry that his memory was faulty, but there'd been traces in this area when he'd done his scan. It was always possible that perhaps the temple had been destroyed rather than merely lost to time. Maybe this hadn't been such a good idea. Damn him for wanting to show off. Even if it was here and just buried, how would they get in?

"Do your friends normally follow you everywhere?" Eva asked as they trudged along.

Michael winced. "Not usually, no." That was another thing that had changed over the years. It used to be that everyone just came and went as they pleased. Others would know where someone was if one was looking for someone specific. Nowadays, with them traveling less and trying to blend in more, they'd relegated themselves to small groups. Still, Gabe and Rafe normally would let him do as he pleased unless they were worried about something. "Anyway, don't worry about them. I'm sure they'll keep their distance." He turned to smile at her, but to his very great surprise, Eva wasn't there.

All that was left of her presence was a hole in the ground.

EVA WAS FALLING. One minute she'd been following behind Michael, more puzzled by her employers' sudden desire to take a trip, and one to where she and Michael just happened to be, than she really should have been, and the next, the ground had opened up underneath her.

Something above blotted out the hole—Michael's head, probably, her brain supplied—and she thought she could hear him calling out her name. There was no way she could answer, though. Her breath felt like it had been pushed from her lungs. She was going to die. Her mother had been right.

Darkness took her. No longer could she see the hole, and the falling sensation ceased. Were her senses that dependent on visual sensations?

She waited for the impact to come, but it didn't. Had she already hit the bottom? Was she already dead? Eva became aware of the twinkling of tiny lights around, flitting about in the black. She could almost swear she heard laughter, the murmur of voices. Eva had never been terribly religious, had never really considered what would happen after death. Where was she? She reached a hand out toward one of the lights, or tried to at least, but she had no sense of her own body.

Eva was unsure how long she hung there with the lights, but she began to panic when they faded. They had seemed so peaceful, and she would have been content among them, or so she felt, if she had to choose. They had seemed like the spirits of children—happy, innocent.

Tears welled up in her eyes, and she was surprised to discover that she could feel her body again, though it felt a little strange. Dying would do that to you, no doubt. Experimentally, she opened one eye to find herself lying beneath some sort of tree-bush thing she'd never seen before, in what was apparently a desert. Her mind struggled to make sense of it.

"Eve," said a familiar voice a moment before Michael entered her field of view. "Are you all right?" She blinked at him, wanting to protest that she wasn't Eve, but something held her back. Michael looked different somehow as well—younger, in some way, like he had in some of her dreams. He had long hair, pulled back at the nape of his neck. Before she could answer, Michael had wrapped his long arms around her, burying his head against her shoulder. He wasn't as warm as usual, she noticed. "Thank goodness, I thought something had happened to you."

A blast of wind blew Eva's hair out of her face as two large birds landed just behind Michael. He pulled back, and as he did so, Eva's eyes widened. They weren't birds at all, but Gabe and Rafe, except both had impressive sets of wings growing out of their backs and everyone, herself included, was apparently wearing some sort of strange desert-wrap clothing. This was the oddest dream she had ever had. Anyway, she must be hallucinating, because there was no way that she could be dead, because nothing she'd ever heard about dying included your living friends showing up as angels.

"Michael," said angel-Rafe. "You found her, good. We're gathering nearby."

Michael turned back to face her, concern flashing in his brilliant eyes. "How are your wings? Can you fly?"

Everyone apparently got wings in this dream. Awesome. "I'm not sure," she said. Her voice sounded different.

Michael took a step back, pulling her to her feet as he went. He shut his eyes, grimacing slightly as two giant golden wings spread out behind him from seemingly nowhere. He gave them an experimental flap as he opened his eyes again, looking at her. "I can carry you if needed," he offered.

Eva eyed Michael's wings. Almost instinctually, she closed her own eyes and felt a slight pain as her own wings released, followed almost by a sense of euphoria. She grinned wildly at Michael.

He seemed relieved. "They look fine. Let's go." Rafe and Gabe took off first, followed shortly by Michael. Eva felt a moment of panic, wondering if she knew what she was doing, but all she had to do was think about flying and her wings responded, boosting her off the ground. Her employers seemed to be leading them off toward an oasis that she could just barely see against the horizon. Eva allowed herself a moment to soar, enjoying the feeling of the breeze beneath her wings.

Her pleasure faded as she caught a whiff of burning...something. She wasn't sure she wanted to identify the smell. Eva glanced back over her shoulder and almost forgot to continue flying. Behind them, a massive fire raged across the sands, charred remains of objects momentarily becoming visible through the roaring flames.

She didn't realize she'd stopped until Michael came back to join her. "Eve?" he asked. "What's wrong?"

Eva couldn't tear her eyes from the inferno. "Is that...?" she whispered.

"Yes," Michael said, following her gaze. "That's all that's left of Eden."

Everything plunged back into darkness, and for a moment Eva couldn't straighten out her thoughts.

"Is she okay?" someone was saying. The voice was familiar but she couldn't immediately place it. She became aware of a sharp pain in her side, of a dull throbbing in her head. She shifted, trying to ease her discomfort.

"Eva? Eva, can you hear me?" Michael's voice again, only now he was calling her by the right name. Another dream? If death really did consist mostly of hallucinations, she was going to spend eternity very confused.

"She's not responding," said Michael to the first voice.

"I'm pretty sure you caught her in time," replied the first. "Are you okay, by the way? That cut doesn't look so good."

Michael murmured something incomprehensible. Eva tentatively opened one eye, wondering what she'd find this time, but it took a moment for her eyes to adjust to the low level of light, the only source of which seemed to be a hole far above them.

"Eva?" asked Michael. She realized that he had her gathered into his chest, one warm hand cupping her head, the other wrapped around her side. She pulled back a bit, looking up at his face, instantly regretting the move as her head began to swim unpleasantly. Besides that, Michael's left temple seemed to be leaking blood.

"I feel terrible," she said. "What happened to you?"

"He slammed his head into the floor when he caught you," supplied Thor. "It was kind of awesome."

Michael glared at him. He turned back to Eva, holding up three fingers. "How many fingers am I holding up?"

"You caught me?" Eva glanced up at the hole, mocking them far above. "How is that even possible? Why is Thor here?"

"How many fingers?" repeated Michael calmly. Eva found it slightly ironic that one could be so composed with blood running down the side of one's face.

"Three," answered Eva. "You don't have wings, do you?"

"I...what?" asked Michael, blinking at her.

"Never mind. I think I'm going insane. I had the strangest dreams. There was this darkness, and all these little happy lights..." Eva raised one hand, thinking she'd demonstrate, though she wasn't really sure how. She should stop leaning on Michael too, but she was afraid she'd just topple over.

"You dreamed about the Void?" Thor's face appeared behind Michael's head, surprise written across his features. "But I thought..."

"I didn't think you were out long enough to hallucinate," interrupted Michael. "You gave me quite a scare, but I suppose it's my fault for taking you out this way. Though hundreds of thousands of people must have passed this way over the years, so God knows why the ground decided to give out for you."

"What's the Void?" asked Eva, though she agreed with Michael's assessment of the odds. Now that her eyes had adjusted, she could see they were in some sort of temple, elaborate carvings crossing its columns and walls. It'd obviously been here for a long time. "How did you catch me? Why is Thor here?"

"Thor is here because he wants to drive me insane," said Michael. "I have no idea what he's talking about. I caught you by jumping in after you, which in retrospect was not very smart at all and actually hurt quite a bit." He glowered at his friend before running one hand down Eva's cheek. "How are you feeling? Can you...?"

"...fly?" interrupted Eva.

Michael stared at her. "Everyone has gone insane but me," he stated to the general room. "I was going to ask if you could walk, but if you can fly, by all means, let's do that instead, because otherwise I'm not really sure how we're getting out of here." He was beginning to sound a little hysterical. Eva wasn't sure she blamed him.

"There's a staircase over there," said Thor, indicating some dark corner with a vague wave of his hand. "The opening's pretty tight, but we can get out that way." He shrugged at Eva's surprise. "What? You don't think I jumped in the hole after you too, do you? I leave such antics to other people."

"Liar," replied Michael. "I've seen some of the things you've done, and I think very few would be classified as 'sane'."

"Is this about the hammer again?" asked Thor. "Because I told you you could have one if you really wanted."

There they were, talking about things she couldn't understand again. Between that and her headache, she wanted to scream. "Yes, I think I can walk," she interjected before Michael could go on with whatever retort he had planned.

Without releasing her, Michael pulled himself to his feet, Thor helping. Eva experimentally put her weight on her legs and was pleased when they held. Michael seemed reluctant to let her go, his hand lingering on hers as she pulled away.

"You really scared me," he murmured, his mouth close to her ear. "Let's not do it again."

Eva managed a smile. "Agreed," she said. Questions still buzzed in her mind, however—what had she seen when she was out? And how had Michael really caught her? As he turned to follow Thor to the staircase, she couldn't help but notice that his shirt had ripped right over the scars on his back.

MICHAEL WAS silent as they climbed out of the temple. Eva didn't seem to be seriously hurt, but what did it mean that she was suddenly talking about wings and the Void? She hadn't previously mentioned anything that could have been attributed to when she'd been one of them. It didn't make any sense. Even if she'd seen him come after her, she should have attributed it to her shock or fear, but it didn't seem like she had seen him at all. It was all very puzzling, and Michael was so into his thoughts that he missed the narrowing of the tunnel as they approached the exit and ran his head into the ceiling.

"Haven't you run your head into enough things today?" asked Thor.

"Apparently not," replied Michael, rubbing his temple. His hand came away wet with blood; he must look a mess. This was perhaps the worst idea he'd had in a long time. He was supposed to be helping Eva with her trip, not putting her life in danger, not revealing himself, and not bleeding all over the place. His shirt would have to be thrown out. After all these years, one would think he'd know better than to let his pride get ahead of things.

They emerged into the sunlight. Michael shaded his eyes with one hand, surveying the landscape. Really, what were the odds of Eva finding the one unstable bit of ground and falling through? It made no sense.

"Do you want to come to my place?" Thor asked. "It's not too far from here. Wash you up a little."

Michael glanced over her shoulder at Eva. She was still looking a little pale. Logically, Thor's offer should be accepted, but something told him that Eva would prefer it if they didn't. She seemed distant. "I think we'd better just go."

Thor nodded and clasped Michael's shoulder. "I did tell you to be careful, didn't I? Try not to beat your face up any more today."

"I make no promises," said Michael. "See you later."

He offered a hand to Eva, but she hesitated for a moment before she took it. Michael briefly debated taking another path back to town, but the odds of one or the other of them tumbling through—again—were astronomical.

"I'm really sorry," he began once they'd safely reached the edges of town. "I didn't know that the ground would be unstable."

Eva was silent for a long moment. Michael began to wonder if she was angry with him. He wouldn't be terribly surprised. Almost falling to one's death rarely did anything for one's mood.

"I thought he wasn't going to be following us anymore," Eva finally said.

Michael wasn't sure he had been, but there was no way to test and explain in a manner that Eva should know about. "Maybe he wasn't."

Eva gave him a look that him know exactly what she thought of that. "You're not being honest with me, Michael."

"About Thor? Listen, I don't know what he's doing. Man's practically a ninja when he wants to be."

She shook her head. "Who cares about Thor? In general, Michael."

That shut him up. What did she want from him? This was, no doubt, why they stayed with their own kind when at all possible. Otherwise people would begin to notice things, begin to ask questions—but Michael had spent years perfecting his façade. He'd never had anyone suspect anything before, though he had to admit that circumstances hadn't exactly been normal recently. There had been entirely too much wing usage.

And if Gabe was right about her being someone reincarnated—and Michael didn't like to think about that too closely—then maybe there was no way to hide it. But he still felt like he had to try. They didn't know for sure, and there were rules.

Eva stopped, turning to look up at him. "I'm going to ask you a question, Michael, and I want you to answer me truthfully." Her large chocolate eyes met his, and it was all he could do to keep her gaze. Michael took a deep breath. "How did you catch me, really?"

For a second he almost told her, but then he pulled his eyes away. "I told you, I jumped after you," he said, knowing even as he did that she wouldn't accept that answer.

Without another word, she turned away and continued up the street, leaving Michael to follow behind her.

Chapter Fifteen

MICHAEL COULD see Eva drifting further away from him. She still surveyed their stops with interest, and kept up conversations with him, but she left opportunities for Michael to tell her what he absolutely could not. With each empty response, she grew quieter. Michael didn't know what to do. He could feel his carefully crafted control, created over centuries, slowly falling apart. Gabe was right; he shouldn't have come. He couldn't tell her the truth—she was still human, after all—but he was beginning to think that if he didn't, he was going to lose her, and he wasn't willing to let that happen.

Not that that made things any easier. Gabe would have his hide either way.

They moved slowly northward, nearing the completion of the trip. Michael watched out the window as the bus they were on meandered through the mountains. Mount Olympus was barely visible, the tallest mountain in the country. Michael had wanted to climb it, see what had happened to the Mount Olympus he remembered, see if there was any sign of what had happened to those of his kind that had made their home there, but it was the wrong season and climbing it now could be a dangerous proposition. He'd have to come some other time.

Beside him, Eva was nose deep in a book. She'd barely said two words to him since they'd gotten on the bus that morning. They were almost to their destination now. He reached over, offering her his hand, hoping that she'd take it, but knowing she wouldn't.

Eva barely looked up from her book long enough to take note of his hand before returning to her reading.

Michael sighed, turning back to the window. He wished there was something he could say to fix things. Maybe he could just tell her one thing—but where to start? Their apparent immortality? Their alignment with the elements, the wings? She'd think he was crazy. He rested his forehead against the cool glass, though it did little to subdue the fire inside him.

They arrived at their destination and checked in at their hotel. Their room was tiny, smaller than most of the ones they'd stayed in thus far. Eva immediately took the far bed, settling down with her back toward Michael. She pulled a notebook out of her bag and began scribbling in it.

There was an amphitheatre nearby that they were supposed to go and see, but Eva didn't seem to be in any hurry to head out. Michael sank down onto his own bed, ignoring the tempting urge to pull out his hair. What was he going to do to fix things?

A knock came on their door. Grateful for any sort of interruption, Michael sprang up to answer.

Gabe stood in the hallway, his hands in his pockets. "May I come in?"

"Where's Rafe?" It shouldn't have been his first question. "Why are you here?" would have been good. "What do you need?" would also have been acceptable. It's just that the two were so rarely apart that he'd, in some manner, forgotten they were separate entities.

The redhead shrugged. "He's taking care of something outside. So, may I...?"

Michael stood to one side so Gabe could enter. Eva looked up, eying Gabe with suspicion. Michael sighed.

Gabe gave her a smile. "How have you been, Eva? Did you finish that book Rafe gave you?"

"That and about four others," murmured Michael under his breath. Gabe shot him a look.

"Hello, Gabe," Eva finally said. She sounded like she was making an effort to be friendly and not managing it very well.

"I'm sorry to disturb you two," Gabe continued when Eva didn't say anything else. "I just need to talk to Michael for a few minutes." His roommate turned and took Michael by the arm, leading him as far across the room as they could get. Eva just blinked her eyes at them and went back to whatever she was writing.

Gabe raised an eyebrow. "What did you do?" he murmured in a low voice.

Michael briefly recounted, in a whisper, what had happened at the underground temple and subsequently, making sure to leave out everything that had happened before. "I was thinking I could tell her about the Void," Michael concluded.

Gabe practically exuded disapproval. "Michael, you know the rules."

"The Void can be passed off as a religious belief. Come on, Gabe, I have to tell her something or I'm going to lose her. Besides, she's practically one of us anyway." Michael glanced over at where Eva was still sitting on the bed. She had been watching them, but when she noticed Michael looking, she turned back to her notebook.

"Maybe you should lose her," said Gabe.

"No," Michael said, much too loud. Both he and Gabe quickly glanced over at Eva, but she didn't even bother looking up. "No," he said, quieter. "I will not lose her, Gabe."

Gabe groaned. "Michael, you *know* the rules. And you know the consequences for going through with this— exile, even death. Not just for you, but for Eva too."

"Where are we going to be exiled from, Gabe?" Michael crossed his arms over his chest. "We haven't had a real home since Eden burned millennia ago. And Rafe's right—no one would know, and I suspect no one would care. The rules were put in place to prevent further Nephilim because they were dangerous and couldn't be controlled, but I know better than that. So who's going to come after me? The only people who even know are you and Rafe, and Rafe's on my side. So, are you going to tell me, after all we've been through, that *this* would be what you kill me over?"

Michael stopped, chest heaving. Gabe could kill him where he stood, if he wanted to. And Gabe had always upheld the rules.

Gabe looked a bit shocked at the question. Then he stood up straighter, setting his jaw. Michael straightened as well, preparing himself for the worst.

"...no," Gabe said finally. "No, I wouldn't."

Michael let out a breath he hadn't realized he'd been holding. "Oh, thank God."

Gabe gave him a withering look. "You thought I was going to kill you right here in the middle of the room, didn't you."

"Of course he did," said Rafe from the doorframe, "because, as I have said many a time, you are terrifying, Gabriel." He walked over, draping an arm over Gabe's shoulders. "Fortunately for Michael, you are also a hopeless romantic at heart."

"Rafe," said Gabe in exasperation, "we are here for a reason, I would remind you. I mean, a reason that does not include Michael thinking I'm going to kill him."

"Well, get on it then," Rafe replied. "If you hadn't been lecturing him on stupid things, this whole conversation could be over already."

Gabe turned and glowered at Rafe until the other man removed his arm. "Anyway, we think Sam's here." He held up a hand, holding off Michael's response. "Rafe lost track of him after you two left, and it was a few days before we had any idea where he might have gone. In fact, if Thor hadn't called, we probably would still be back in the States trying to pick up the trail."

"Yeah, thanks for the babysitter, by the way. But I thought Thor didn't know who it was that had arrived after me."

"He didn't, but we suspected that it was probably too much of a coincidence to be anyone else. Anyway, we're reasonably sure now, so I want you and Eva to stay together at all times. Rafe and I will be around if you need us."

"Can I tell her about the Void, though?" asked Michael. "I think the remainder of the trip will be more pleasant for everyone."

Rafe nudged Gabe in the side. Gabe sighed. "Do whatever you want," he said. "I don't care anymore."

"Speaking of Eva," said Rafe, "where is she?"

Michael and Gabe both looked at him. "What do you mean?" Michael asked. "She's right—" He turned, indicating her bed, but it was empty, the notebook abandoned along with her bag. Michael felt his heart drop into his stomach. How long had she been gone? Where had she gone?

"She wasn't here when I got here," Rafe said.

Gabe looked as worried as Michael felt. "Quickly," he said, then turned and left the room.

EVA HAD SLIPPED out of the room in an attempt to maintain her own sanity. She couldn't take it anymore. She had just watched Gabe and Michael converse in low tones and knew that they were talking about things that she, again, wouldn't understand. And she was sick of feeling like she had no idea what was going on.

She was beginning to think the whole trip had been a mistake. What did Greek mythology have to do with early Christianity anyway? All she'd learned was that things here were a lot older than anything they had back home and that good-natured, cute guys could be just as scummy as other guys.

She slipped outside, knowing she was being a little unfair. Michael probably had his reasons for keeping things from her, but she couldn't forget her visions from the temple. Part of her felt like as close as she and Michael seemed to be getting, he shouldn't keep secrets from her. And she knew he was—it was as clear as day each time he told her some lie. It hurt in a way she hadn't known it could. This was why it was important to focus on her studies and not worry about relationships.

And the worst thing of all was that she still wanted him. With a mangled sigh, Eva buried her face in her hands.

Why did people follow him around? Back at school, it hadn't been like this. She'd gotten the impression from Gabe and Rafe that they saw him only very occasionally, but here it seemed like every time she turned around either they or Thor was lurking around, distracting Michael. Maybe she should have come alone anyway, her mother's worries be damned, because then at least she would be focused on what was important and not be an exile from her own room. Every group of friends had their joint experiences, she knew, but never had she felt so alone.

There was a small garden just outside the hotel. Eva stared at it for a while, hands deep in her pockets, but got the urge to wander. Maybe it'd help her clear her head. She'd spent so much time being upset over the past few days that it was draining all her energy, and maybe some time away from Michael would be good for her.

She passed a couple on her way out of the garden. Eva took one last glance at the hotel, pausing just for a moment, then chose a direction and began wandering along the street. She took a deep breath. Maybe just a stroll around a few blocks, see if she could find any shops to duck into just for a moment. She remembered that they'd passed a market on their way to the hotel, and if nothing else, perhaps she could go smell the spices for a while.

Of course, it didn't help that she was terrible at directions, and Michael normally directed them to wherever they were going. Eva shook her head, pushing all thoughts of Michael out. She was relaxing. She was having a Good Time. She was learning.

Eva reached the end of her block and turned left randomly. This street didn't look much different than the other, but it was a small town, so she probably couldn't get herself too lost. People lounged in doorways and off of patios, chattering among themselves in what Eva assumed was Greek. Maybe she should have tried to learn a little of the language before she came, but she'd been so focused on her classes. Who knew if she would have retained any of it anyhow.

The buildings were a jumble of sizes, each topped with a red tile roof. They were vaguely laid out in straight lines, and most of them were rectangular in shape, but there was no uniformity to their positions relative to each other or the street. Still, there were plenty of trees and the occasional burst of color, and the overall impression was one of calmness and serenity.

By some miracle, Eva managed to find the market she'd seen earlier. It was a bustling place and, for a moment, it seemed like the entire town had to be there. There were individual stalls, with people selling a variety of food—vegetables, spices, meat, often still identifiable as the animal or fish it had started out as—and occasionally, things like jewelry and clothing. It really showed how much smaller the world had gotten, Eva thought as she fingered a tomato, which she was pretty sure wasn't from Greece.

Several of the stall owners called out to her, sometimes in Greek, sometimes in English, but she'd merely come for the atmosphere, though she did pause at several booths to admire their wares.

"Come and buy a pretty ring, pretty lady," said one merchant selling jewelry as she passed. Eva paused, giving the man—more of a boy, really—a little smile. She should get something nice for her mother. After examining the wares at the table, she selected a silver chain with a small charm, and gave the boy the asked-for amount of Euros.

"You're supposed to haggle," said a man she hadn't noticed next to her in heavily accented English.

Eva blinked at him.

He gave her a lopsided smile that seemed oddly familiar. "They mark the price up for tourists," he clarified.

"Everyone, really," said the woman beside him in. She didn't have as much of an accent and was significantly younger than the man. "But the locals know that they shouldn't accept it."

"Are you locals?" asked Eva. They both looked like they could be from the Mediterranean, except something was a little off.

"At one time, yes," replied the man, his smile widening. "Now, we just visit. I am Mathias, this is my wife, Efthalia. You are lonely; where are your companions? Surely a young woman like yourself would not be traveling alone."

"Oh," replied Eva, "they're...busy."

"Come with us," said Efthalia with a little shake of her head. "We will go to a *kafenion*, spend some time until your friends are available. It will not do to be alone all day, no? We know of a nice one just down a few blocks. It will be our treat."

Eva clutched her purchase to her chest, eying the couple. Indecision warred within her. On the one hand, she was lonely, and she would love someone to talk to for a while that had nothing to do with her or Michael or anything else, and if they'd lived nearby she could get a better idea of the local culture. Plus, they seemed nice, and she was a little hungry and a *kafenion*—kind of a mix between a coffee shop and a pub, Eva had discovered—would be a nice, public place. That's what they always warned about internet dating, right? To do it somewhere in public where other people would be around in case something happened. On the other hand, her mother's warning rose up. Greece was a fairly civilized country, yes, but that didn't mean that there weren't slavers or prostitution rings or other such unpleasantries lurking in the shadows. It was bad enough that she was wandering around on her own, but to wander off with strangers? There was always the possibility that they were harmless. There was always the possibility that they were not.

"I did not get your name," said Mathias when she didn't immediately respond. He offered a hand to her.

Eva realized she'd been staring and shook her head slightly. She took the offered hand, which Mathias squeezed almost uncomfortably tight before releasing it, and said, "I'm Eva." Caution won out. "Thank you for the offer about the *kafenion*, but I should really be getting back to my friends before they worry."

Efthalia sniffed. "Some friends, if they let you go out on your own. Are you sure you wouldn't like a nice drink? We are free the rest of the afternoon. We have no plans really, just to enjoy our time."

Eva shook her head, though she would make Michael take her out for food when she got back. Maybe she'd even try to be friendlier. It wouldn't do to end the trip on a bad note. "Thank you, but all the same, I should be going."

"We will walk you back to your hotel," offered Mathias. "Make sure nothing happens."

"That's really not necessary," replied Eva. She had a sudden premonition of danger, the hairs on the back of her neck standing up.

"We insist," said Mathias firmly.

There didn't seem to be any way to lose them, so Eva reluctantly accepted their help and the three headed out of the market. Efthalia began to chat merrily about nothing in particular, her voice soothing and melodic. Occasionally, she would reach out and pat Eva's shoulder. Eva kept ahead of the other two, in a hurry now to get back to the hotel and to more familiar territory.

She led her escorts back along the path she'd taken to get there, which, in retrospect, seemed fairly circuitous, following small details she remembered from her initial trip. She kept up a brisk place, half-hoping that the couple would decide she was too much work and continue their day elsewhere.

Efthalia continued talking the whole time, still touching Eva every now and then. Eva found it was making her a little sleepy, not unlike her lecturers back home, and her skin crawled a bit every time Efthalia laid a hand on her. She shouldn't have wandered off alone— all she wanted to do was get back to Michael and get away from these two.

When they reached the street that Eva was pretty sure was the one next to the hotel, Mathias paused, a blank look coming over his face. Efthalia also stopped, her eyes on her husband, though she didn't stop talking, and she laid her hand on Eva's arm again, but left it there this time.

After a moment, his eyes cleared and he smiled at Eva. "Let's go this way," he said, indicating a street that Eva didn't really remember being there earlier. She frowned at it, wondering if she was more lost than she thought she was.

"But I came from this direction," she replied, waving vaguely. She was almost back now.

"This is a—how do you say it?—short cut," replied Mathias, and, without waiting for a response from her, he turned and headed up the street.

Eva sighed, rubbing one temple. Maybe she'd take a nap, then go get something to eat. Her thinking felt muddy. She took a few steps to follow Mathias, then paused. Surely it had only been one turn from this street to the street with the hotel, if she was remembering correctly. It was always possible she wasn't—she took a few more steps, then stopped again. She had come an awful long way along that first street before she turned.

She continued after Mathias for another minute or so before something occurred to her. "I didn't tell you which hotel I was staying at," she said.

Mathias stopped, turning to face her. He looked younger now, different somehow, and he gave her a lopsided smile that was so familiar. "That's true," he said. "You didn't."

Eva felt Efthalia's hand move up onto her shoulder. A deep drowsiness descended upon her, and then all was black.

Chapter Sixteen

"I can't believe that, after all these years, you can't hold a transformation," said a familiar voice. Eva winced, her consciousness crashing back with alarming speed. She was going to have the worst headache later.

She was being carried, she realized, over someone's shoulders. A creaky door was forced open, the stale air almost making her choke as they entered some sort of building. Eva debated opening her eyes, but it seemed like too much work. She was exhausted.

"Shut up," said a different, familiar voice. "Not all of us work through subterfuge like you do. I don't normally need to resort to transformations to achieve my end goals."

"Lot of good that's doing you at the moment."

"Can't you work your powers silently? If I had to listen to you drone on for any longer, I was going to hit you." He grunted, and Eva found herself deposited onto a rather cold metal chair. She couldn't get up the energy to sit up, let alone anything else. What had happened to her? "What did you do, anyway? I swear, it's like carrying a bag of rocks." Strong hands pulled hers behind her back, tying them together with something rough. Eva winced.

"You can thank me later," the first voice said. Now something rough was being secured around each ankle, and still Eva couldn't seem to get her body to respond to her. "She should be snapping out of it soon, anyway."

"Well, can't you speed it up?"

The owner of the first voice scoffed. "You know I don't work that way."

"You'd think she'd be able to do it herself. Oh well." The second voice moved off, and Eva could hear two sets of footsteps echoing across the floor. Another door opened, then closed a moment later, and Eva realized she was alone.

It was a few minutes' struggle to get her eyelids to respond, and then to get her neck to hold her head up. She felt like she'd been run over by a truck, but as far as she could tell, she hadn't been hurt. She'd been left alone in an empty room with a lone slit of a window in the door they'd come in through. Fluorescent lights lined the ceiling, giving the entire place a strange, unnatural glow.

Eva tugged experimentally at her hands, but they were too well secured to break free, even if she hadn't been feeling so drained. Sighing, she leaned back in the chair as best she could, resting her head on the back. This is what came of wandering off on your own, she supposed, though it wasn't really what she had expected.

The second door scraped open again and Eva whipped her head up so fast it made her dizzy. To her very great surprise, Mathias and Efthalia walked in, which did not fit the voices at all.

Efthalia smirked at Mathias. "See, what did I tell you?" she said in her lightly accented lilt. "She is awake."

"Let me go," said Eva. "My friends will not take kindly to this."

"You're really in no position to be making demands," Mathias said, running one hand through his hair. The motion was at odds with his appearance. Eva frowned, knowing something was wrong with the scene in front of her. She could almost feel what it was, but the knowledge sat just out of her grasp. "Your friends, well, we will worry about them later."

"I'm serious," said Eva. She pulled against her bindings again, wincing as the rope cut into her wrists. All of a sudden, the knowledge she needed snapped into clarity, even though it didn't seem to make much sense. "This isn't funny, Sam, let me go."

Her senses told her she was right, though she didn't know how. Mathias stared at her, blinking, then let out a laugh. "Lily's right again," he said in his normal voice. "Well, this will be easier then." He rolled his shoulders and, before Eva's eyes, morphed from a middle-aged man into the Sam she was familiar with from school.

Eva gaped at him.

Behind him, Lily went through a similar process, her features slowly smoothing out as she became younger, her hair returning to its normal copper hue. "Of course

I'm right," she said, sounding a little put out. "I am generally aware of Lights' powers, after all. Besides, your transformation was failing while she was still awake." Squinting, she reached one finger into her eye and extracted a contact, revealing the brilliant green eyes Eva was used to. "God, I hate these things."

Sam leaned down so his face was level with Eva's. "This doesn't change the situation, though, Eva."

Eva looked away from him, staring at the blank, peeling wall. She tried to reconcile her basic knowledge of the world with what she'd just seen. People couldn't just change their hair, their age, on a whim. What the hell was going on?

Sam pulled her face back towards him. "So why were you just wandering alone? Made our job a lot easier, though I was hoping I'd get to take a few swings at Michael. Still a little mad about the lightning, you know. You get sick of him already?"

"What on earth are you talking about?" asked Eva. "How was the lightning Michael's fault? No one can control the weather."

Sam laughed and stood, letting go of her face. "I noticed you didn't answer the important part of that. Finally figure out how much a jerk he is? I must say, you're much faster on the uptake this time around."

This was getting her nowhere, and the longer she sat here, the more a feeling of dread began to creep up her spine. "What do you want, Sam?" she asked wearily.

Sam stood all the way up, stretching his arms over his head. It would have been a nice view if it weren't for all the crazy involved. "We tried to do this the easy way, Eva. I knew you'd come back for Michael. It was nauseating, how close the two of you were. All I had to do was wait and watch, and get to you before he did. And then, all you would have had to do was give me the time of day, but no. You were so wrapped up in your studies. What's the point? None of those idiots have any idea what they're talking about, and they're too stupid to realize that the people who could tell them are walking around running a bookstore in their very own town."

"What?" said Eva. What did Gabe and Rafe have to do with anything?

"Oh, come on," replied Sam, sounding exasperated. "How often do you think three people named Michael, Gabriel, and Raphael hang out?"

For a second, Eva forgot her current situation. The idea was just...so bizarre. And yet... "You're saying they're the archangels? The actual archangels?" The thought rang true, and it would explain those scars where Michael would have wings, and why the three had such history.

Sam ignored her question, beginning to wander the room in front of her. "I should have taken Gabriel and Raphael into account. I should have known they'd find some way to muck up my plans. But my point still stands, Eva. If you'd just come along on your own, spent time with Lily and me, then all this unpleasantness could have been avoided."

Eva opened her mouth to reply, but found she couldn't think of anything to say. She couldn't decide whether or not Sam was insane, but at least someone wasn't keeping something from her.

Sam knelt down in front of her again. "You could have come with Lily, you know. That would have made this a lot easier too. But no, we had to chase you halfway around the globe. So here we are, Eva. You forced me into this. If you had just listened to me earlier, we would all be a lot happier. And more of us would be leaving here alive."

Eva's blood ran cold. "What do you mean?"

Lily, who'd been watching this whole display in a bored manner from across the room, was alert again as well. "Yes, what do you mean?"

"I want this confrontation, Lily. I want to be able to end this," Sam replied.

All the pretense dropped from Lily's face. Eva had never seen raw emotion from her before, and she looked livid. "What did you do, Sammael?"

Sam shrugged, seemingly unconcerned with Lily's reaction. "I merely left them a little clue, that's all." He spread his arms wide, taking in the room at large. "Look at this place. All concrete and steel. Objects taken from the earth, my specialty. Michael won't be able to do a thing with his fire. It will be like shooting fish in a barrel."

"You idiot," Lily spat. "You've invited your enemy into your home! We have Eva; that's what we came for. We should go. Leave the angels for another day. You're going to undo your own plan."

Sam's eyes flashed. "I'm going to crush them once and for all, Lily. I'm sick of them undoing all my hard work, and I will not give them another opportunity."

"I'm out," said Lily. She turned, heading for the door.

"Don't you dare," hissed Sam. "Come on, Lily, I know you want a shot at them too. Wouldn't you like to bring Gabriel down? Feel your hands around his throat?" His voice had changed into his normal, charming voice, the one that slithered into your mind without your knowledge. Eva watched the exchange closely. It was like listening to Thor and Michael, or Michael and Gabe, except now she felt like she almost understood.

Lily's shoulders stiffened and she didn't turn around. "That is unlikely to happen. Gabriel is a formidable opponent."

Sam crossed the room to her, running a hand lightly down her back. "So are you," he murmured. "If you wish, I can even make him vulnerable for you. I know his weak spot, after all."

Lily turned, meeting Sam's eyes. After a moment, she nodded. Sam smiled, then turned and made his way back to Eva. "Here's the short of it," he said. "I need you, one way or another. I shouldn't have let you go the first time. I spent centuries beating myself up over that, and I will not make the same mistake again." He patted Eva on the cheek, smirking when she shied away from his touch. "Well, I have some preparations to check." He headed toward a second door in the back of the room and disappeared from sight, leaving Eva and Lily alone.

Eva squirmed in her chair, trying to see Lily better. "What do you get out of this?"

"Hmm?" Lily's mask was back in place. "I don't know what you mean."

"It seems obvious that Sam needs you a lot more than you need him. So what do you get out of this?"

"Oh, Eva," breathed Lily. She came over, kneeling next to Eva's chair. "Hopefully I get some excitement. A chance to use powers that I have little need for anymore. A chance to feel what it was like to be powerful, once again." She paused, then reached a hand out toward Eva's cheek. Eva tried not to flinch, though Lily's hand was as frigid as ever. "Do I have an issue with Gabriel, as much as Sam seems to think I do?" She shrugged. "It doesn't really matter. It has been so long since there's been something to fight over that I am willing to take any fight now, just to remember what was."

Understanding flitted just out of Eva's reach, so she asked, "Why are you always so cold?"

A flash of pain darted across Lily's face, but it was gone as quick as it had come. "I am not meant for the light," she said.

"I guess it wouldn't be worth it to ask you to untie me," Eva said, hoping anyway. But Lily smiled slightly, shaking her head. "Who does Sam think I am?"

The man in question chose that moment to reappear. Lily made a big show of standing up and moving away from Eva, but Sam didn't seem to care. "Do you understand the plan?" he asked as he crossed the room.

He stuck his hands in his pockets, appearing more relaxed than Eva had seen him in a while.

"Of course," Lily replied. She tossed her head, sending red curls flying.

Sam moved his attention back to Eva. She stiffened, but he didn't get any closer. "What to do with you while we wait for our company? Quite frankly, I'm a little disappointed with how slow this whole process is—I need you to be of use, after all, or why have I been bothering with that religious crap all these years?—but I think I know a way to speed things up. Lily?"

The redhead eyed him. "Are you sure that's a good idea? She'll see everything, not just what you want her to see."

"I don't see what harm it will do," replied Sam. "She's already compromised; this will confirm my theories if I have to start over."

Lily didn't look like she agreed with this assessment of the situation. "I hope you're right," she murmured as she stepped closer. Eva stared up at her, feeling the dread climb back up her spine. Lily wouldn't meet her eyes. Her hands closed on either side of Eva's head, holding her tightly enough to hurt.

Eva screamed as the visions began to invade.

MICHAEL STUMBLED over a tree branch as he rushed through the garden across from the hotel, his senses alert. There'd been a remnant of her on the street—she'd obviously not been there very long—but that was it, and he couldn't sense which way she'd gone. He could hardly focus on the task at hand. What if something had happened to her? What if he never found her? With a moan, he sat down on the grass heavily.

He felt Gabe before he saw him. "Find anything?"

"Not yet," replied Gabe. "You should go back to the hotel. You're not in any condition to do this."

Michael gave a bitter laugh. "You know I can't do that."

Gabe shrugged. "Worth a try."

Michael leaned back, covering his face with his hands. "God, how did I let this happen?"

A smaller man than Gabriel would tell him it wasn't his fault, but the redhead just sat next to Michael on the grass. "We don't know what happened to her. She could stroll back, happy and healthy, any minute now."

"Nobody believes that."

"I admit that it seems a little too mundane, considering the circumstances, but that doesn't make it less of an option."

Michael was silent, staring at the clouds gently meandering by. On any other day, he would have found it relaxing. Now it just made his nerves wind up tighter. "You know we're not going to get out of this without having to reveal ourselves. Sam will want—and force—a fight."

Gabe looked at him out of the corner of his eye. "She may not be conscious."

"I can't believe that. He'd want her to see, and I'm not willing to put her in further danger by removing her ability to react to her surroundings." Michael sighed.

"Nothing's gone right this trip, but I can't see how it could have been fixed. I think she'd attracted Sam's attention long before any of the rest of us met her."

Gabe pulled out a stalk of grass with his long fingers. "You'd have to go back further than that. If we hadn't moved there, hadn't opened the store, would Sam have moved there anyway? Don't dwell on it, Michael. You can't second-guess every decision you make. None of us can see the future."

That didn't really make him feel better, but Gabe was right. He'd go insane trying to predict if a decision would lead to trouble years in the future.

Rafe's head appeared from around a tree trunk. "This looks highly effective."

"Anything?" asked Gabe.

"Thor didn't answer, so I left him a voice-mail. Damn Viking can never keep track of anything, can he?" Rafe shook his head. "But beyond that, no. I checked the room again, to see if Eva had left any clues as to where she was going, but I've got nothing."

Michael sat up, rubbing at his temples. It was all he could do to keep his panic in check. "Let's go back to the street. Maybe all three of us together will be able to sense something." If they didn't find something soon, he was going to crack.

Rafe offered a hand to each of his roommates and pulled them up. The grass had been damp, leaving the back of Michael's shirt wet and clingy, but he found he couldn't be bothered about it. Besides, a little distraction would probably help his sanity.

A couple was lingering on the street when they arrived, but when the three men continued to stare intently around for several minutes, they up and left in a hurry. Michael closed his eyes, trying to sense something that he hadn't earlier. Eva hadn't been here longer than fifteen minutes at most, and he could just barely detect her as it was. He scanned the area immediately around again, hoping against hope for some inkling of a trail, but there was nothing.

He opened his eyes. Rafe was to his right, his brow furrowed in concentration as he glowered at nothing in particular. He probably couldn't sense anything at all. Michael had always thought it odd how terrible Rafe's capacity to sense things was when his power gave him the ability to enhance most of the basic five senses if he put his mind to it. Gabe was to his left. The redhead met Michael's gaze and shook his head.

"Well, she didn't come back to the hotel," mused Rafe, rubbing his chin. "But we don't know if she went through the garden or along the street."

"Might as well try the other side of the garden," said Michael. A side entrance to the garden was closest; Michael headed in that direction. This was crazy. What the hell did Sam expect them to do? He didn't believe for a second that Sam wouldn't want some sort of confrontation. Michael shook his head. No, he shouldn't think like that. That's what had gotten Eve killed. He'd underestimated Sam, assumed he knew all his tricks, and in the end, he'd been too late.

As deep in his thoughts as he was, as Michael passed through the gate something gave him pause. It was fainter than the trace on the street, but it was unmistakable. "Sam," he said.

Gabe nodded. "And Lily."

Michael tilted his head. "Strong enough?"

"I think so." Gabe stepped past the gate and turned to the left, his roommates following behind him. It was slow going; there was a bit of a breeze—Michael almost got hit by a shirt that blew off a clothesline—and the trace wasn't that strong. Although it was probably lucky that they'd found Sam and Lily's trail at all. With the two of them together, they left just enough behind.

So it was with some surprise that they discovered that the trail led them straight to a market and, more specifically, a jewelry booth. The vendor eyed them curiously as they blinked at him in bewilderment.

"I am so confused," said Michael as he halfheartedly examined the booth's wares. It was mostly silver trinkets, plated only, probably, judging from the price.

Rafe didn't seem much better informed. "Well, Lily likes pretty things, which, actually, would make me think she'd want to be as far away from this booth as possible."

"Shh," said Gabe. He closed his eyes, taking a deep breath. "Eva was here too."

Michael shivered. "At the same time?"

Gabe nodded. He opened his eyes, blinked once at Michael, then turned and began to weave his way out of the market. Michael ran to catch up with him.

"I don't understand. They met here? I can't believe Eva would willing go with them."

The redhead paused for a moment, then turned and headed in a different direction. "Something's weird with their trail," he murmured so quietly Michael could barely hear him.

"Not weird enough that you can't follow it, right?" asked Rafe. He sauntered through the crowds, looking completely at ease. Michael could see he was worried through the little details—his hands stuffed in his pockets, that weird vein in front of his ear that tended to twitch—that a normal person would never notice.

"No," said Gabe distractedly, "but it overlaps the trail we came in on. We should have picked it up first." He scratched his head. "I hate it when things don't make sense."

"You're probably going to hate the rest of today, then," replied Rafe with a wild grin.

Gabe just looked at him before he turned back to the duty at hand. This trail led them almost all the way back to where they had started, but just before it reached the hotel, it veered off down a narrow, dark alleyway. The alleyway dead-ended after about fifty feet. There was no sign of a struggle.

The trail ended abruptly. There was no sign of any of the three of them leaving. Michael could sense Sam and Lily, but if Eva had been here as well, it was only for a short while.

"Okay," said Rafe, rocking on his heels. "Now what?"

"Well, they didn't just vanish into thin air. That'd be a neat trick, but to my knowledge, nobody's managed it yet." Michael ran his hand down the back of his head, scanning the alleyway with his eyes. There were no doors at ground level. There was no easy way to access the higher stories. That didn't mean that they hadn't gone that way, but it would probably require wings, and carrying another person when flying made everything harder. It would have been noisy, and the buildings were occupied, which would not make it a convenient hideout. "This doesn't make sense," he said out loud.

"It's probably Lily's doing, somehow," replied Gabe. He began to move about, rifling through some stray leaves and trash that had wandered into the alley. "Maybe she's figured out some way to mask presences or something along those lines."

"That's terrifying," said Michael. "But now that you mention it, when I talked to Thor that first time, he was only aware of one other arriving after Eva and I did. Assuming that she came with Sam, that fits with your theory. Goddamn!" Michael kicked at the brick wall. It hurt like hell, but at least it was something to focus on other than his rising panic. "Do you realize what that means? They could be anywhere, and we'd never know. They could sneak up on us before we had a chance to hear them coming."

"For now, all it means," interrupted Gabe, "is that they left this trail on purpose, knowing we'd find it." He stood, his eyes meeting Michael's. "Michael, I need you to calm down. This is probably going to be a very long day, and I know how your temper can be, and I think if we're going to get through this we're all going to have to be as rational as possible. Do you need me to help?"

"Yes," replied Michael. "That would be good, I think."

Gabe crossed the alleyway and placed his hands on Michael's shoulders. Instantly he felt calmer, Gabe's water dimming the fire inside of him. Michael took a few deep breaths to collect himself.

"Better?" asked Gabe.

"Yes, thank you."

"How about you, Rafe?"

"Bah, your strange water thing doesn't work on me and you know it," came the answer. "I will just be anxious like a normal person in this situation. Anyway, I found something." Rafe offered a scrap of paper to Gabe.

The redhead took it and held it with both hands. Michael peered over his shoulder. It was an address copied down in a messy hand. If Michael's understanding of the layout of town was correct, it was somewhere on the fringes.

"I miss the old days," Michael said. "Things were less complicated. If you didn't like somebody, you just told them so and dealt with it."

Gabe stuck the address in his pocket. "Nobody ever told me they didn't like me."

"That's because you're terrifying," replied Rafe with a grin. "Shall we go? There's three of us and two of them; this will be a piece of cake."

Michael didn't really agree with that assessment. He always felt a little sluggish under Gabe's influence, but even so, he felt worried and a little scared. It was one thing for them to take on Sam and Lily, but it was another thing when their enemies had Eva held hostage. Logically, he knew he hadn't been directly responsible for putting her in danger, but Sam and Lily had still managed to take her out from under his nose. She was only human. She wouldn't be able to protect herself.

"Please try to show a little restraint, Rafe," said Gabe. He glanced at Michael. "Well, it's probably best to get this over with. It's been lovely spending time with you two, and I hope if we return to the Void it will be in the least painful way possible."

All humor dropped off Rafe's face. "For the love of God, Gabriel, don't talk like that. We are going to be fine and Eva is going to be fine, and if anyone returns to the Void it will not be us, and I don't want to hear anybody say otherwise." He rolled his shoulders back. "Right, off we go."

Without another word, Rafe strode out of the alleyway and promptly turned in the wrong direction. Michael and Gabe exchanged a look before they followed after him. As they turned, Michael couldn't suppress the shudder that ran down his spine.

Chapter Seventeen

EVA'S NERVES BURNED. Images, too many to process, flitted across her field of vision, flashes of people and places she didn't—couldn't—recognize. There were sounds, feelings, memories associated with each one, and Eva knew that if the torrential flow didn't stop it was going to overwhelm her, destroy her, wipe her from history. It was too much.

After an eternity, Lily released her head, taking a step back. Eva's head fell forward without the other woman's support, and a few teardrops dripped onto her pants. The images didn't clear out even with Lily's intrusion gone. They continued to swarm in her field of vision in a confusing and completely unhelpful manner.

"I think I broke her," said Lily, but her voice was muffled as if she were very far away. It was a struggle just to pull her head up, and then Eva could just barely make out the silhouettes of her captors. The foreground of her vision was still filing through images. Eva blinked.

She was in the Void again, surrounded by tiny, cheerful lights—no, she was one herself. Contentment settled over her, and she wheeled through the emptiness. Another light joined her, and they spun around each other, their glee only increasing as they continued their activity.

Then, all of a sudden, something pulled her away, away from the other lights, away from the Void completely, and she found herself sitting under a tree, completely confused as to how she had gotten there, where "there" was, or what she was supposed to be doing. Eva took the time to examine herself—her skin was darker than she remembered it being, her hair curlier. She had a set of giant black wings growing out of her back.

She was in some sort of forest. It was damp and full of plants she didn't recognize. "Hello?" she called. Her voice was deeper, the way it had been in the visions in the temple. No one was around, and after the joy of the Void, she felt entirely alone. Her calls scattered some birds, but no one answered her.

She'd been in the jungle for some time. Eva could tell that, though she had no idea how much time had passed, nor did she have a clear idea of what she'd been doing with herself in that time period. She settled down against the trunk of a tree, leaning her head against its smooth bark. She much preferred the Void, and wondered what had happened to cause her to leave it. Had it been a conscious decision or not? The longer she stayed in the jungle, the more she became aware of things, emotions, feelings, sensations.

There was a noise off to her right. Eva continued sitting, but she straightened up, looking in the direction of the disturbance. A hand pushed a branch aside, and another like her entered her field of vision. He seemed as surprised to see her as she was to see him.

"Hello," he said.

"Hello," she answered.

For a moment, they did nothing else. Then Eva slowly stood, stepping closer to the new arrival. He looked like she did, with black wings. Every other creature she'd come across in her forest had been different. They could not understand her.

"Are you alone?" he asked after a moment.

"I am," Eva answered. She resisted the urge to reach out and touch this new arrival, to check if he was real. "Did you come from the Void?"

He nodded. "I hear others like us are gathering east of here. Would you like to go with me?"

Eva looked about her forest. It was not an unpleasant place, but she did not belong. "Yes. I am Eve."

Her new friend held out a hand to her. "I am Sammael."

Through the haze of the visions, Eva heard the present-day Sam. "It can't be helped now. We need to prepare. They should be here soon." The juxtaposition was almost dizzying. Ancient Sam lacked the anger and the menace that lurked beneath the surface of the man who stood before her now.

The images spun before her eyes. Eva took a few deep breaths, willing them to slow down again, to let her see what they contained. Her brain dug sluggishly through them, trying to force order.

They were in Eden. Eva wasn't sure how she knew, but she could tell that there'd been a significant jump in space and time from the previous vision. The missing time swirled in the peripheral, providing information without coming to the foreground.

Eden rose out of the desert, its palms waving high in a breeze that danced playfully across Eva's cheeks, and she immediately recognized it as the garden from her—Eva's—dreams. It was as lush as any painting she'd ever seen, with one major difference—there were those like her everywhere, as varied in appearance as the humans they would later attempt to blend in with.

Things had been tense lately. They'd discovered creatures like them, except less experienced, living in small nomadic groups. Rumors of them came in from the far corners of the land, where restless ones occasionally wandered. They had no wings, did not seem to have ever possessed them, and were affected when her kind went out among them. Some responded with fear, violence—some with awe.

Eva could not see what the fuss was about. There were many creatures on this planet. Simply because a type had been found that was the closest to what they were did not merit such a disruption of the peace. The other creatures deserved to be left alone, to do what they would. They had all they needed here in Eden.

She heard footsteps behind her. They were familiar, years together immediately identifying their owner. "Where have you been, Sammael?"

He wrapped his arms about her waist, nuzzling his chin into her shoulder. "Don't be like that, Eve. You know I find this whole thing fascinating."

"We're asking for trouble." Eva stepped away, turning to face Sammael. "Can't you see that? When we arrived here, it was almost like being wrapped back into the warmth of the Void, but now there is strife everywhere. No one can agree on anything."

"There's nothing wrong with a little discussion." Sammael ran a hand through his ebony hair. "Besides, there is such an opportunity here. Where did these creatures come from, who are so like us and yet so different? They don't feel like they came from the Void. We could teach them, lead them. Think of what we could do. Their numbers are significantly higher than ours. Their gestation period is less than a solar cycle, you know. With that sort of power, we could get so much more done."

Eva shook her head. "Get so much more what done? What's wrong with what we have here?" She spread her arms wide to encompass Eden as a whole. "We have everything we need. We are happy."

Sammael took her hands in his. "Eve, please, try to understand. I'm not complaining about the life that we have here. But we have to think about the future. We've

noticed that other creatures grow old, that their life eventually leaves them, but that is not so with us. Who knows how long it will be before our life leaves us too? Will you really be content to sit here for however long, with no changes?"

"Yes," she answered. "I don't understand why you are not."

"I think we can make things better." An ugly look crossed Sammael's face. "There are some who disagree, of course. They'd rather leave the others alone, or teach them our skills instead. What utter nonsense. We need to work together, not raise competition in a species more numerous than ourselves."

Eva pulled back. "You worry me when you talk like this. Let it go, Sammael. Let us just ignore them, and let them do what they will."

Sammael released her hands and rubbed the back of his neck, stretching out his wings. "Sometimes I think you are right. But when I hear that Michael, it just makes me...I don't even know how to describe it. It's an emotion I am not familiar with, but it makes my blood boil."

"Let it go," repeated Eva. She ran a hand down his cheek and Sammael relaxed into it.

"Yes, you're right," he murmured.

Another time shift. Later, again, Eva imagined. Things looked less lush, the inhabitants of the garden seemed more on edge. Not a lot, not enough that a casual observer would notice, but compared to the last vision, the difference was noticeable and disturbing.

She hadn't seen Sammael for some time. It had been several days, and Eva was beginning to think that perhaps he had decided to wander without telling her, or that he was acting on one of the strange rumors she heard circulating. He'd been quiet lately, keeping more information to himself. She did not think the change could mean anything beneficial.

Something was unsettling about just sitting around. She stood, looking about the garden. She hadn't done a good job of interacting with the others. Some she recognized merely by sight, but she didn't know anyone's name. Perhaps, in the current climate, it was time to change that.

Except she didn't know what to do. Perhaps, when they'd come into this world, the others had come in groups. She had been alone. Sammael had found her, had initiated the contact. Any of the others she had met had been through him. Well, how hard could it be? Eva squared her shoulders and went for a walk.

By the time she reached the well in the middle of the garden, she had made no progress, but there were several of them gathered here. Eva hung back, hiding behind a tree, watching as one took the contents of a container of water and had the liquid spin in the air around him. How was that possible? Pulling her eyes away, she scanned the crowd, looking for a friendly face, someone she wouldn't feel too shy to approach, and then she would introduce herself, ask after Sammael, find out what was happening.

"Hello," said a voice behind her.

Eva turned. The man behind her had long, chestnut-colored hair tied at his neck, and his wings were an odd golden color she had only seen a few times. "Hello," she replied.

"Can I help you?" he asked. "You look lost."

"I am not lost," Eva said, taking a bit of a dislike to him. "I am just..." Part of her wanted to explain her quest, but now, confronted with another being, she felt she'd rather keep it to herself. "...watching."

"Yes, I can see that." He smiled widely. "You don't have to watch from so far away, though. Gabriel doesn't mind an audience."

"If he did, he would practice somewhere else," said a second voice. Eva spun to find another behind her, this one dark with soft gray wings. "Don't mind Michael, he has no manners. I'm Raphael."

"Eve," she answered, glancing back at the one named Michael. Sammael often complained about him to others, often while he thought Eve was out of earshot. However, judging from some of the theories she heard from her companion, she thought he was a bit hypocritical to be so upset about somebody else's.

"Did you just arrive from the wastes?" Raphael was asking.

The one with the water joined them. "No, she's been here for a while. Tends to hang out with Sammael." The tall, red-headed man wrinkled his nose.

"Oh," replied Raphael, the word thick with meaning. Eva bristled.

"Do you always jump to conclusions about people so automatically?" she asked. "Sammael accompanied me from the forest I came into being in through the wastes to Eden, so I feel a connection with him, but that does not mean that he thinks or speaks for me."

Michael laughed. "There you go, Raphael. Now, Gabriel, Eve here was enjoying your little show."

Gabriel looked down at her. After a long moment, he finally smiled. "Are you a Water?" he asked.

"Am I a what?" asked Eva, eyes widening.

"Your power," answered Michael. "What do you pull on?"

"...my what?" Eva was right to go out on her own; apparently there was much that Sammael hadn't been sharing. She would have words with him later, if he ever returned.

The three men glanced at each other. "Well," said Gabriel, "it seems that each of us has some limited control over a portion of nature. It was discovered purely by accident some cycles ago, but as far as we can tell, each one of us possesses this ability."

"To move water without touching it?" asked Eva.

"Not necessarily," answered Raphael. "Gabriel is a Water, but not all Waters work the same way. And there's things other than water. I'm an Air, and Michael here is a Fire."

"Oh," replied Eva, thoroughly confused. "How do you know?"

"Experimentation, really," said Michael. "Though I've found that it's somewhat obvious after you figure it out."

"You'll figure it out," added Raphael. "Well, good luck to you, Eve. Maybe we'll see you around again."

The three of them walked away, heading in a direction opposite than the one Eva would need to take to get home. Just before they disappeared under some trees, Michael looked back and gave her a smile and wave.

Eva stood there, filled with new knowledge and emotion and unsure what to do with any of it.

"Where are they?" came the voice of the modern Sam through the images. "What's taking them so long?" It took Eva a moment to remember where she really was, what was really happening, but then the visions, Eve's memories, took her again.

Eden looked lush again, greener than ever, but there was a stronger undercurrent of discord. Eva sat near the well again, twirling a flower around her fingers.

"Here you are," said Sammael. Eva thought the cheerfulness sounded a bit forced. "Are you ready?"

"I'm not coming," she answered.

Sammael let out a moan. "Eve, we talked about this."

"And I told you in no uncertain terms how I felt about it. You have been keeping things from me, Sammael, and I do not appreciate it." She dropped the flower at her feet and stood. "I think perhaps it would be best if we went our separate ways."

For a moment, seeing the look on his face, she wished she hadn't said it, but then he tucked his hurt away, smoothed his expression. "Are you sure that's wise? You haven't had to deal with the others of our kind very much. I have protected you."

"I do not need protecting." Eva sighed, crossing her arms across her chest. "Listen, Sammael. It's not that I do not appreciate what you've done for me over the cycles, and it's not that I do not appreciate our time together, but we've grown apart. You spend your time off doing...whatever it is you've been working on. I am more and more left on my own as it is, and I have been dealing with the others. Some are misguided, yes, some are scared or confused, but they are not a danger. I cannot condone your plans. I do not believe we should be meddling in the development of other creatures, even ones so like in appearance to ourselves. You said it yourself—they do not feel of the Void, so why should we concern ourselves? If we continue to consider impeding their path in this world, it will only end in pain."

Sammael gripped her upper arm, his fingers digging into her skin. Eva flinched. "I am *sick* of your endless resistance on the subject. We are going, and that is final."

Eva pulled against his grip. "I am not yours to command, Sammael. Not now, and never again."

He hissed, but before he could reply another voice broke in. "What are you doing?" Eva pulled her glance away from Sammael to find Michael leaning up against a nearby tree, the ease of his pose belied by the tenseness of his muscles. "Have you started to treat your equals as you would treat your subordinates?"

"This is none of your concern," Sammael replied, his voice low. With him distracted, his grip on Eva's arm loosened. Eva took the opportunity to free herself and fluffed her feathers in his face as she separated herself from him, moving so the well was between them. Sammael's face darkened. "We are not done, Eve."

"But we are," she answered, examining her arm. Already, dark bruises were starting to stand out against her flesh. Eva closed her eyes, laying her good hand over the injury. She could feel the light of the sun beaming down on them. Reaching out, she flowed some of its power into her arm, relaxing as she felt the damaged tissue revert.

"You're a Light," breathed Michael. Eva could hear the awe in his voice.

Eva removed her hand, the skin underneath now unblemished. "Yes," she replied. "You knew, didn't you, Sammael? That's part of the reason you tried to keep me all to yourself. But perhaps you should keep better watch on that which you're trying to hoard."

A dark shadow passed over Sammael's face, but then, almost as if it had never been, it disappeared, his normal smile brightening his face. He extended a hand towards her. "I'm sorry, Eve. I don't know what came over me. Let's go home, talk this over."

"There is nothing more to talk about. I have made my decision. If you continue on your current path, you shall do so alone."

"You shall not talk to me that way," Sammael answered. He took a step forward, but Michael pushed off his tree, inserting himself between the other two.

"There will be no violence in this haven," he said. Eva blinked. There was such power in his voice. Sammael faltered, then, without another word, turned and disappeared into the surrounding trees.

Tension she hadn't realized she'd been harboring left her. Eva sank onto the ground, burying her face in her hands. There was a hole in her chest, deep and raw, and when she pulled her hands away, she discovered they were wet.

Michael hovered over her, seemingly unsure of what to do now. "I am sorry," he said softly. "I couldn't help but overhear the beginning of your argument. I think it's noble of you to want to stay out of their path, but I fear it's too late."

Eva wiped her eyes with the back of her hand. "Don't say that like you're any more innocent than he is. I am aware of your stance on the matter."

He gave her a wry smile. "I am not trying to deceive you. I am as incapable at staying out of matters as your Sammael is, and so are many others of our kind. That you have managed to do so is to your credit." All cheer left his face. "And I suspect your message of doom is also appropriate. Nothing good will come of it, but people are too invested now to turn back. Something will happen, and there is no way to stop it."

"Surely that is not true," Eva replied. "Surely there is a way we could remain at peace."

Michael shook his head. "I think, if it were not these other creatures, then eventually it would have been something else. Maybe we would have gained a few hundred more cycles of quiet and contentment, but eventually something would have come along to divide us. We are too long-lived, and there are those who wonder why we were forced out of the Void, what our purpose in this place is, and they are determined to find it."

"And do you believe that? That our fate is tied to these others?" Eva slowly pulled herself to her feet, using the well to help steady herself.

Michael shrugged. "I cannot be sure. Only time may reveal the answers we seek." He offered a hand to her. "Come."

She shied away. "What?"

"Where else will you go? You will not go back to Sammael." Michael continued to hold his hand outstretched. "No one will force you into our cause."

Eva blinked at him, loath to trust someone again. It had taken her so long to realize what Sammael had been doing. Still he was right; she would not return to Sammael, not while he stayed on his current course, and she had nowhere else to go, and despite Michael's unproven confidence, there was something wholesome about him. Hesitantly, she took his offered hand.

Michael gave her a brilliant smile.

Eva could practically watch time pass by, staying stationary as the years spun through Eve's memories. There were additional voices in the room with Lily and

Sam now, but she was too deep in the visions to make them out.

It was dark when the memories stopped rushing by. Eve had been asleep very recently, Eva could tell, but something had awakened her, a deep undercurrent of malice. Michael was curled next to her. It was hard to reconcile the mindset of this Eve to the previous one; several years must have passed.

She reached over, grasping Michael by the shoulder. "Wake up," she whispered in his ear.

Michael stirred beneath her touch, but instead of waking up he rolled over, snuggling against her side. A slow panic began to gather in her stomach. "Michael," she said louder. Eva glanced around at the surrounding trees, her imagination giving rise to creatures lurking within. She gave his shoulder a hard shake.

Blinking, he pushed himself up onto his elbows. "What is it, Eve?" he asked groggily.

"Shhh," she said, cocking her head, listening. There was no evidence of anyone nearby, no sounds of encroaching danger, but still all her nerves stood on end.

Michael appeared to be listening as well. He tensed, then slowly rolled onto his feet. "Stay here. I'm going to go consult with Gabriel. Don't go with anyone you don't know." He stood, staring out into the night. "Does it seem darker than usual?"

It did. The dark was deep and inky, obscuring all but the closest objects. Normally Eva had no trouble using the moon and the stars for light, but tonight, she could barely make out their glow. She wrapped her wings about her. "Hurry."

"I won't be long." Michael faded into the night, leaving Eva all alone.

She sat there for several minutes before some instinct told her she didn't want to be there. For half a second, she thought perhaps it had been her nerves, and that she should wait for Michael to return, but her hunches had been too reliable to her out in the jungle for her to discount them now.

As she rose, her feet seemed to pick a direction on their own. She kept her wings up, hoping their darkness would help shield her from the eyes of whatever lurked in the night. There was a low rumble behind her and she forced herself to keep walking. It would do no good to draw attention to herself.

She hadn't gotten very far when there was a bright flash of light from behind her as one of the trees caught on fire. It crashed to the ground, throwing burning embers into its surroundings. Eva's heart dropped into her stomach. It wasn't very far from where she and Michael had been.

Screams and yelling began to permeate the night. Eva turned away from the chaos and continued walking into the night.

Eva lost track of the images swirling around her. It was hard to tell where she ended and Eve began, if there was even any difference in them at all. Snatches of many millennia crossed her vision, almost faster than she could reconcile them into her understanding of the world. Eden burned and was destroyed. Religions, cultures, people rose and fell and were forgotten by history. She had been there through it all, Michael at her side.

She hadn't realized how much she had come to rely on him over the years. Despite all they'd been through together, she sometimes forgot how he'd always been there. Others of their kind often separated for a few hundred years at a time, rotating partners, but they had been a permanent fixture.

Years of ancient history gone through, Eva found herself in a considerably more modern location. They were in the south, in the New World, though Eva suspected that, very long ago, she had been here before, perhaps when she had first arrived from the Void. The early days were hard to remember—she'd been barely conscious at the time, hardly an intelligent being. Wherever she had started out, it had taken them a long time to reach Eden.

She and Michael had been slowly examining the world. After the fall of most polytheistic religions, many of their kind had isolated themselves from the humans in an attempt to reclaim Eden, but they had grown too restless over the years. Even Eve, who had had no compulsion in that early war, could no longer just sit. She and Michael had needed stimulation, returning to the world after a few hundred years. Humans had just been coming out of a dark period and seemed content to make over the world as best they could, and Eve and

Michael had been determined to see what they could accomplish on their own.

The New World—America, as it was starting to be called—was an interesting mix of cultures. There were the natives, some of who still had direct contact with some of their kind, trying to coexist with the invading Europeans. And they were invading, even if they were, for the most part, attempting it without outright warfare. The landscape was slowly being rearranged to fit with their purpose, and the South had become sprawling farmland.

The memories spun down into a single timeline. Eva glanced around the parlor she was sitting in at the inn they'd been staying at in New Orleans. Michael had gone off with Gabriel and Rafe to do...well, she wasn't exactly sure what, exactly, but it hadn't seemed terribly interesting at the time. Now she'd almost wished she'd gone, if only so she wasn't alone and bored. More and more recently she had taken to wishing they had someone else traveling with them. While she loved her boys, they lacked some sensibilities, and gender differences were as alive and well in this time as they had been earlier.

With a sigh, Eva extracted some stationery from her bag and began a letter to Brigid. She hadn't seen the other woman in a few centuries, but rumor said she'd been on the move lately, and perhaps she wouldn't mind coming along with them for a while.

There was a knock on the door. Eva looked up, hoping it was the boys back again, but it was only a servant. He took a step into the room, giving her a slight bow. "My apologies for the interruption, Miss Basurta, but you have a visitor."

A visitor? Before Eva could ask who was calling, a man appeared behind the servant. He removed his hat in greeting, and her breath caught in her throat.

"Good afternoon, Eve," Sam said, giving her his familiar smile. "It's lovely to see you. I had not been aware you were in the area."

The servant seemed flustered at Sam's attitude. "Mr. Payne would not wait," he clarified.

It had probably been close to a millennium since she'd last seen him, but it wasn't long enough to stop old emotions from stirring up. "Why are you here, Mr. Payne? I thought I made my feelings on the matter of our acquaintance quite clear the last time we spoke." Still, curiosity raised its head, as it often did whenever they encountered another of their kind. So many had disappeared while they had been in isolation, and she yearned to fill that void with knowledge of what had gone on in the world.

The servant looked even more uncomfortable. Eva couldn't blame him. Sam was intimidating, even without his wings released.

Sam gave the servant a winning smile. "She's lovely, isn't she? Actually, Miss Basurta, I came to apologize."

Eva was so surprised so couldn't immediately answer. Sam had never apologized in the entire time she had known him. Oh, sure, he had said the words, but he had never meant them. There was something different here, though, some undercurrent to his words she couldn't decipher. "Apologize?" she echoed finally.

He fingered the brim of his hat. "I've had a lot of time recently to think about what you said so long ago, and I think you were right. I'd like to make it up to you."

Nothing could ever make it up. There had been so much destruction, so many deaths. No amount of guilt or sorrow could remake the world the way it had been before. Eva looked away, running her fingers along the edge of her stationery. Still...there were so few of them left. If Sam had truly repented, she would be mistaken to continue to cast him away.

"Come join me for dinner," Sam was saying, looking at his hat now instead of her. "It's the least I can do for now. I have a plantation a little ways out of town."

"And what of my companions?" she asked.

"They are, of course, invited as well," Sam said, "though I doubt they would be eager to accept my invitation. Still, I will leave it. And now, if it's not too presumptuous of me, would you care to join me for a walk?"

Eva hesitated, but there was no spark of intuition to influence her either way. On one hand, she should probably wait until Michael came back and talk to him about the situation, except who knew when that would be. She had been considering a walk after her letter anyway, and at least this way the servant would be aware of whom she had gone out with and would be able to tell the others when they returned, as opposed to her running into Sam on the street where there no witnesses.

With Sam you were never really sure if you were getting the truth. She should go and see if she could figure out if he meant what he was saying. It would be easier for her than the others; there was too much bad blood there, and neither Sam nor Michael could contain their tempers for long when near the other. She, at least, had some happy memories.

Making her decision, Eva slid her half-finished letter into the drawer of the desk. "I would, yes." She rose, accepting the offered elbow, and the two of them descended down to the street.

New Orleans would one day be a grand city, perhaps on the scale of London or Paris. Eva would have to return one day to see what would become of it. For now, it was still a little rough at the edges, as many of the New World cities were. The European settlers were just beginning to push west and explore the land President Jefferson had secured for them some decades past.

Sam led her up the street, remaining almost uncharacteristically quiet. Eva was unsure how to broach the topic. "So," she said finally, "you live around here now?"

"I came over a couple centuries ago," Sam answered. "It was getting harder to survive over in Europe. I tried Asia for a time, but it didn't really sit well with me. I considered Africa, Australia, but after these continents were rediscovered I thought I'd try my luck over here." He reached up, straightening his hat. "I spent some time farther south, came up when the European settlements started to take hold. I'm spending about thirty, forty years in a place before I move on. I figure I'll just continue moving west as the continent opens up."

"And you are...alone?"

He gave a wry smile. "We can't all have friends as close as what you've managed. I've spent some time with different people over the years, but...no, I haven't found any true companions. I'm afraid I screwed that up early on." He sighed, shaking his head. "And we have long memories. There are many who won't forgive me for my part in Eden."

Eva didn't doubt it. "You taught us all violence. You taught us lies and treachery and death. I am not terribly surprised."

"You were always so blunt." Sam chuckled. "I really should have listened to you, back then, but I was so blinded by what I saw as our potential. Look where it got us in the end anyway—the humans proved to be rivals even with our attempts to subjugate them."

"Your attempts," Eva corrected.

"I was speaking generally, but fine, my attempts," replied Sam. "We probably just sped up their development in the end." He paused, looking thoughtful. "I almost feel like those who came over here did a better job with the whole thing, until the Europeans showed up."

Eva had heard some of the stories of the human sacrifices and the fear the people had for their gods and found she could not share Sam's opinion, though that didn't really surprise her. She wasn't sure they'd ever been on the same side of anything when it came to dealing with the humans. "Yes, well," she said vaguely.

They reached the edge of town and started off down a farm road. Cotton flourished on either side of the dirt path, though there was no one currently in sight.

"My plantation's just up a little ways," Sam said, gesturing generally to the north of where they currently were. "If you'd like, I could show you the grounds. The roses don't really like to grow in this climate, but I've managed them somehow." He gave Eva a brilliant smile.

She had to laugh. "Hm, I wonder what your secret is," she murmured through her grin.

"A very good understanding of the earth," replied Sam. "A green thumb. I have some lovely ivy growing up the side of the house too. I think my servants are gossiping behind my back about my deal with the devil or something along those lines."

"Did you tell them that you were the devil?" asked Eva, then sobered. She needed to remember why she had come out this way. Sam was dangerously charismatic when he wanted to be.

"I've still got fifteen years left here, I would prefer not to be run out of town," Sam replied, then seemed to notice the change in Eva's attitude. "I do like it here," he continued. "I like the climate. It does get a little muggy in the summer, yes, but other than that, I think I may like it better than anywhere else I've spent a decent amount of time."

"You said you'd been thinking," Eva said, deciding perhaps that it would be best to get to the heart of the conversation before she was any more distracted. "Why now, after all these years?"

Sam tilted his head back, using his free hand to steady his hat. "For so long, there was another culture to try, another group to interact with, but it's not so any more. People are starting to move about, and it's dangerous to try to continue the charade. We may be difficult to kill, but a well-aimed rifle would do the trick. It's best not to risk it. So I've come down to try and live among the people, but it's really very hard." He turned to face her. "How do you do it so well?"

"I beg your pardon?" replied Eva.

"Don't you ever want to teach them a lesson? When someone's carriage splashes you, or when someone talks back to you? How do you keep your wings hidden, your powers under wraps?" Sam stopped, and Eva obediently stopped with him. "I mean—I was worshipped and feared as a god. How am I supposed to adapt to this mundane existence?"

Eva had never seen him so honest. "It is hard," she admitted. "I know the others have had the same problems. But after a while, it becomes easier. You start to see them as people too, worthy of respect." She paused, brushing at her skirt. "I think, perhaps, that we are not really all that different in the end. Different enough, certainly. It would not do to be found out in this day and age as something so alien. We will never be the same as them—we found that out with the Nephilim— but I do believe we will be able to coexist peacefully." She looked at the confusion on Sam's face. "I know that does not really help, but that is the best advice I can give you. Perhaps it was not as hard for me; after all, I was never worshipped as a god."

Sam snorted, the action at odds with his gentlemanly appearance. "Don't give me that, Eve. You have an entire major religion believing you were the first woman, created by God Himself. How you and Michael pulled that off, I shall never be sure." He shook his head. "'Adam' indeed." Eva opened her mouth to protest, but Sam cut her off. "Oh, I know Michael never really went by that, but the point stands."

He began walking down the path again. "Anyway, I do appreciate your advice. I guess I will just need to give it time, though I worry that I am going to snap one of these days. I will just need to find another way to give in to my stress, I suppose."

The house rose up out of the surrounding fields. It was much as Sam had said, fashioned out of red brick, a variety of different rose bushes blooming happily along the front edge, a dark green ivy curling up one end of the house.

"I do mostly cotton," Sam was saying. "Some tobacco. Dreadful stuff, really, I don't know why it's so popular. I have an orchard with a variety of fruit trees on the back part of the property. And I keep some animals—a few sheep, some chickens, nothing terribly exciting."

"I'm impressed, Sam. You've really managed to accomplish quite a bit." Eva leaned over to smell one of the roses. "I guess that's the appeal of settling down in one place for a while. Maybe we'll get there someday."

"Actually, I wanted to talk to you about that." Sam took one of her hands in his, pulling her around to face him. "Eve, I've always regretted driving you away. Do you think you could find it in your heart to come back and stay with me for a while?"

Eva looked away, real grief welling in her chest. "I'm sorry, Sam, you know I can't. It's been too long and too much has happened in that time period."

"Please, Eve," Sam begged. "I am so lonely."

She shook her head. "No, Sam. My heart no longer belongs to you."

A dark look flashed across Sam's face a moment before disappearing. "Ah, yes, Michael. How could I forget." The bitter disappointment in his voice was evident.

Eva reached up with her free hand to cup Sam's cheek. "Don't be like that. You and I are old news. Don't let something like that cloud your future."

Sam sighed and nuzzled his face into her hand. "I wish I could be as pure as you, Eve, but I'm afraid there's something dark that lurks within." He took her free hand in his. "I'm sorry, I shouldn't have asked, but I wanted to know if there was any hope for the two of us." He dropped one of her hands and led her around the side of the house with the ivy climbing up it. This part of the yard was in complete shade from the towering house. "Old sentimentality occasionally raises its head."

"Don't give up hope," Eva said, trailing a little behind him. "I think, in time, people will be willing to forgive."

"Oh no," he replied, turning to face her. "There are some of us who will never forgive me."

Then his hands were around her neck, choking off her breath. Eva gasped, attempting to bring up her arms to fight him off, but something—the ivy perhaps?—held her immobilized.

"I didn't mean to pull up the past, Eve," Sam said, almost carelessly, as Eva's vision began to swim. "After all, what if you had said yes? It would have ruined all my plans." He chuckled, low in his throat. "Though perhaps I could have improvised. Oh well. The original plan stands."

Bright spots of white began to speckle her vision as she tried desperately to get some air into her lungs. She reached out for the sun's light, but couldn't reach it through the shade. In a last, distressed attempt, she released her wings, but Sam had bound her too tightly. The pain as the vines crushed them only served to heighten her sense of panic more.

And then, there was nothing at all.

Chapter Eighteen

MICHAEL STARED AT the metal door in front of him. The address on the sheet of paper had turned out to be a rundown industrial building, fashioned out of concrete and metal sheeting.

"What are you waiting for?" asked Rafe from behind his right shoulder. "Let's go in there and kick his ass."

"I can't help feeling that this is a bad idea," said Michael. He was a little surprised at his own reluctance. Normally he would have torn the door off its hinges at this point. "The hell did you do, Gabe? I feel really off."

"I just wanted to make sure you were thinking clearly," replied the redhead. Rafe gave him a look and he sighed. "I admit I may have overdone it, but there's nothing to be done about it now."

Rafe rolled his eyes. "Lovely. Great. Can we go now? I would just like to point out that we are pretty sure that Sam has killed in the past and that perhaps leaving defenseless hostages in his care is a bad idea."

"Look at what he's done," Michael said, ignoring his roommate. "This structure plays to his strengths. Metal, earth. Plus it will make it so we can't fly."

"I hereby forbid any further strange water tricks, Gabriel." Rafe shook his head. "You have completely drained all action out of him, and there is entirely too much thinking."

"What's done is done," replied Gabe. He walked around Michael and put his hand on the doorknob. "Well, here we go." With that, he squared his shoulders, turned the knob, and opened the door. Rafe followed him inside, leaving Michael to bring up the rear.

Once inside, his attention was immediately drawn to Lily and Sam, standing in the middle of the room, their arms crossed across their chests. Eva was tied to a chair just behind them, but something was off. She seemed drugged—her eyes fluttering open and closed at an unsteady rate—though he doubted Sam would bother with something like that. At least she didn't seem to be physically harmed, but that didn't necessarily mean anything.

Gabe halted a good five feet away from the other two. Sam and Lily didn't seem to be fazed by their arrival. That made Michael nervous. He glanced around the room, searching for some sort of trap, but there was nothing to be found.

"Took you guys long enough," Sam said after a long silence. He uncrossed his arms, shoving his hands in his pockets. "I thought I was going to have to come out and get you. Trail we left wasn't too hard, was it? It wasn't supposed to be that much of a puzzle."

Gabe peered past Sam to Eva, cocking his head. "What did you do to her?"

Lily and Sam glanced at each other. Sam shrugged, and Lily's glance slid over to Eva. She seemed uncomfortable. "Sam had me induce Eve's memories."

"What?" asked Michael, aghast.

"What?" echoed Gabe. "How could you do that? You're likely going to drive her insane from too much information."

"But you know what this proves?" said Sam with a terrible smile. "It means she *is* Eve, because there wouldn't have been anything to induce if she wasn't."

Some of the familiar spark began to kindle in Michael's stomach. "You idiot," he breathed, balling his hands into fists. "What good is it to prove that if she can't function afterwards? Whether she was or not, it was no right of yours to force those memories back on her."

Sam sighed, rubbing a hand down the back of his head. "Hmm. My bad."

There was the fire he was familiar with. It stamped down on Gabe's calming influence and roared into life. It took all Michael's willpower to keep from closing the distance between them and shoving his fist into the other man's stupid, smirking face. "You've never had any respect for any living thing other than yourself. Even now, you're only using Lily for your own ends."

"Lily's and my arrangement is none of your business," replied Sam. "We are, at the moment, working towards a common goal. It is little different than some of the things you've done over the years, Michael." He held up a hand, blocking Michael's reply. "But that does bring me to the matter at hand. If you'll agree to a certain arrangement, we're willing to back off, and everyone gets to go home nice and safe."

Michael glanced at Gabe. The redhead shrugged. "And what would that arrangement be, out of immense curiosity?" Michael deadpanned.

"It's very simple," Sam said with a half-grin. "Eva stays here with me. You three head back to wherever you want and don't get in our way. Everybody's happy."

Rafe snorted. "Except, oh, I don't know...almost everyone. Seriously, Sam, have you lost what little semblance of sanity you had left? First of all, Michael will be miserable if we leave here without Eva, and then Gabe and I are going to have to deal with an irate pyromaniac for who knows how long. And as for Eva, provided you haven't fried her brain and she regains consciousness, what makes you think that she—Eva or Eve—is going to go along with anything you have planned when she hasn't shown any inclination of doing so in the last seven thousand years?" He eyed Lily. "And Lily, well. Lily is Lily."

Irritation broke through Lily's perfectly maintained mask for a second. Michael almost smiled; Rafe had always had the ability to get under her skin.

Sam's eyes flashed. "Is that a no, then?"

Michael glanced at Lily, then at his roommates, and finally, drew his eyes to Eva's limp form. She seemed to occasionally be mumbling under her breath, her eyelids still fluttering erratically. How long had she been like this? He shouldn't have let Gabe calm him down. Maybe if they'd followed the trail faster, maybe if he'd been more decisive, he could have prevented her from having to suffer this pain.

"How do you feel about this?" he asked Lily. "Is this what you want?"

Surprise cracked through her mask. She had to be at least a little unsure if she was breaking so easily. "Well," she said. "It's more a question of…"

Whatever Lily had been about to say was drowned out by a large, bone-jarring crash from behind him. Michael's heart dropped into his stomach and he turned to find a rather large hole in the ground where Rafe had been only moments earlier.

Lily looked horrified. "What the *hell*, Sam?"

"Rafe?" called Gabe. He and Michael slowly inched towards the edge of the hole. Michael peeked in, then pulled his glance away. All he could see of his friend was one hand. The rest of him was buried beneath a small mountain of dirt and stone and concrete, and it didn't seem to be moving. A stream of sunlight beamed down onto the rubble from where the ceiling had been a moment before.

"There," Sam said, sounding rather pleased with himself, "vulnerable. Just for you."

"You didn't even give him a chance to defend himself," said Lily.

"Rafe!" Gabe called again, a desperate edge to his voice.

Michael was frozen to where he stood. Surely he couldn't be gone, just like that, not after so many years together and so many worse threats than this. He refused to accept it. Any second now, Rafe would stir and pull himself out of the dirt and make some terrible quip about the whole situation. Michael stared at the hand, willing it to do something, but it continued to lie still.

"Oh, like you've never stabbed anyone in the back, Lilith," Sam said.

"That's not the point!"

"Gabe?" Michael asked, placing a hand on his roommate's shoulder. The redhead tensed under him, muscles tighter than Michael had felt in anyone in a very long time. This was not good. Gabe had to be the calm one, because someone had to be the calm one, and Michael was never ever the calm one. He couldn't think of anything else to say.

He had the slightest warning to get out of the way as Gabe released his wings. Michael stumbled backwards and landed hard as his roommate extended them to their full wingspan, taking up most of the width of the room. Once again, Michael was insanely grateful that they were on the same side.

Sam and Lily released in response, Sam giving Lily a look out of the corner of his eye. "Stick to the plan, now."

Lily glowered at him, but instantly a dark mist began obscuring the room. Crap. Michael pulled himself to his feet, releasing his wings as well. He winced as they extended. He'd been using them too often lately. He needed to leave them out or leave them in and stop tearing up the skin on his back, but it wouldn't do to be the only person in a fight without them out. Michael took a few hesitant steps back until he could feel the wall with his hands.

He could hear Gabe off in front of him, searching frantically through the darkness for their opponents. Michael would need to stay away from him. If Gabe decided to just direct water about, well, that would be very bad indeed.

There was a low buzz in the back of his mind, the beginning of an anger the likes of which he hadn't felt in a very long time. Sam would pay for what he'd done. Michael would make sure of it.

Unfortunately, in the dark, they had the advantage. Lily could see through it without any issues, meaning she could just walk up to someone and use some of her more problematic powers on them without them seeing her approach, and Sam didn't need to see, just upend the floor from underneath them like he had to Rafe.

"Why this cowardly behavior, Sam?" called out Gabe, a dangerous undertone to his voice. Michael shivered. "Why not fight it out like equals?"

Sam chuckled, somewhere off on Michael's right. "What good does that do me, Gabriel? I'm not here to prove anything. I just want to be rid of you, and it behooves me to do that in the way where I am least likely to suffer damage."

Carefully judging the distance, Michael shot off a burst of flame in the direction of Sam's voice. Lily's dark was unnatural, failing to properly light up as the fire passed through it, but Michael did catch a glimpse of Sam's startled face as the fireball impacted his wing just above where it connected to his left shoulder.

Michael could hear Sam shuffle out of the way, letting off a string of curses. The ground beneath Michael rumbled, and he had only a moment to throw himself to the side before the section of floor he'd been standing on slammed upward, leaving a significant dent in the ceiling. *Shit.* That would have hurt.

Michael froze where he was, ears alert. All his nerves strained, commanding him to go charging into action, but someone had to be the calm one, and though he didn't know what the hell he was doing, it didn't seem to be Gabe, so he'd have to try. At least there was still no water, but Gabe seemed to be moving rather rapidly around the room, probably mapping sources, so no good would come of that.

Out of nowhere, Lily appeared in front of him. She gave him a look and a slight smile before moving on, making no attempt to attack him. Was it a trick? He strained his ears, trying to hear her approach, but everyone seemed to have stopped moving. Lily didn't have to let him know that she was there. What was she trying to say? That she was purposefully leaving him alone?

Even if she was, Michael couldn't count on her to change sides. If Lily decided there was nothing else for her here, she would be gone before any of the rest of them noticed.

This thinking thing was troublesome.

Well, screw this sneaking-around crap. No one could see anyone to do anything, Eva was liable to get caught in some crossfire because no one would be able to tell where she was, and it was taking entirely too long for Michael's tastes. He pushed himself to his feet just as Gabe let out a yell from off on his left. There was a crash as something—or someone—slammed against the wall, some of the concrete breaking off and tumbling to the floor. Another crash followed soon afterwards, and then the darkness in the room began to thin.

A pipe squealed as it broke through the wall, concrete flying far enough to hit Michael as he made sure he got as far away as possible from the now flying water. Through the fading mist he could make out two people locked together—Gabe and Lily, judging by their sizes—though he couldn't tell what was happening.

"There are pipes everywhere," murmured Sam from just behind his left shoulder. Michael let out a yell and stumbled away from the other man, who, of all the mad things that he could possibly be doing, was smiling. "Gabriel's not the only one you have to worry about with them."

As if to demonstrate his point, Sam gave a wave of his hand just as a section of pipe pulled itself out of the ceiling and flung itself at Michael's head. Michael managed to duck out of the way, and the pipe ended up smashing into the wall behind him.

"Really, I'm pleased to see you're still thinking more with your heart than your mind," Sam said, placing his hands on the wall behind him. The concrete broke apart, shards flying across the room.

Michael flung up his wings to protect his body, wincing as the concrete tore at the feathers. Stupid concrete wouldn't burn. Stupid metal wouldn't burn. He'd have to generate his own fire and he was still feeling a little woozy from whatever Gabe had done earlier.

"Watch it, you're going to hit Eva," he hissed as he lowered his wings. He reached down, sending a chain of fire across the floor at Sam. It was easier to direct the fire along things, and he would need to conserve his energy.

Sam dropped the floor out from underneath Michael's trail of flame. As Michael watched it disappear into whatever lay beneath the building, he couldn't help but wonder how long the structure would continue to stand, with the current rate of abuse. "See," Sam said, "this is what I mean. You must have realized that I would have the advantage in here, and yet you all came charging in anyway like the predictable idiots you are."

There was another crash from behind them and Michael turned his head at the sound. Gabe had Lily up against the wall, his hand around her throat, but she had a death grip on Gabe's forearm, and, from the glow in her eyes, she was probably doing more damage than he was.

There was a groaning of metal before the ceiling collapsed on the two combatants, sunlight streaming in from outside. Michael wheeled back around to find Sam glaring at him. "Will you please focus on what is important?"

Michael stared at him, mouth hanging open. "Did you really just drop a ceiling on your ally?"

Annoyance flared in Sam's eyes. "I'm not here to get a lecture on proper battleground etiquette from you. I am here to crush you, and where is the fun in that if you are not even paying attention? You're so worried about everyone else that you turn your back on the enemy right in front of you."

"You really are twisted." Michael stretched his wings out. "This is why Eve will never come back to you. You have no respect for the living. You have no respect for anyone that is not you, not even her. You just see her as some sort of trophy to be won, a tool to be used, with no concern for her feelings, her wants, her desires. And that is why you will always lose." Without waiting for the other man's response, Michael dove at him, latching onto Sam's upper arms with his hands. The anger boiling inside, he set his hands alight. Flesh, at least, did burn.

Sam howled. He flailed at Michael, but he wasn't in a good position to connect with any force. Michael held on, furrowing his brow in concentration, increasing the strength of his flame. Maybe this would finally be it. Maybe today would finally be the day where one of the two of them wouldn't walk out of the fight.

Something slammed into the back of Michael's head. Ears ringing, he collapsed onto his knees, losing his grip on Sam.

Panting, Sam kicked at him. The air smelled slightly of charred skin, and when Michael gingerly felt the back of his head, his hand came away wet with blood.

"So what if you're right," Sam growled, still trying to catch his breath. "Eventually she will come around. And if it's not in this lifetime, then maybe it will be the next time. I just need to keep trying."

Michael winced at the throbbing in his head. "Keep trying what?"

Sam wasn't listening to him, though. He shakily pushed past Michael, stumbling a little as he went. Michael stared after him before pushing himself weakly to his feet. Too fast, apparently. His vision spun, forcing him to use the wall for support. He took a few deep breaths before going after the other man. He couldn't really figure out what Sam was up to, but it seemed imperative that he keep him from whatever it was.

Sam seemed to be gaining strength as he went, heading across the room towards where Eva still sat tied. She had quieted, and, luckily, seemed to be unharmed. Michael felt a dizzying moment of relief before the meaning of Sam's words finally presented itself.

"God, Sam, stop," he said. "Is that what you thought in New Orleans too? No matter how many times you kill her, it's not going to change her."

Ignoring Michael, Sam slashed at the ropes holding Eva to the chair. She tipped forward, Sam catching her before she hit the floor. He slung the unconscious woman over his shoulder, then paused, glancing over his shoulder at Michael.

"I guess we'll see," he said, before disappearing through the door at the end of the room.

It took a second for Michael to realize what was happening. What had Sam hit him with, anyway? He hesitated for a second, wondering if he should check on Gabe, but there was nothing he could do even if his friend was still alive, and there was one life, maybe, that he could save.

Moving as quickly as he dared, Michael reached the door, pulling it off its hinges. Beyond was a corridor heading parallel to the wall, and straight ahead lay a staircase. Sam would go closer to his element, Michael was fairly sure. He didn't have time to think. Charging ahead, he threw himself down the staircase, using his wings to slow his descent.

The staircase opened into a large room, nearly identical to the one above it, save for the fact that the floor was made of dirt. Sam had deposited Eva in the middle of the room and had his hands wrapped around her throat.

Fear seized his heart. Using his momentum from the staircase, Michael threw all his weight into Sam, sending the other man flying. A spasm of pain shot through his head and it was all he could do to keep standing as he gathered flame in his hands.

Sam recovered faster than he expected. Fury dancing in his eyes, he regained his balance and pulled another pipe out of the wall, this one still spurting water. Fortunately, the pressure didn't seem to be very great, though Sam solved that disappointment by flinging the pipe at Michael.

He dodged, but he wasn't moving as quickly as he had been, and the pipe caught his right wing. Something bent wrong and broke, and pain shot up into his shoulder.

"Fine," growled Sam. "I thought it would be fitting for you to fail at protecting her, yet again, but maybe I'll finish you first and then finish what I started."

Michael retreated before Sam's approach. He wouldn't be able to surprise him like he had before, and there was very little to burn down here as well.

He half-tripped over the pipe, then bent down, picking it up in his hands. Sam froze, eying him warily. Michael held it for a second, transferring his energy into it, then flung it back at his opponent.

Sam had been too close; the scalding pipe hit him straight in the face. He went down and Michael pressed his advantage, gathering his fire back into his hands. As Sam sat up, Michael drove his hand up against Sam's chest.

"Too slow," murmured Sam. The ground underneath Michael erupted, smashing him into the ceiling. He dropped back to the floor, pieces of the ceiling coming with him, letting in the sunlight from above. A large slab dislodged itself and crashed down onto his chest. Pain exploded through his body and he struggled to get air into his lungs. Something was terribly out of place.

Sam slowly pushed himself to his feet, leaning down so Michael could see his face. Michael shoved weakly at the slab crushing his ribs, but it wouldn't move. "I almost like this better," Sam said. Michael noted with a small bit of amusement that Sam's hair was burning, though the other man didn't seem to notice. "There's nothing you can do now if I decide to go and finish off Eva. I'm tempted to do that, but on the other hand, I'm not sure how long you're going to last, and I want the last thing you feel to be the despair of you being helpless, the last thing you see to be me, finally and ultimately winning."

Michael chuckled. It was a mistake; a new wave of pain, stronger than before, rocked his body. "Do you want to know what Gabe theorized was the reason for reincarnation?" he choked out.

"I know the theories," Sam snapped.

His ribs protested as Michael drew another breath. "Someone will only return if there's something that ties them here." It was getting harder to force the air into his lungs. "If I return to the Void today, if Gabe and Rafe go too, what do you think will pull Eve back?"

Rage flashed across Sam's features. "I will."

"I don't believe that, and I don't think you do, either. We'll all be together, happy, and you can just stay here, miserable, alone, powerless, for all eternity."

Real fear flickered in Sam's eyes for a moment. Then, with a growl, he dropped another section of the ceiling on Michael's chest.

Fire, not the kind he'd felt his whole life, burst through his body. He gasped, but now no air at all was reaching his lungs.

"At least I'll be free of you," said Sam.

Michael's vision began to dim. This was really it. He had lost, and no one was going to come save him. There was no one left. A strange sense of acceptance entwined with sorrow took him.

A bright light erupted in Michael's fading awareness. Minor curiosity flared, but what did it really matter, where he was going? He wondered who he would find there, if they would remember who they'd been in their time here, if they would remember him.

A slim hand rested itself on his shoulder. "Michael," said a voice.

This was odd. He didn't remember any voices from his first time in the Void.

A second hand laid itself on his other shoulder and, quite surprisingly, his strength began to return to him. His vision cleared and air, sweet air, returned to his lungs.

"Push the concrete off," commanded the voice gently.

There didn't seem to be any reason not to try. Gathering his strength, he shoved at the slab. The hands on his shoulders tightened, and to his very great amazement, the concrete began to slide, a little at a time. Michael managed to force it off completely after what seemed like forever.

He lay there, breathing heavily, as the world clarified around him. He wasn't dying anymore. Someone had saved him.

Eva leaned over him, her hands still on his shoulders. Michael blinked up at her, but instead of his eyes meeting her warm, chocolate ones, they met eyes as green and bright as his own. Brilliant, glossy, black wings sprouted out of her back.

"...Eve?" he asked hesitantly.

She chuckled. "Yes and no. Let's worry about that later. I've healed what I can at the moment, but you're still not in that great of shape. Don't let him get at your ribs."

Sam. Michael had completely forgotten about him. "Why isn't he attacking?"

Eva pushed him up into a sitting position. Sam was hunched over partway across the room, hands clutching his face. "I temporarily blinded him." She gave Michael a slight smile. "He was the idiot who let the sunlight in."

Michael's head swam, trying to make sense of what exactly had happened in the last few minutes.

"He can hear everything we've been saying," Eva murmured into his ear. "I'm out of practice; I don't know how long the blindness will last. You'd better move fast. I don't have the energy to re-inflate any more lungs."

With Eva's help, Michael hauled himself to his feet. His head still throbbed, his ribs still ached, but he seemed to be able to move without too much trouble, though he felt like a strong breeze would blow him over. Now that he was upright and coherent, however, he could tell that Sam hadn't been having as good a time of it as he had thought. Sam was considerably more charred than Michael had believed, and he seemed to be having a hard time keeping his arms up where he wanted them.

"I don't have to see to find you two," he said, his breathing labored. "All I have to do is hear you."

"There's still time to walk away from this, Sam," Eva said. "If you promise to go your own way and stay out of ours, this can end today."

Sam laughed low in his throat. "It will never end. It can't, not until things fix themselves."

Eva flapped her wings once. "You know, I spent a long time thinking, Sammael, about the beginning, when it was just you and me. And I came to the conclusion that it wasn't meant to be. We weren't meant to find each other. We weren't meant to be together. Things fixed themselves when we reached Eden and went our separate ways. All this time, you've been trying to revert things to an unnatural state."

Sam straightened, his burned arms dropping to his sides. "No. You're wrong."

"Am I?" replied Eva, crossing her arms.

"I will fix things," Sam said, though it sounded like he was mostly talking to himself. "I just need to keep trying." He took a deep breath, raised his head, and threw himself at Eva.

Eva struck him with her wing, driving his attack to the side. Sam stumbled, blinking in surprise. Then he growled, balling his hands into fists.

The ceiling above Eva creaked ominously. She managed to get out of the way before the concrete collapsed, moving so gracefully Michael could barely keep his eyes off of her. As she dodged, her eyes met his, and a connection he hadn't felt in centuries jolted back through his mind. His resolve strengthened. He would let nothing happen to this woman.

As Eva kept Sam distracted, Michael crept around behind him, moving slowly in an attempt to avoid detection, though he wasn't sure how Sam would hear him over the crashing concrete. Michael winced as a flying pipe came far closer to Eva than he would have liked. No matter what Eva thought, there was no way he could allow this to continue. Sam was a danger to them, and Michael wouldn't spend the rest of his life, however long that was, looking over his shoulder waiting for Sam to strike him or his loved ones.

Michael gathered his flame just below the surface of his skin. Sam's attention was concentrated on Eva, though his attacks were becoming increasingly erratic. "It's not fair!" Sam screamed as another chunk of ceiling missed its mark. "I was winning! How *dare* you regain your powers now!"

"I have you to thank for that," Eva replied. "Who knows how long it would have taken if my memories and powers had continued to return at the rate they had been? You sped the process up immensely." She grinned. "Too bad you couldn't leave well enough alone, or this could have been all over by now."

Sam's shoulders tensed. "It will be soon."

"I agree," said Michael. He latched onto Sam's wings, igniting the feathers. Sam shrieked and attempted to tear his wings free from Michael's grasp, but Michael held on.

"Michael!" called Eva in warning. He ducked as a chunk of what looked suspiciously like staircase flew through where his head had been and ricocheted off of Sam's burning wing. The other man hissed in pain, more hunks of concrete detaching themselves from the walls. Michael wouldn't be able to dodge them all and continue to hold on. He closed his eyes, bracing himself for the impact and pushing more of his energy into his flame. The fire was spreading now, crawling almost lazily down Sam's back.

The blows never came. After a long moment, Michael opened his eyes to discover Eva standing behind him, her wings spread to encompass both of them. There were tears in the corners of her eyes, but she gave him a half-smile when she noticed him looking. "I'm okay." The smile disappeared. "If he drops the ceiling, you let go and get away, do you understand? It will do nobody any good to get trapped beneath that."

Michael personally thought the ceiling looked like it was going to collapse on its own. Sam thrashed underneath his grip, moaning in pain. Guilt welled in Michael's throat. Maybe he had gone soft over the millennia, but it seemed a little heartless to burn one's enemy to death.

A creak above halted any further philosophizing. Eva grabbed him by the shoulder and pulled him away as a large section of the ceiling above dislodged itself and tumbled down. Even halfway expecting it, Michael barely made it out of the way. Sam was not so lucky.

For a moment, it was unnaturally quiet. One ebony wing still peeked up through the rubble, blazing almost merrily.

Eva took a deep breath. Michael glanced at her. Her wings were torn and there was a large streak of dirt down one cheek, but other than that, she seemed unharmed. "You're going to have to check," she said. "I'll get burned."

He almost didn't understand what she meant, but then he glanced back at where they had been moments before. There was no movement, and as Michael crawled over the piles of destroyed concrete, he wondered what exactly he wanted to find.

Michael didn't think he was up to lifting any more slabs, and quite frankly, wasn't sure he wanted to see what was underneath. He searched around until he found an arm, wrinkling his nose at the stench. Half of the skin on the arm was charred black, the untouched skin unnaturally pale against it. Tentatively, Michael reached down, laying his hand on a patch of exposed skin. Despite the proximity of the smoldering feathers, there was no warmth left in it.

He left out a breath he hadn't been aware he'd been holding. Stepping away, he shot a ball of flame at the remains. They couldn't be leaving evidence around, and the wings would fade by themselves.

Eva watched him closely as he made his way back to her. She met him as he cleared the rubble, wrapping her arms around his waist. "It couldn't be helped," she murmured, laying her head against his chest. "It's better this way. Maybe he can finally find some peace."

"I hope so," Michael answered, sliding one arm around her back. It felt nice to have her so close again. "But...who are you?"

She looked up at him. "I'm Eva," she said. "But, heartmate, I was also Eve, and I guess in some ways, I still am and always was." She paused, furrowing her brow. "I'm not really sure how to best explain it. In my heart, in my head, in my memories, there's no difference between the two."

Michael gathered her close, burying his face in her hair. "I've missed you," he murmured. "I wasn't complete without you."

Eva's grip tightened on his waist. "It's my fault. I should have known, back then, not to go alone with Sam. I was so desperate to help him that I let my feelings get the better of me. I'm so very sorry, Michael."

"It's okay," he answered. "We're together now."

They stood there for a long time. Michael hadn't felt so whole in years. She still felt like Eva, yes, but he could recognize Eve in her now as well, and her presence soothed his soul.

It was Eva who pulled away first. "Did you come alone?" she asked. "Where are Gabe and Rafe?"

Michael's heart dropped. He had almost forgotten them. "I—they're..." He paused, trying to gather his thoughts. "Yes, they came with me, but I...I don't know if they're okay." He ran one hand down the back of his head. "Sam got to them, but...I didn't have time to check."

Eva's eyes widened in horror. Michael took one of her hands in his, leading her back toward the staircase. He dreaded what they would find, but he owed it to his friends to do what was needed if the worst had happened.

A warzone greeted them at the top of the stairs. A good majority of the floor was missing, as well as considerable portions of the walls and ceiling, pipes drooping out of holes throughout. They probably wouldn't want to stick around too long. Michael assumed this place was fairly out of the way, but it wouldn't do to have to explain what had happened if someone came by and started asking questions.

Gabe was easy to find. In fact, judging by the disturbance of the rubble, someone had dragged him out from underneath the concrete. He was pale, large bruises dotting his skin, and one wing was bent in an abnormal direction, but he was breathing. There was no sign of Lily. Michael shook his head slightly; he was never going to understand that woman.

Eva knelt next to the redhead, placing a hand on his chest. She closed her eyes. "He doesn't have any life-threatening injuries. Concussion, a couple of broken bones, some internal bleeding but not in any critical areas. I'm going to wake him up."

Michael settled on the floor next to Eva. After a moment, some color returned to Gabe's cheeks and his eyes fluttered slowly open. He groaned and started to push himself into a seated position.

"Not too fast," warned Eva. "And watch your wing."

Gabe blinked at her, but he listened, wincing when he accidentally brushed the broken wing with his elbow. He looked between Eva and Michael, then slowly turned, surveying the remains of the building. "Sam?" he asked.

"Dead," answered Michael.

His roommate nodded, looking down at his hands. "Rafe?"

"We haven't checked yet," murmured Eva.

Gabe took a deep, ragged breath. "Okay," he said.

"Can you stand?" Michael asked. At Gabe's nod, he hauled himself to his feet first, wincing as something twinged in his side, before extending a hand to help the redhead.

"You look terrible," Gabe said.

"Gee, thanks," said Michael.

The three of them slowly made their way across what was left of the floor to where Rafe had fallen through. One section was missing completely, necessitating a jump across a small chasm. Michael stayed close to Gabe's side, catching him when he stumbled.

The hole was in a different spot than the basement room where Sam's remains lay; there was no way to reach the bottom except to jump in.

Michael glanced around at the three of them. He and Gabe both had broken wings, and Eva's feathers were torn. "Can any of us fly?"

"We're going to have to," replied Eva. "We can't leave him down there." She gave her wings an experimental flap. "I'll go first." Without waiting, she strode to the edge of the hole and disappeared.

"I'm not staying up here," said Gabe. He disappeared after Eva, though his landing was considerably louder than hers had been.

Well, he wasn't going to be any help getting them out, so they might as well all get stuck in the hole. Michael jumped down after them, not even bothering to try to slow his fall. He landed hard on a sloped pile of debris and stumbled, but managed to keep his feet.

Nothing had changed from earlier; one hand was all that could be seen. For a moment, no one moved, but then Eva shook her head and stepped forward, dropping to her knees. She reached out, hesitated, then set her shoulders and finished the motion, laying her hand against Rafe's.

Her shoulders dropped and Michael's heart dropped with them, but then Eva turned and flashed him a smile. "He's alive."

"Hurt?" asked Gabe.

Eva shook her head. "Not too bad, no. Seems like he blocked the worst of it with an air shield."

Michael laughed, then flinched as his ribs protested. "Lazy bastard," he said, without any malice. "Couldn't dig himself out to give us a hand."

Working as a team, it took them several minutes to get the largest pieces off of Rafe. They came across the other hand, and then not long after, uncovered his head.

"Oh, thank God," said Rafe. "I was beginning to worry that none of you were coming back." He grinned up at Eva. "Hello again, you."

"Just as worthless as when I left you," Eva said, smiling. Rafe laughed and pulled her into a bear hug. After a moment, he released her, turning to grin at Gabe. Whatever he saw on Gabe's face must have shaken him, though, because the smile disappeared almost immediately. He pulled himself out the rest of the way and stumbled over the rubble to the redhead, wrapping his arms around him. Shakily, Gabe returned the gesture, burying his head in Rafe's shoulder. Michael turned, giving them their privacy.

"Hello," said a voice from above. "Why are you in a hole?"

"You damn Viking," said Rafe, shaking a fist. "Why don't you answer your damn phone?"

"Well, gee, I'm sorry," said Thor from his perch on the edge of the hole. "I wasn't aware we were supposed to be striding into battle. That isn't something regular people are doing in this day and age. I like what you did with the place, though."

"We can't really take credit," replied Michael. "Now get down here and help us out."

"If I must," said Thor, grinning.

It took a few trips to get everyone out. Eva tried to heal people as best she could, though she was tired and out of practice. Then wings were retracted and people were cleaned up as much as possible before they wandered back out onto the streets. Michael draped one arm over Eva's shoulders, pulling her in close. "Not really the finding yourself you were looking for, was it?"

She chuckled. "It was a more eventful trip than I was hoping for, but I can't say that I mind terribly." She wrapped her arm around Michael's waist, entwining her fingers through one of his belt loops. "Certainly explains why my theories were at odds with the professors'. Who knew I was hanging out with a bunch of archangels in my free time?"

"We are a terrible influence," agreed Rafe.

"Sadly, yes," said Gabe. "No matter how much I try to make it otherwise."

"The important thing," said Eva, "is that we have many more years for you to try."

Michael smiled, giving Eva's shoulder a little squeeze. "Yes. Yes, we do."

Chapter Nineteen

EVA PULLED HER bag up her shoulder, heading across campus. It was frigid and the sky was threatening rain, but she found that she didn't really mind. Things were finally starting to fall into place, and she felt freer than she had in a long time.

It was mostly dark by the time she pulled open the diner door. Light and warmth spilled out onto the street. Eva stepped inside, looking around. She spotted the boys in a booth near the back. Rafe saw her at the same time, waving a hand in greeting.

"You're always so excited to see me," she said as she slid into the seat next to Michael, dropping her bag on the floor next to the booth. "It's very flattering."

"I can't help it," Rafe said. "You're like a new friend and an old friend all rolled into one. Apparently I was sicker of these two than I realized."

"Haha," said Gabe from behind his menu.

"Anyway, you're just in time. Gabe was going to tell us his latest theories on reincarnation."

Gabe lowered his menu to glare at Rafe. "I was *not*. And if you can't keep things I tell you in private to yourself, I am going to stop telling you things."

Rafe grinned, leaning his head on one hand. "Gabriel, you have been saying that forever."

"I mean it this time," Gabe said.

Eva shook her head, leaning into Michael's side. He wrapped one arm around her shoulders.

"How was your day?" he asked.

"Excellent. I got all my paperwork turned in, so I can start taking my new major-specific classes next semester."

"Good for you," Gabe said. "I kind of like the idea of using your powers for good in a perfectly acceptable human manner."

"Yep, no more angel essays for me, thank God."

"Hey," said Rafe, nudging Gabe in the shoulder, "if you like the idea so much, I've got a job for you—fireman. The hat, the boots, the uniform." Rafe waggled his eyebrows. "It'd be perfect."

Gabe rolled his eyes and returned to his menu.

Rafe turned to Eva, giving her a pleading look. "Help me out here."

"I'm sorry I left you alone with these two for so long," Eva said to Michael. "It's a miracle you're still sane."

"I was reaching the breaking point," replied Michael, grinning. "I was about two days away from doing something really drastic."

"More drastic than burning Rome down?"

"Hey," Michael said, "a lot of that was—"

"You'd better not be blaming that on me," said Thor. He slid a chair over from the neighboring table, plopping down into it. "Sorry I'm late. Did I miss anything good?"

Rafe muttered something about 'damn Vikings' under his breath. Thor stole his menu.

Eva smiled, taking a moment to enjoy just being there, being surrounded by friends, having an idea of what she was going to do with her life for the near future, and finally understanding herself.

"Did you talk to your mother?" Michael asked quietly while Thor and Rafe started arguing over the menu in the background.

Eva nodded. "She's thrilled to have a doctor in the family. She's already started bragging to all her neighbors." She smiled wistfully. "I guess she was right— I was doing the wrong thing with my life. I just didn't know it or how to figure it out. Plus, having you at my side certainly seems to be improving her mood. Though I suspect she wants grandkids."

Michael rubbed the back of his head, looking uncomfortable. "We could adopt, I guess? I mean, if you want to."

Eva leaned up, kissing him on the cheek. "Not something we have to worry about right now."

Rafe had won the menu war. Eva gave Thor hers.

"What did you decide?" Michael asked him.

"Oh, it's grand," Thor said, sitting up a little straighter. "I am going to become a private eye. I leased out a little shop and everything. 'Midgard Investigations.'"

"Do you know anything about private investigation?" Gabe asked.

"It can't be that hard," Thor replied. "From what movies have taught me, mostly you just follow people around talking to yourself."

Gabe frowned and Rafe looked like he wanted to laugh, but didn't want to give Thor the satisfaction.

"I figure if he ever gets bored, Michael can come on as my partner."

Michael snorted. "Now there's a terrible idea."

"I don't know," Thor said, "this place seems a lot less flammable than Rome."

Michael looked thoughtful, like he was considering the idea. Eva elbowed him in the side.

"Not to ruin the moment," Gabe said, "but has there been any news of Lily?"

Thor and Michael both shook their head.

"I don't think we need to worry, honestly," Eva said. "I mean, she was practically sabotaging Sam the entire time she was here, giving me information that ran counter to what he was and making sure I knew Michael. I don't think she's going to bother us." Eva frowned. "I mean, I guess she could have been showing Sam that I knew Michael, but I don't think that was it."

"Not to mention that she could have done a lot worse to you in Greece than she did," Michael added.

Gabe pursed his lips. "I guess."

"You worry too much," said Rafe. "Relax, Gabe. We're home, we're all in one piece, and the store survived our absence." He glanced at Thor. "Though we did seem to come home with some extra baggage."

Thor stuck his tongue out at Rafe.

They were saved by Pat coming by to take their order. Eva took Michael's hand under the table, wrapping her fingers around his. His hand was nice and warm again; for the first few days after the confrontation in Greece, he'd been cold, and she'd been secretly worried about him, that he'd used up too much of his internal fire. Luckily, he'd recovered without issue.

Thor glanced at Eva once Pat had gone. "This may be a bit forward of me, and feel free to tell me to go jump in a lake if it is, but do you...remember anything? Like, from in between?"

"Between Eve and Eva?" Eva shook her head. "I have Eve's memories, and they stop when she—I—died, and then my memories as Eva pick up almost immediately. There's nothing else."

There was silence around the table. Eva had had some of this conversation with Michael, and again with Gabe, but there were so many unanswered questions. Had she returned to the Void when Eve died? Had she lived out other human lives between Eve and now? It seemed unfair that she didn't have at least some answers.

When she thought too hard about it, it hurt her head. Back in Greece, when Eve had died in her memories, Eva had thought she'd gone too, and there had been nothing for what seemed an eternity. But then it was like waking up from a long dream, and she'd been herself, but Eve had been there too, like a lost part of her she hadn't realized she'd been missing. Eve's memories had filed themselves away like any of her own, and her powers—which she realized now that she had already been regaining to some degree, even before—were as instinctual again as they'd once been. But if her memories and powers had continued progressing at the rate they had been before, would everything eventually have happened in the same way? She had no idea.

She wouldn't complain, though. Everything felt right, and she wouldn't trade any of it away.

"Hey," Rafe said after a moment. "Have I told you the story about the Ark?"

Gabe visibly flinched. "Oh, no, Raphael."

"It is an excellent story and I don't know why Gabe is so uptight about it." Rafe settled into the cushion, leaning one arm across the back of the booth behind Gabe. "It involves daring escapes, ancient mysteries, and a stunningly handsome hero."

"Are you talking about me or you?" Gabe asked. He'd crossed his arms over his chest, but otherwise looked resigned to his fate.

Eva was distracted by Michael nuzzling her ear. "I've heard this before," he murmured. "I can think of better things to do while we wait for our food."

"I've heard it too," Eva replied softly, cupping his cheek with one hand. "But I like how the vein in Gabe's temple starts to throb about the time Rafe gets to the actual building of the Ark."

Michael laughed, pulling her closer. He tilted her head up, gently kissing her. The urgency was gone, but it still filled Eva with warmth. She returned the kiss, running one hand through his hair.

"God, they're like newlyweds," said Rafe. "Kind of makes me want to go set things on fire."

"I can help with that," Thor supplied.

Rafe ignored him. "How long is this going to last, anyway?"

Michael pulled back, smiling down at Eva. "If we're lucky, forever."

The End

ACKNOWLEDGMENTS

First of all, many thanks to my husband, mother, and sister for being constant sources of support, for reading my first drafts, no matter how rough, and never being afraid to tell me exactly what they think even if I sometimes have to go have a bath and eat some chocolate afterwards.

Many thanks to my many writer friends who read many iterations of drafts. Your insights are always helpful, and I value them highly. And thank you to the non-writer friends who read it as well. Your take as a reader rather than a writer was important to my fine-tuning.

And, of course, much appreciation goes to the ladies at Turtleduck Press, especially Siri Paulson, my editor, who is never afraid to let you know when you are making no sense or waxing too poetically on the sad state of library chairs.

While writing a book is a singular task, creating a book takes many people, and I am so pleased to have all of you on this journey with me.

ABOUT THE AUTHOR

Kit Campbell has never met a mythology she hasn't liked. This sometimes leads to issues, such as the occasional Norse God of Thunder showing up in the Garden of Eden. She adores weaving in the possibilities forgotten magic can bring to a story, and enjoys making up new creatures, such as large, venomous monsters that hunt in packs.

Kit's stories have been published in half-a-dozen anthologies, and her YA novella, *Hidden Worlds*, was released by Turtleduck Press in 2010. *Shards* is her first full-length novel.

Kit lives in Colorado in a house of ever-increasing chaos. She can be found around the internet at kitcampbellbooks.com, @KitCampbell, and on Goodreads.

ALSO AVAILABLE FROM TURTLEDUCK PRESS

Fey Touched
a novel by
Erin Zarro

Two sisters.

Asha is the Queen of the Fey, genetically engineered immortal humans who feed on human souls to survive. But she's running from her people. When she is found by her enemy, one of the Hunters of the Fey, she expects to die. Yet he's oddly intrigued by her, and Asha finds herself falling in love with him, hoping she can find safety and the home she's been seeking. Then she's kidnapped, and everything changes.

Fallon is a Hunter. She's looking for her long-lost sister, using an addictive drug to search through the stream of time. Her addiction leaves her dangerously exposed to her enemies but, consumed by her search, she doesn't care...until her fellow Hunters start dying from a mysterious illness. She is torn between duty and desire, and must find an answer before they all die.

What Fallon doesn't know is that Asha might just be the key to saving them all, if only she can find her.

And time is running out.

A novel of the Dream'verse

Captain's Boy
a novel by
KD Sarge

Donte spent his teen years orphaned and homeless in a snowbound smuggler's port. Now he's a university student. The hot meals are nice and everything is warmer on his new planet, but life among people is so much more complicated. With only two friends—young Jordan whom Donte tutors and the fiery Selene who shares his table in the coffeehouse—Donte has things somewhat under control, but still he struggles with both unfriendly and friendly people, and he can't shake the feeling that he's getting it all wrong.

None of that matters after Jordan is stolen by slavers. Donte enlists Selene to help rescue the boy, and when Jordan is taken off-planet Donte and Selene follow. But determination and luck can only get them so far, and the closer the pair come to Jordan, the nearer they get to Donte's deepest fears, and a past he'd worked to hide from everyone—especially himself.

Donte knows all too well the horrors Jordan faces, but when his secrets are dragged into an open courtroom, will Donte find the strength to speak the truth and save the boy?

www.ingramcontent.com/pod-product-compliance
Lightning Source LLC
Chambersburg PA
CBHW032134190626
46814CB00005BA/1693